MISSING THE MOMENT

MISSING
THE MOMENT

Grace Thompson

This first world edition published in Great Britain 1995 by
SEVERN HOUSE PUBLISHERS LTD of
9–15 High Street, Sutton, Surrey SM1 1DF.
First published in the USA 1995 by
SEVERN HOUSE PUBLISHERS INC of
425 Park Avenue, New York, NY 10022.

British Library Cataloguing in Publication Data
Thompson, Grace
  Missing The Moment
  I. Title
  823.914 [F]

ISBN 0-7278-4761-9

Typeset by Hewer Text Composition Services, Edinburgh.
Printed and bound in Great Britain by
Hartnolls Ltd, Bodmin, Cornwall.

Chapter One

Charlotte Russell looked around her at the untidy workroom where the few employees were doing various tasks in a desultory manner. Uncaring as well as untidy, she thought bitterly. Once, Russell's Bookbinders and Restorers had been a proud family business, but since the disappearance of her father, Eric Russell, and his brother Peter's accident, motivation and efficiency had dwindled.

For a while they had allowed things simply to tick over, believing against all common sense that Eric would return. Now, after an absence of seven years, all hope had gone. Charlotte knew that her mother had never given up believing that her husband would come back to her and she continued to watch each day for a letter from him explaining his absence and announcing his imminent return. Charlotte and her younger sister Rhoda had encouraged her in that belief, wrongly it now seemed, as Harriet Russell continued to waste her life waiting for that distant day when everything would be all right once again.

They knew he hadn't died. Every year Eric sent them a Christmas card, one to Charlotte, one to her sister Rhoda and one to Harriet. The cards arrived in August and each was sent from a different holiday resort. Harriet insisted they showed no one the cards and refused to discuss them. They all agreed they were simply a way of informing his family that he was alive, without giving away his whereabouts.

As far as everyone else in Bryn Melinau knew, Eric Russell had suffered a breakdown and wandered off, having lost his memory. To anyone who asked, Harriet explained in details that were pure invention, how all this had been due to his terrible experiences during the war. A few wondered how Eric could have suffered anything so serious in Aldershot, which was where he had spent the war, but no one questioned it. Like Harriet, they accepted the fabrication.

Now, in the sadly neglected workroom that had been her father's pride and pleasure, Charlotte swallowed the disappointment she felt each time she came there, and prepared a smile for her uncle.

Uncle Peter was looking through the pages of the monthly accounts ledger and from his face she knew he was not concentrating on the figures he had before him. He cared little for what they told him, like everyone else, she thought with mild anger. Then a frisson of pain crossed his face and at once she felt remorse. Uncle Peter was almost constantly in pain and if he hadn't given so much of his time trying to gather together the threads of her father's business, he might now be living a more relaxed and comfortable life.

When she had made her own cursory examination of the book and gathered the letters to which she would reply at home when her mother wasn't around, she kissed her uncle and refastened her coat and scarf.

"I'll have to go. Sorry I can't stay longer, Uncle Peter, but you know what Mam's like if I spend too much time up here." She smiled. "Got to make sure dinner's ready. Mam's out with Kath Thomas – you know, her from the boarding house on the bridge. She hates it if she comes back and I'm not in. Specially when it's as cold as today."

She saw the relief in Uncle Peter's face as he pushed aside the heavy ledger and moved himself away from the desk, where a curve had been cut to accommodate his wheelchair.

"I won't be far behind you, Charlotte. I'll be glad of something hot, the heating doesn't cope with this weather very well and my hands are a bit stiff."

"You're all right, aren't you?" At once she was concerned. "Shall I ring the doctor for some more tablets? Or ask him to visit?"

"I'm fine, just a bit chilled like the rest of us. January is a cruel month."

They discussed some of the work that had arrived and took pleasure in the more unusual tasks that offered a challenge; like the Victorian flower prints that needed restoration. Then, with regret, Charlotte left the office. Her uncle had reached for the order books and was scanning the pages with some dismay, but his concentration was already waning as she turned away from the factory doors to walk the half mile to her home.

She turned to wave, but Peter wasn't looking. From his desk he was staring out of the window, with its view of the small tributary to the river below. Through the seasons, he followed the progress of the several families of herons who lived there, and loved to watch

3

for the darting colour of the kingfisher. She suspected that he spent more and more time watching the birds and less time dealing with the day-to-day running of the small bookbinding firm that had once given Charlotte and her sister Rhoda a very comfortable standard of living.

If only her mother would allow her to spend more time at the office and not resent every moment she was away from their large and solitary Mill House home, this comfortable standard might continue.

Peter Russell was unable to give the same amount of energy to the family business that he once had, and even with his assistant, Jack Roberts, he simply couldn't manage to keep ahead of the daily routine. It didn't help that neither Uncle Peter nor her mother Harriet, would admit that a problem existed, Charlotte thought with a resurgence of simmering anger and frustration. Why wasn't she allowed to help?

She wished once again that her mother were less dependent on the support of her daughters. If only her sister Rhoda hadn't married so young . . . If only she, Charlotte, had married Joe Llewellyn the first time he had asked. If only. What a stupid expression that was. What an utter waste of time thinking about "if only". No one could turn back the clock. She and her mother knew that better than most.

Since her marriage at the age of seventeen to Brian Carpenter, Charlotte's sister Rhoda had continued to spend a great deal of time at the family home. Charlotte was grateful. Rhoda kept her mother from sitting and brooding about their father's disappearance and Uncle Peter's accident and its consequences. With Rhoda free to spend hours of every day with

4

her mother, Charlotte was able to go to the small bookbinding factory and help for a few hours most days to keep the firm alive. Now, with Rhoda and Brian on holiday, things were even more difficult, with her mother wanting her at home every moment of the day. Charlotte was despairing of ever getting the overdue letters typed and the monthly accounts delivered.

Around her the Welsh hills were locked in the grip of winter; the colours sombre, yet with a bleak beauty. Their greys, blues and purples deepened to black like an intricately woven tapestry, enlivened here and there with the rich greens of the conifers that rose through the darkness of the season and provided a reminder of better days. The sky was low now and threatening snow. She looked down at the river that looped its way around the town of Bryn Melinau and likened it to molten metal frozen into stillness. It seemed hardly to move and was silent in the bleak landscape, forbidden to disturb the hush of winter.

On the hill that gave the town its name, the hill on which seven mills had once stood, the ruins of those ancient buildings showed a rich green, where ivies defied the season of somnolence, retained their rich colour and gave protection to many of the small birds that went about their constant search for food in anxious, fluttering silence.

The day was without warmth and she pulled her scarf up over her dark hair, which she wore in a sleek under roll just free of her shoulders. Up here, high above the Welsh town of Bryn Melinau, the wind cut into her head like a chilled knife. Her long, slender legs strode out a little faster to warm herself but soon slowed. She was never in a great hurry to reach home these days.

Charlotte's hazel eyes looked around her: she was fascinated as always by the richness and variety of the countryside. The road was a narrow one with hedges on each side, and birds were busily searching for food. A flock of goldfinches swooped across the hedge and up again like a scattering of gold and red confetti. A charm of goldfinches: she remembered the collective noun with a smile. A bullfinch with its startlingly red breast stood on a branch, impatient for the new shoots to emerge so he could enjoy them. She smiled in pleasure. Even in this darkest of months there was the knowledge that in weeks food would be more plentiful and the birds would be busy nest-making.

The smile faded. When would *she* be able to start nest-making? Never, unless something happened to release her from fulfilling her mother's need for her constant attention. Rhoda couldn't be relied on to amuse her mother indefinitely. Her younger sister would soon have a family of her own and then it would be she who would again be expected to forgo any plans of her own to fill her mother's hours.

It was past midday. She was later than she had promised. She knew her mother would be standing at the gate, watching for her return, almost tearful with anxiety and impatience. She would be wearing her fur coat and matching hat to protect her against the chill of the January day. Harriet Russell never stepped outside the door without first checking she was suitably dressed to impress.

As she turned into Heather Gardens with its few

select and isolated properties, Charlotte was unable to hold back a sigh. She knew she was fortunate to live in such a beautiful place, but at twenty-three, she wondered with increasing frustration, when was she going to start living a life of her own? It was January 1950. The war had been over for almost five years, yet, in spite of the magazines she read telling her that this was an era for fun and a time when anything was possible, she foresaw only years of sameness stretching before her. That is, unless she married Joe Llewellyn.

Since they were children, Joe had proposed on a regular basis. It had almost become a joke, but not quite. In his quiet way, Joe was persistent, and it was apparent to all who knew them that one day they would marry. For Charlotte, Joe was a safe future and she loved him, of course she loved him. But something held her back from facing her mother and arranging a firm date for her marriage to "that bicycle repair man" as Harriet called him.

Facing her mother was the main problem. Charlotte blamed the disappearance of her father for her mother's fragile state of mind and for her own predicament; her mother was, like Charlotte herself, a victim of circumstances. Inwardly, she bitterly resented the fact that at twenty-three she was still having to accept her mother's rules.

But was she being completely honest in blaming either of her parents? Why was she stepping back from a commitment, accepting her mother's dislike of Joe as a reason to delay? Wasn't the true reason for her hesitation not her mother's but her own uncertainty? Was she holding on to Joe while waiting for something better, more exciting?

Marrying Joe wouldn't change much, she admitted to herself. She knew that fun was not a priority for Joe Llewellyn, who ran a business selling and repairing bicycles. He had returned from the army and resumed his life and his living, which had been in the care of his Auntie Bessie Philpot, with hardly a ripple to reveal the four years' disruption.

She sighed again. Joe loved her and she loved him – she supposed. The doubt brought guilt and confusion back to her mind and she pushed it away. She and Joe would make a good partnership. She had been trained well for marriage, never having worked outside the home, apart from the few hours she stole to spend at the family's bookbinding factory. She would organise Joe's home, serve well-cooked and economically sound meals, deal efficiently with his finances and give him a secure and contented base from which to go out and earn the money to keep them. It was what every young woman wanted from life. So why did it sound so abysmally dull? What was wrong with her that she wanted more?

In sight of the gates of Mill House, she paused. The large house had been built against the ruin of one of the old windmills and was solid and secure and, to her rebellious heart, like a prison. Her mother was waving, impatience showing in the gesture. Charlotte looked back along the road she had walked. The premises of Russell's Bookbinders and Restorers was out of sight but she felt the familiar tug of resentment that took her away from an occupation she enjoyed back to the routine of attending her unhappy and highly strung mother.

"Hello Mam. Sorry I am to be late. There were some interesting books that Uncle Peter wanted me to see. Victorian flower paintings they were. Become a bit 'fluffed' they had. I love watching him working on old and beautiful things."

"I'm sure." Harriet Russell's voice was high-pitched, sharp, belying the tight smile on her face. "And there's me standing in this freezing cold wind watching for you to come home."

"You could have waited inside, Mam," Charlotte admonished. "It's only children who think you can make someone come quicker by stretching your neck around corners!"

"You don't know what it's like, sitting here all alone for hours at a time, waiting for a knock at the door or a note to tell me your father's safe and on the way home."

Charlotte didn't reply. Her mother could hardly have been alone for more than half an hour. References to her absent father were frequently repeated and, after seven years, had become almost meaningless. Harriet bustled past her, disapproval tightening her once pretty face, and went into the kitchen where a vegetable stew, flavoured with oxo cubes, made the previous evening by Charlotte, simmered on the gas ring. Today was a meatless day. The rationing meant that meat was only available three days a week and on one of those days it had to be corned beef.

"I had to see to all this." Harriet waved her arms, encompassing the whole kitchen. "I thought you'd never get here on time. It will probably be awful. I haven't your knack of making these peculiar meals." She threw her coat and hat down carelessly. With a sigh, Charlotte picked them up and began putting them on the coat hanger near the front door. She would put them away later.

"Put it upstairs, Charlotte." Harriet spoke petulantly, as if everyone was out of step with her standards and desires. "If someone should call, it looks so slovenly with clothes hanging about in the hall, dear. Bring down my tablets, will you?" her mother called moments later.

"I already have them," Charlotte said, with a grimace of childish satisfaction. Her mother frequently asked for them when Charlotte had already started down the stairs.

"Thank you dear. You are a gem." Her mother smiled at her and Charlotte forgave her for the small irritations and smiled back, all acrimonious thoughts gone. She could always see in the small, thin face, the woman who, until the family disasters had occurred, had been so different. This present situation, one that had changed her mother from the beautiful, lively party-giver into an unhappy, possessive person, surely was only temporary. Even after all this time, they all pretended it was only a bad period that had to be lived through with as little resentment as possible. Charlotte told herself she must forget her own ambitions until her mother had returned to her previous independent self. Impulsively, she gave Harriet a hug.

Peter Russell's arrival was announced with the tooting of a car horn and Charlotte saw the grimace of ill

10

humour close up her mother's face. Quickly checking on the dinner, she slipped off the apron she was wearing and opened the front door. Jack Roberts, book-keeper and her uncle's assistant, was helping her uncle out of the car and into his wheelchair. The car belonged to Uncle Peter but since the accident, it was Jack Roberts who was his obliging and amiable chauffeur. She waved at them both, watching as Peter turned his wheelchair efficiently through the gate and propelled himself around the house to the ramp set against the back door. It would be easier for him to enter by the front door, but Harriet refused to have the wooden ramp in view. Peter's disability was something she tried to forget.

Peter looked tired: his eyes were heavy and deeply shadowed with lines of pain. She asked her mother if it was time for another visit to the hospital but Harriet shrugged away all talk of Peter's illness as she always did. Ignore it and it will go away, seemed to be her attitude and nothing Charlotte said could change her mind. Perhaps she would ring the hospital herself and make the necessary appointment. As long as her mother didn't find out. It wasn't that Harriet didn't care about her brother-in-law, Charlotte knew that. Her mother was so afraid of trouble she preferred to pretend it wasn't happening.

The small Welsh town, Bryn Melinau – Hill of Mills – was built on the lower slopes of the hill on which there were the remnants of no less than seven mills.

Joe Llewellyn's workshop was the first – or the last – building on the main road simply named Main Street. There was no through road. The road ended soon after it had crossed the road bridge, narrowing, then becoming nothing more than fingers of tracks stretching more and more tenuously up onto the hill. Some tracks wound easily upward and were passable by bicycle and a few tough farm vehicles, but few cars could manage the steep gradients beyond Mill House, the home of the Russells.

Bryn Melinau was a backwater, surviving for only as long as its young people stayed and accepted its limitations. For hundreds of years it had been a thriving place where farmers for miles around brought their grain for the seven millers to process.

But now the small town had outgrown its usefulness but remained, an area where people lived while they worked in other places, the railway a slender thread that made it possible. It was feared that the town's population would soon shrink lower than a viable number of inhabitants as an increasing number of young people moved away to find more lively and profitable communities.

Some of the people in the isolated villages used bicycles as their only means of transport. With shops delivering everything; bread, grocery rations and vegetables, besides heavier items, this did not present a problem. Which was why Joe did good business selling bicycles and repairing them, with people coming from other towns and villages, drawn by his expertise, fair prices and reliability.

He was painting the front of his shop with cheerful red paint when he saw Charlotte approaching. He smiled, put down his brush and wiped his hands on a rag. Perhaps today was the day to inform Charlotte of his plans.

"Charlotte! This is a pleasant surprise! Let you off the hook, has she? The Dragon?"

Charlotte felt the usual lurch in her heart as his dark eyes creased in a welcoming smile. Why did she ever have doubts? It was only when she was away from him that she began to wonder if perhaps life had something more to offer than marriage to Joe and a comfortable domesticity. She backed away from the kiss that showed on his face. "Joe," she admonished, "someone might see!"

He turned her away from the street and guided her into the porch where, near the front of the window, she could see the display of children's scooters and three-wheelers.

"Afraid in case you lose control, are you?" he teased. "Glad I am that you're here. I was going to call and face the Dragon after closing." He pushed open the shop door and as she passed him, stole a kiss that was aimed at her mouth but which touched her cheek. "*Duw*, your cheek is like ice. Come on, I'll get a cup of tea to warm you. Weak it'll be, mind, my ration is almost gone. Where have you been?"

"Only doing a bit of shopping," she said. "Mam is resting."

"I reckon she does too much of that. But good on her if it means I can see you."

They went into the shop with its smell of rubber, oil and new leather, and into the small "office" which was only a partition in a corner. Joe put the kettle on to boil on a single gas ring which was set in a shallow biscuit tin. Charlotte looked around the orderly display in the shop and noticed an addition to the stock. A man's bicycle stood

13

against the wall, not a new one, but one that she recognised.

"That bike, doesn't it belong to Brian, Rhoda's husband?"

"It did, but not any more, love. Rhoda asked me if I could sell it for her. She doesn't like cycling and she doesn't want Brian to do anything that doesn't include her. More like your Mam than your Mam, that one!" He attended to the kettle that was hissing impatiently. "I gave her six pounds."

"You won't make a profit on that, then!"

"Of course not. She's practically my family, isn't she?" He glanced towards the doorway before kissing her briefly. She responded to his second kiss and clung to him, hidden from anyone passing by the partition.

"Poor Rhoda," she said. "I don't think she and Brian are all that happy. Why else does she spend so much time with Mam? With a beautiful house like theirs down by the river, you'd think she'd want to stay home. Glad I am that she doesn't, mind. With her keeping Mam entertained I have a bit more freedom!"

"Forget about the Dragon. Come here." Joe held her close and thoughts of her mother and Rhoda were forgotten in the warmth of his love and desire. Their kisses created a need in them which, until they were man and wife, had to be ignored. But for both of them the sensations made marriage a more urgent consideration. Charlotte feared the weakness of her body, heightened by her unhappiness and the need to escape. She stepped away, avoiding looking at Joe, knowing he would see the longing in her hazel eyes, unable to trust herself to refuse if he began his persuasions.

To sharpen the mood, guide them away from dangerous waters, she began telling him about the work her uncle was currently doing and her worries about the slackness of the way he was dealing with the orders and accounts. But she could see that Joe had something on his mind and was not really listening to her.

"What is it, Joe?" she asked. "Is something wrong?" The fear of him leaving her made her cling to him again.

"I'm thinking of making a few changes," he said, his lips touching her sweet-scented hair.

Charlotte moved away again, the pulse in her throat powerful and alarming. Forcing her mind away from her treacherous body, she looked at the neatly lined bicycles set up on their blocks. "Changes?" she asked. "What changes? The display is good. If you bring any more items from the stores you'll make it look cluttered and people will be less inclined to come in and look around." He didn't reply and she stepped away from him, glad of the distraction. "I think you should fit a mirror over near the door, mind. So you can watch the shop when you go out the back. People aren't as honest as they once were."

"I don't mean here, in the shop." He handed her a cup of tea and they sat on one of the boxes which held lamp batteries. "I'm selling up. Moving out altogether."

Fear shrank her heart. Was he saying they were to part? The thought of him leaving was a painful one. But alongside it was the other fear, of living with her

15

mother far into the distant future, without a prospect of leaving home and starting out on her own life. The ubiquitous guilt made her turn from him as if he could read the selfish and unloving thought on her face. What was wrong with her? Was it lust she felt and not love? Wasn't she capable of true love, in which the happiness of another was paramount?

"What are you going to do?" she asked in a low voice, surprised at how calm she sounded.

"I want you to come and see something. Can the Dragon spare you for half an hour?"

"What about the shop? You can't close it?"

"Oh yes I can," he said and she heard the smile in his voice as he touched her chin and turned her to face him. "In a couple of months' time it will no longer be mine."

"You've already sold it?"

"Come and see what I've bought in its place."

Ignoring her protests and refusing to tell her anything more, he led her further down the road to the centre of Main Street, where a shop that had once been a butcher's stood empty, the window starkly, coldly white with marble slabs. The name Maldwyn Prosser was sculpted in the centre of the marble edging the window front and still showed the glitter of gold paint.

"You're never going to be a butcher, Joe Llewellyn!"

"That's right. I'm never going to be a butcher. This will be a shop selling motor car spares and oil and polish and all the accessories a growing market of motorists can possibly need. What d'you think?"

"I don't know what to think."

"There's something else I want you to see." He

16

unlocked the door and they went inside. In spite of being empty for several months, the place was clean and fresh. Newspapers covered the newly washed black-and-white tiled floor. Joe guided her through the shop and up the scrubbed wooden stairs to three rooms above. One room was a kitchen. Further stairs led to two more rooms with views across the road and over the town in one direction and across fields towards the river that wound itself around the town, a protective moat, in the other.

"This," Joe said, kissing her gently, "is for us. I want us to marry and make this our first home. I have enough money to buy what we need. Nothing swish, mind, just the essentials. It'll only be a start. In a few years we'll be moving on from this. I have great plans for us, Charlotte, my pretty one. Great plans."

Joe had spent several days clearing out the remnants of the previous occupier and scouring the floors with vim and a hard scrubbing brush, helped by his Auntie Bessie Philpot. He stood back and waited for her enraptured reaction. Instead he got his face slapped.

"Thank you *very* much!" she stormed. "So this is my life is it? All planned out for me and arranged down to the last breath I take, by you and Auntie Bessie Philpot!"

"I thought you'd be pleased!" He was so shocked he hadn't felt the blow for several seconds. Now he rubbed his cheek and stared at her, wide-eyed. "Most girls would be thrilled to have such a surprise."

"Surprise? Shock more like! Why didn't you ask me what I wanted? Oh, lovely this is, you and your

17

Auntie making all the decisions for me! Don't you think I've had enough of people telling me what to do? All my life I've been told what's best for me! Mam does that all the time! Well, when – and *if* – I get married, Joe Llewellyn, it will be when I decide, and where I live will be a shared decision. *Right?*"

"You want time to think about it. I understand that. But don't be too long, the wallpaper is being delivered tomorrow and I want to get started. If you don't want to live here then I won't bother to decorate. *Right?*"

"You've even chosen the wallpaper? This I don't believe." She pushed him out of the way and clattered down the hollow-sounding stairs and out into the street. She felt humiliated. She could see her life drifting from a possessive mother into the hands of an equally possessive husband.

Possessive mother. She had never admitted that before, but that was what her mother was. Possessive. It had taken this foolishness of Joe's to make her see it. Now she had seen it, could she do anything to make sure it didn't continue? She clenched her teeth in a grimace. She could try!

Joe called at Mill House that evening. He crossed his fingers as he knocked on the door, hoping it would be Charlotte and not her mother who opened the door. He gave a wide smile when he saw Charlotte in the light from the hall.

"Sorry. The wallpaper was a joke," he said. "If you don't want to live above an ol' butcher's shop, well, we'll rent it out and find ourselves somewhere else. Come with me tomorrow, my pretty one, and we'll

18

start looking at rooms to rent." He stepped towards her and she ran into his arms.

"I'm sorry Joe. I think the flat will be a perfect home for us."

"Marry me, Charlotte. Don't let's wait until it's all right for your Mam. It will never be all right with your Mam, we both know that. Come with me now and let's discuss our plans."

"It isn't that easy. I'll have to – "

"Who is it, Charlotte?" Her mother's voice made Charlotte pull back from Joe's embrace. "Time you closed that door. The house will be like a cold store!"

"It's Joe, Mam," Charlotte called back.

"Oh."

"Her disapproval of me nearly rips the paint off the door!" Joe chuckled.

"Well," Harriet continued from within the house, "tell him it's very late."

"It's very late," Charlotte joked.

"Tell her we're getting married in three weeks' time and are going to live in a marble hall!" Joe whispered.

Giggling at the butcher's shop being described as a marble hall, they kissed until they were breathless, laughter fading and passion bringing them to a pitch of desire. Then at Harriet's increasing insistence, they said a reluctant good night.

"Tomorrow midday, then?" Joe said, pressing her to him in a way that made her body flood with longing. Charlotte agreed and after one final kiss, rejoined her mother.

"Mam," she said, her face glowing with the suddenness of the decision, "Joe and I are getting married."

"We'll talk about your future, dear, as soon as your father comes home and Uncle Peter is well again."

"Mam, you're not listening. We're getting married and we're going to live above the butcher's shop in Main Street."

"And you think I should take you seriously? Marry that – repair man, and live above a butcher's? Reeks of death, a place like that. No one would ever visit you. Such funny ideas you get, Charlotte. Go and fetch my tablets, will you, dear?"

"I brought them down earlier, here they are." The small victory was without joy.

Charlotte and Joe met as arranged, but Charlotte had lost the impulsive excitement of the previous evening. Her mother had seen to that. Unable to admit her mother's part in her switchback attitude to Joe, she told herself the excitement had only been the relief of making up their quarrel, and knowing he hadn't been so insensitive as to choose the paper to go on their walls.

"I'll have to wait a while, Joe. Until Mam gets used to the idea of my moving from home."

"You wouldn't like me to move into Mill House would you? So she can live my life for me, as well as hers and yours!" This time the joke was a sour one and a glance at his blazing eyes brought out the worst in her. The quarrel was worse than any they'd had. His last words as she stormed off were:

"If you won't make the break and marry me, then get yourself a job. Do something to prove to yourself you aren't spineless. Because that's what I think you are, Charlotte Russell! Spineless!"

She stopped and turned back. Joe prepared for more abuse but what she said was:

"All right! I *will* marry you! We'll go now this minute and talk to the Vicar!"

Sobbing, kissing, apologizing and swearing undying love, they went to the vicarage of the church and made an appointment to discuss and arrange their wedding.

The following morning, two hours later than she had promised to be home, she stepped through the door of Mill House in a state of euphoria. It was done. The long-delayed decision was made and this time she wouldn't be persuaded to alter it. There was nothing her mother could say to make her change her mind. She was strong because she loved Joe.

"Mam," she said as she entered the house, "I don't care what you say. I'm going to marry Joe. I'm past the age of consent and it's all fixed. Right?" Then she saw that her mother was crying. "Mam? What is it?"

"Constable Hardy has just called. Your Uncle Peter has been taken into hospital. Oh, Charlotte! What will become of us? I'm sure he's going to die! Thank goodness Rhoda is away, she's like me, so sensitive she'd be unable to cope. I'm so glad I've got you here. I don't know what I'd do without you here to support me. What were you saying, dear?"

"Nothing, Mam. Nothing important."

Chapter Two

Joe's Auntie Bessie Philpot had arrived for work at Mill House while Charlotte and Joe were discussing their future. The gates had just come into her view as the ambulance was leaving. She had watched the ambulance drive past and a frown crossed her plump face as she glanced towards the gates of Mill House. It seemed to have come from there. And there was nowhere else apart from the Russells' factory. A walker perhaps? Daft beyond, they were, walking the hills in January!

Could it have been poor Peter Russell? Then it might have been Harriet. Grizzling herself into an early grave for sure, that one! Whatever, she would still be needed to do the Friday cleaning. Curiosity hastened her footsteps as she pushed through the gate and hurried up the drive.

The door of the house was closed and she withdrew her key from the pocket of her ancient tweed coat. Then she thought it wiser to knock, just in case there was someone left at home. Even after all the years she had looked after the Russells, Harriet could be very sharp when she thought someone had overstepped the boundaries of respectful behaviour! There was no reply and she opened the door and called, "*Bore da*, Mrs Russell, it's only me, ol' Bessie Philpot come to sort you out." Humming tunelessly, she bustled into the kitchen and began to gather the dusters and brushes she needed.

She started as always with the bathroom, and, still humming, she washed and shone the surfaces and wiped the linoleum, leaving the room clean and smelling of disinfectant. There had been no sign of anyone being home. Perhaps the ambulance *had* been leaving Mill House. Well, it was an ill wind. She would treat herself to a sly cup of tea before anyone turned up. Mrs Russell watched her like a slave master, making sure she didn't get less work than she paid for, and she guarded her ration of tea and sugar like an old ogre. *Pisio crics* it was when Mrs Russell made it. Although cricket's pee was probably stronger! The opportunity of getting away with an extra tea-break was irresistible.

The humming stopped as she went into the kitchen and put on the kettle, muttering to herself as usual about the cranky kettle that wobbled on the jet and the state of the ancient stove with which the family managed. For people who considered themselves a bit above the rest, they had no idea about some things. Tatty ol' stove and battered pans . . . talk about fur coat and no knickers! While she waited for the water to boil, she went into the parlour to see if there were ashes from last night's fire to lift, box for the ashes, dustpan and brush and floorcloth in her arms. She started with shock. Mrs Russell was there, sitting in a chair staring out of the window. She had a blanket around her and her face showed signs of tears.

"I – just put the kettle on, now this minute," Bessie said briskly after a moment of embarrassment. "Peeked in and saw you I did, and thought – a good strong cuppa is just what she needs by the look of her. I was worried it might have been you or Mr Peter in that there ambulance I did. *Duw*, there's a shock this time of the day. Who was it then? Have you heard? Some *twp* ol' walker was it?"

"It was Peter," Harriet whispered.

"Never! And you not able to go with him?" In sepulchral tones she added, "There's a pity." Going into the kitchen to deal with the kettle she called back, "Have to wait for Charlotte to come back, I suppose. Get a taxi, go on. I'll wait by yer till your Charlotte comes home. Still with my Joe, I expect."

"She isn't with your nephew! She went shopping." Even in her shocked state Harriet corrected any inference that her daughter was involved with that awful bicycle repair man.

"Shopping in an empty butcher's shop they were then. Funny the way some folks carry on, isn't it?" Bessie said, quickly adding, "Two sugars is it then? We need it for the shock, we do."

Bessie Philpot was a buxom woman, looking younger than her fifty-eight years, with a smooth, pink complexion and hair that was still fair, although untidy and fly-away. She was the town's express news reporter, spreading the latest goings on in the houses where she cleaned. The people down in the town loved to hear the latest gossip about "them up there" in the larger houses on the hill. It was Bessie's life-long commitment that they wouldn't be disappointed.

This was some carry on for a start. Peter Russell, poor dab, taken to hospital, and his sister-in-law, who depended on him for providing them all with a living, sitting here crying tears that were for herself and not for him. Bessie sniffed as she remembered when he'd had the accident that had crippled him. Harriet, his only relative since his brother had wandered off in a miasma of lost memory, never went near him all the time he was in hospital. There's a family for you!

She added saccharin to Mrs Russell's tea and stirred two heaped teaspoons of sugar into her own. Didn't deserve sugar, she didn't. Selfish ol' snob that she was, treating her Joe as if he were dirt.

"There you are, lovely, drink this down and it'll warm the cockles of your 'eart," she smiled, handing Harriet her cup.

After her three hours' work was finished, Bessie repeated her offer to stay while Harriet went to the hospital to be with her brother-in-law. When she had made Harriet admit that she wasn't going to see him, Bessie smiled a satisfied smile. Now she could say with honesty that Mrs Russell admitted she wasn't going to visit him and stand beside his sick bed. Poor dab.

The walk down the steep hill and through the town was punctuated with brief visits to some of her friends to impart the disgraceful news. Kath, who ran the boarding house near the road bridge, Vi and Willie Walters who ran the café and her closest friend and next-door neighbour, Bertha Evans, were all equally shocked, bemusedly agreeing with Bessie when she added that it was no more than they might expect of a woman who changed her beds twice a week.

When she reached home, Bessie sat and enjoyed

a snack and a cup of tea, then set off to do her collections. It was Friday and she needed to get around as many of her catalogue customers as possible, before the wages were doled out and the spare used up. Missing a weekly payment was the lot of those collectors who called last and Bessie made sure it was rarely her. No time for a proper chat on Fridays. "Headlines only" was her golden rule.

The cottage in which she lived was one of a pair close to the smaller, older bridge upstream of the town, simply called Bridge Cottages. Bessie lived with her nephew Joe in number one and her friend Bertha Evans lived in the other with her slow and amiable daughter Lillian. Across the river from them, high on the hill, Mill House could be seen.

Downstream of the town was the coracle station where the small, fragile river craft set out to catch the salmon that leapt the distant falls and came up to spawn in the shallower water beyond Bessie's cottage, where the river widened.

Bessie's first call that cold January evening was on Kath Thomas who lived at number one, Main Street. One of Kath's lodgers was Jack Roberts who helped Peter Russell at the bookbinding factory. Bessie picked up the weekly shilling-in-the-pound payment and an order for some matting and a new kettle, and hurried on.

At five o'clock it was very dark outside. She carried a pair of men's shoes under her arm, an order from Vi Walters for her husband Willie. Wrapping her coat around her legs, poking the darkness with the thin beam of a torch, she left Kath's warm room and set off for her next call.

Vi and Willie lived just around the corner, down-stream from Main Street, in Betws Villas, nicknamed Tatws Villas, as Willie ate only chips and Vi survived on a diet of mashed potatoes. Best she went there first and got rid of the shoe box. But they were good payers. No, she would be better starting with some of the other, less reliable ones. She eventually decided to go first to the furthest call. That way she would be heading for home, a cheering thought on such a dark, bitterly cold night.

At seven o'clock she turned for home. She hadn't called on all her customers but the cold was biting into her hands and the shoe box was a nuisance to carry. She decided to go and have a cup of tea, then call back on some she had missed.

Leaving the lights of Main Street behind her, she turned onto the narrow path and hurried through the darkness towards Bridge Cottages. The river was on her left and now, with the bushes and grasses bare, she could see occasional glimpses of the steely cold water. The torch was inadequate for the lonely path and she was glad when she saw the light shining out of Bertha's windows like a welcoming beacon. No light in her own; that meant Joe wasn't home.

While she was still some distance from the twin gates, a sound made her stop. Curious as always, she twisted her torch in the direction of the sound. Perhaps it was Joe. He could carry these damned shoes if it was.

"'Oo is it?" Then she gasped as her torch showed two men struggling on the ground, grunting and hitting out at each other. In the flurry of arms and legs she failed to recognise them. Trying to appear brave, she called out:

"Stop behaving like a couple of tomcats! Get on 'ome with you or I'll fetch a copper!"

The men separated and moved in opposite directions, one limping heavily to his left. In vain she waved her torch, searching for a sign of them. She felt the chill of fear. They could see her but she couldn't see them. She told herself they had done as she had said and gone home, yet apart from the quiet murmur of the river, the night was without sound. Surely she would have heard them running off? "I know who you are, so don't think I don't!" Shaking the torch to try and persuade it to give more light, she walked along the path towards the cottages, wishing Joe was there, trying to give an impression of nonchalance, strongly aware of being watched. She felt a vulnerable spot in the area of her shoulder blades and very much alone. The night was as black as her coal hole. Her gate and Bertha's lights seemed a long way off.

She began to hum to cheer herself but her voice sounded unnaturally loud. She stopped and the silence was unnerving. Fighting they were, no doubt about that, and one was hurt, favouring his left leg he was, for sure. Increasing her pace, she began to prepare the story she would tell Bertha, poor simple Lillian, and Joe.

The eerie silence was broken by furtive rustling in the dead grasses and wild flowers on the edge of the path. Fallen branches, made brittle by the frost, snapped like miniature guns. Her heart tightened and she waved the torch around again in a futile way. She couldn't go into her empty house.

"Bertha?" she called, running now towards the lit windows. "Open up the door, will you? It's me, Bessie." She was touching the gate, feeling safety was only a few steps away, when she felt an arm grab her from behind. She took a deep breath to scream, but before she could make a sound her head was thrown sideways with a blow that knocked her senseless.

Joe was disappointed. Because of her Uncle Peter's illness, Charlotte had put aside their marriage plans without discussion. He understood of course, but it was difficult not to feel resentment. He wondered if there would ever be a time when she didn't put her family duties before him. Tonight there had been yet another abandoned arrangement. She had left a note with his Auntie Bessie to cancel their trip into town to see a film. Perhaps he'd write up his accounts so he'd be free on Sunday. Mr Russell would be better by then, sure to be. Perhaps they could go out for the day.

He whistled as he approached the pair of cottages, his bicycle wheels making a crisp, crunchy accompaniment on the ice-bound earth. His auntie would be settling down for an evening listening to the radio. Two of her favourite comedy programmes were on on Fridays. *Up the Pole* with Claude Dampier and *Over the Garden Wall* with Norman Evans. Perhaps he'd listen to Norman Evans himself. He was quite a turn.

He realised there was no light showing and thought with dismay that she had gone out collecting and had stayed with one of her friends for a gossip. He didn't fancy an evening on his own. He paused, wondering if there was any point in cycling back up to Mill House to talk to Charlotte. He shrugged and walked on, propping his bike against the wall ready for the next day. He almost fell over as his foot caught against something near the gate. He staggered and swore, thinking someone had deposited some rubbish on the path. Then he went closer and realised he had been tripped by the coat of someone lying on the icy ground. His first thought was that it must be a drunk. He lifted the limp body and turned the head so he could see by the light from Bertha's window and was startled to recognise his aunt. As he moved her she began to groan.

"Auntie Bessie! What happened? Frozen you must be lying there. Are you ill?"

"Dying, boy. Dying."

"I heard one of them call the other one 'Jack'. And that's all I remember," Bessie told the doctor when she had recovered and was sitting in Joe's favourite armchair being served tea by Bertha Evans from next door. "Big they were, mind. And not a word from them apart from one of them saying 'that's enough' and 'Jack'." She sighed and passed her cup to Bertha for more tea. "*Duw*, if Joe had been off to the pictures instead of coming home for his tea I'd have died of the cold for sure."

"Jack?" Bertha queried. "Do we know a Jack?"

"There's only Jack Roberts who works with Peter Russell in the bookbinders, but you can count him out," Joe said. "One of life's gentlemen is Jack Roberts. Not the sort to go fighting down dark footpaths and hitting poor helpless women."

"I don't think I know another Jack," Bessie

frowned. "He must have been a stranger. No one round here would behave like that."

"There are several families that have been up in court for fighting, mind."

"Yes, but only good, honest drunks. Not wicked beaters-up of helpless women."

"And thieving," Joe added.

"Damn me!" Bessie moaned. "I bet they were after my collections. Where's my bag? It's gone!"

"It's here," Joe laughed. "You were hanging on to the strap for grim death. Had to prise it away from you one finger at a time!"

"Not much there, and I can't go back for second calls, not tonight, I'm too shook up." She lowered her voice to its lowest and said, "There's a pity." She looked at Joe hopefully. "I'll never get it all tomorrow. You know what some folk are for spending it all on a Friday."

"All right, if Bertha will stay and keep an eye on you," Joe sighed, after a pleading glance from his aunt. "Give me your list." Quickly finishing the snack Bertha had set out for him, he shrugged on his coat and mounted his bicycle.

Low clouds made the moonless night even darker. Leaving his cycle and walking down one of the back lanes was like walking into a cupboard. There were few street lights to disperse the gloom once he left Main Street and Joe wondered how they had ever managed when there were no lights at all. For the long years of the war it had been forbidden to show a light, yet they had managed.

A man appeared in front of him suddenly and Joe couldn't hold back a gasp of fright.

"Sorry to frighten you, mate," the man said. "I wonder if you can tell me how I get to Barry?"

"The buses aren't very frequent at this time of night. Your best bet is the train." Joe directed him along Main Street to the edge of the town and the station. The man thanked him and faded once again into the darkness, appearing as a brief silhouette when he reached the street light on the corner.

Joe wondered if the stranger was one of the men who had been seen fighting. Trying to remember what he could about the man, he decided he was young, perhaps early twenties. He was about Joe's own height, five feet ten and although he must allow for the man having been dressed in several layers against the cold weather, he had the impression the man was heavily built. His accent suggested he came from somewhere not too far away, Cardiff perhaps, or Newport. Although having asked for Barry it seemed possible he was from there. Not much to go on. If only there had been some light.

After calling on all the houses on Bessie's list, he cycled home. It was getting late, almost ten o'clock, but as he was about to turn right off Main Street onto the narrow path he changed his mind and rode over the bridge, heading for Mill House. Perhaps there was better news of Charlotte's Uncle Peter.

Charlotte opened the door and they allowed themselves a brief moment before Joe was invited in to the house.

"Don't let him stay too long, dear," was Harriet's greeting.

"She doesn't talk to me, have you noticed?" Joe whispered. "Talks *about* me she does, as if I'm dull, daft or deaf! Treats me worse than poor Lillian; she only shouts at her! Any chance of a cup of tea?" he said aloud. He went to follow Charlotte into the kitchen but was stopped by Harriet.

"No, come here. You can talk to me while Charlotte sees to the tea."

Guessing it was an attempt to stop him spending a few minutes with Charlotte alone, he grinned at her, then sat dutifully in front of Harriet.

"How is Mr Russell then?" Joe asked. "I'll call in to the hospital on Sunday if he isn't home by then, shall I?"

"Rhoda and Brian are abandoning their holiday and they'll be home. Charlotte insisted they were told. They'll be there with Charlotte, so there's no need for you to bother."

"We'll go together then. We can go on our bikes."

"Charlotte will be going with Rhoda and Brian. In their car."

"There's nice. We'll all visit together, he'll like that for sure." Joe still smiled but there was determination in his dark eyes. "Rhoda and Brian. Me and Charlotte. Right?"

"Yes, well, very nice." Harriet admitted defeat.

"I'm coming with you to see your uncle on Sunday, Charlotte," he said, as he took the proffered cup. "You and me, Rhoda and Brian. We could stop off somewhere after and have some tea. What d'you think?"

"I can't be too long, Mam will want to hear how he is." Charlotte looked at her mother, at the tight lips, and wondered what had been said. "Perhaps another day, Joe."

34

"Sunday. You and me," he said firmly. "We have a lot to talk over, you and me." He was emphasizing the fact that he and Charlotte were a couple. Sooner the Dragon got used to the sound of it the better.

He told them where he had been and about the attack on his aunt.

"Auntie Bessie? Is she all right?" Charlotte asked.

"Will she be able to come in on Monday to do the washing?" was Harriet's question.

Rhoda managed to look tearful, brave and distressed without disturbing her carefully applied make-up. Expensively dressed hair immaculately groomed, she turned heads as they walked through the green-tiled corridors of the hospital.

"She should never have been told," Brian muttered to Joe.

"I agree," Joe said grimly. "Charlotte has enough to do without having Rhoda around flopping a fit every ten minutes!"

"I'll pretend I didn't hear that, Joe!"

Peter Russell was still very ill, but he was pleased to see the four young people. He looked different. His face was still swollen from the kidney infection that had brought him there, and he had an air of weariness about him. Charlotte was startled to see how old he looked. Even in a wheelchair, he had always been lively and alert and full of exciting plans for the future. Recently that had changed and she wondered if this was a result of the illness or if the situation regarding the business was more serious than she already feared.

He seemed a bit vague, his eyes losing focus in

35

middle distance; occasionally he seemed unaware of their presence in the room. Charlotte asked several times if there was something he was worried about, but he shook his head and forced his tired eyes to smile. "Terrible headache, that's all," he told her.

Rhoda took one look at him and burst into tears. For the rest of the visit she sat on a chair further down the ward being consoled by Brian. Occasionally she would come and kiss her uncle, then tears would again overwhelm her and she would clutch Brian for more comfort. Peter smiled at her behaviour and said:

"She's always been the more sensitive one."

"Pain in the arse more like," Joe whispered to Charlotte.

"You're the one we all rely on, Charlotte," Peter added. "I can always depend on you. In the house and at the factory you are our 'Girl Friday'." With Rhoda out of the way he seemed to rally and said, "Take the business. You're the one to help sort it, you know. Been up there lately? There's still a bit of a backlog on the monthly statements going out."

"I keep trying to go up there and get the accounts up to date, but Mam doesn't want me to leave her. You know what she's like. And with Rhoda away it's been more difficult than usual. Don't worry about it, Uncle Peter. It'll soon get sorted once you're back at work. Until then I'm sure Jack Roberts is doing his best. He's so reliable. Lucky we are to have him."

"Yes." There was something in the way Peter said the single word that make Charlotte wonder if there was something she hadn't been told. Her uncle seemed unwilling to talk when Rhoda returned for another tearful session, and after a while he asked

36

Rhoda and Brian to wait outside while he talked to Joe and Charlotte.

"It's the business," he began. "There's a lack of money and if I take any more out the firm will have to close. Don't tell your mother, she can't cope with any more at present."

"What d'you mean, take out any more money?" Charlotte asked. "You only take your wages. Are you saying there isn't enough for you to take wages?"

"I had to repay some of the shares owned by Jack Roberts last month and today he came in and asked that I repay the rest. I don't know what to do." He stirred in the bed, leaned on his elbows and tried to pull himself higher on the pillows with his strong arms. "Sorry to tell you two all this, but there isn't anyone else. Talk to Jack, will you? Ask him to wait for his money, just for a year. We'll be solvent again by then."

When they left the ward Rhoda demanded, "What did he tell you? He isn't going to get well again, is he? Oh, poor Uncle Peter. What will we do when he's gone?"

"Like mother like daughter!" Joe whispered.

"Stop this, Rhoda," Charlotte said firmly. "Uncle Peter is improving and hopes to be home with us again in less than a week. What he wanted to talk to Joe and me about was business. Business. You know, the stuff that fills your pockets but bores you stupid."

They walked to the nearest café for a much-needed cup of tea, but Rhoda wouldn't stop sobbing.

"I know you aren't telling me the truth. People always want to protect me."

By the time they parted, Joe and Charlotte to cycle

home, Rhoda and Brian to go by car, Charlotte felt exhausted.

"I wonder why Jack Roberts wants to take his money out of the business," Charlotte said. "He bought himself in as a partner just after the war. I thought he was content."

"He is sixty-two. Perhaps he wants to retire and do something with his life before his health gives out."

"But take out all the money when he knows it's so difficult?"

"You have to do what's best for yourself sometimes, and for Jack Roberts the time has come for him to break away and do something else. Perhaps he wants to travel. It's getting easier every day now to go abroad."

"I doubt that. He seems the type to stay home. He's involved in so many things. The youth club, the church and the choir. No, there must be a more serious reason. Why could he need money so badly he'd risk ruining the family business?"

"Gambling? Women? Debts? There aren't that many possibilities," Joe mused. "I've never heard of him backing horses, there doesn't seem to be a woman in his life and what debts could he incur? He lives in one room in Kath Thomas's boarding house and once his rent and board are paid he doesn't have anything more to pay for. He walks to work so he doesn't even have to find a bus fare!"

"Best we talk to him," Charlotte said. "If I can persuade Mam I have to go to the office for a while!"

"I'll come with you. Perhaps if we went to see him at home this evening . . . After he's been to church would be a good time?"

It was raining, a cold, steady drizzle that had continued without ceasing all day. They both had waterproof capes but the water splashed up from the road as well as pouring from the skies and they were soaking wet and chilled when they returned to Mill House.

"No sympathy you'll get from me," Harriet sighed. "Deserve to be uncomfortable, refusing a lift with your sister and going all that way on a bicycle. But then," she added, "what can you expect if you waste your time with a repair man?"

At her boarding house near the road bridge, Kath opened the door to them at seven that evening and invited them in.

"How's your poor auntie, Joe? There's a carry on. Two young men onto one helpless woman. What a disgrace."

"Young, were they?" Joe frowned. "I wonder if one was a tall, well-built man of about twenty?"

"Now how can I answer that, boy?" Hands on hips, she glared at him as if he were stupid. "I never saw nothing. It's your auntie you'll have to ask!" She looked at him as they entered her private sitting room and asked, "Why you asking? Got anyone in mind, have you?"

"Not really, but I saw someone later that night, a tall, young chap. He asked the way to Barry and I directed him to the station. Stranger he was."

"Best you tell Constable Hardy then. He's been here asking if any strangers have stayed recently. Told him no, but he'd want to know about the man you saw."

Kath was a round-faced woman with pale skin which shone, Joe thought, as if she polished it along with the furniture. Dark eyes shone too, beneath shaggy brows, and thick brown hair framed her thin features in luxuriant waves. An attractive woman, but one who seemed uninterested in finding a second husband to replace her Cedric, who had died at Passchendaele. Joe asked if Jack Roberts was in, although from the position of the chairs and Jack's glasses resting on the table beside one of them, it seemed likely Jack had recently vacated it. Perhaps Jack was the reason she had so long refrained from remarrying, he mused.

"Down for a cup of tea he'll be in a minute. Just gone up to take off his Sunday-best suit," Kath poked her head out of the living room door and called, and from above they heard Jack's quiet, polite voice reply.

Jack Roberts was a rather handsome man, grey hair still thick, face smooth, with skin that always looked slightly tanned, even in mid-winter. His mouth had a generous fullness and was topped by a slim, carefully shaped moustache that gave him the look of an ageing film star. He was not tall, about five feet six inches, and sturdily built, even a little overweight, yet with an elegance about him that made women turn their heads and hope for a smile. Men found him pleasant company and children flocked around him whenever he visited families on church business.

His greeting to Charlotte and Joe was warm and friendly.

"There's lovely to see two charming young people

when I thought my day was over! Called to let us know how Bessie is doing, I expect?"

"Well, yes, partly that," Charlotte explained, "but also because Peter asked us to talk to you."

"Oh. Business!" Kath said, rising from her chair. "I'll make myself scarce then, is it?"

"Perhaps we could go to my room." He quirked an eyebrow at Kath for permission.

"Go on, I'll bring up your teas in about ten minutes."

Jack Roberts' room was as neat as the man. Shelves held an orderly row of books, including theology, and bibles in both Welsh and English. A rack of shoes, all neatly polished, was visible below a curtain which, presumably, hid his clothes. An old trunk stood in a corner piled with freshly laundered sheets and pillow cases. Ready, Charlotte supposed, for the Monday morning change of bedding.

A chair was facing the electric fire and, at its side was a table, on which was an open book. Nothing was out of place. Yet it was a friendly room, neither formal nor uninviting.

Charlotte came straight to the point. "Uncle Peter's worried about your wanting to take your investment out of the firm," she began, when they were all seated. "It's an awkward time and well – " She looked at Joe for support.

"He wondered if you could be persuaded to wait, just a few months, a year at the most, until the firm is in a better position to cope with it. Question of cash flow," Joe went on. "I know, being in business myself, just how much money you need just lying idle

41

as it were, to cover slow payers and the expense of holding stock."

"He buys too much at a time," Jack Roberts said, smiling.

"To get better prices," Charlotte said defensively.

"He carries too much stock. It isn't better prices if you have to have a bank loan to cover the money lying idle. There's a need to consider all aspects you see."

"Are you saying he isn't running the firm properly?" Charlotte was beginning to feel loyal anger rising and she looked again at Joe, wanting him to protest.

"He runs the firm as it has always been run, my dear. But that's no longer enough. A change is long overdue."

"What do you mean? Russell's is famous for quality work. Most of our work is done by hand. How can you change that?" Charlotte demanded.

"During the war all firms had to change their attitudes and their methods. The number of books your father produced was drastically reduced. He had to go over to making booklets and pamphlets of government information, anything he could get. When the war ended, most firms grabbed back much of the business they had lost and, well, your father was gone by then and your uncle is too much a gentleman for the fierce tactics needed to fight for his share."

"What do you think he should do?" Joe asked quietly.

"I've only been with him for five years so I don't think I should presume to – " He smiled gently at Charlotte. "It's for your uncle to decide, my dear."

"And you won't consider leaving your money

where it is, for a few months at least?" Joe asked. Jack shook he head sadly.

"I don't consider my money is in the best place any longer. Besides, if you can keep a secret, I'll tell you what I plan to do with it." He tapped the side of his nose in an unmistakable gesture and tiptoed to the door. Opening it, he smiled and said, "Thank you Mrs Thomas, our tea. You are very kind." Taking the tray, he firmly closed the door against her and put the tray down on a small table.

He didn't speak for a while, listening until he heard the creak of the stairs as Kath, finally giving up hope of some interesting eavesdropping, went back to her kitchen.

"There's a young man who I have known for many years who needs help. I think, with a little financial assistance, he will do well. I want to be the one to put him on the road to a successful future. He has a family that, without my help, will live in abysmally poor conditions. *With* my help, they will have a good home and a business to keep them solvent."

"Relation, is he?" Joe asked.

"No," Jack replied with a smile, "just someone in need."

"That's commendable, Mr Roberts," Joe said, "but in helping them you will possibly see Peter Russell and his family having to sell up their home."

"They will never be as desperate as this young man and his family. As for Peter Russell's problem, I think Charlotte here could turn the business around in less than a year."

"Me?"

"Why not you? Surely you aren't one of these who think a woman's place is in the home? I'd have thought taking over your father's business was what you were best suited for, my dear. What about you, Joe, don't you think Charlotte has a head for business?"

"I think Charlotte could do anything she set her mind to do." Joe smiled proudly at Charlotte and she felt a warm glow of love spreading between them.

"I couldn't," she said, but her eyes were filled with excitement. Perhaps this was what she had been looking for. A business to build, and one about which she already knew a great deal, thanks to the hours spent with first her father then her uncle. Then the glow faded. "Mam wouldn't be willing, for a start."

"Think about it, and," Jack whispered, "not a word about what I told you."

"Then you can't help Mr Russell?" Joe asked.

Jack shook his head. "I am sorry."

It was as they rose to leave that Charlotte saw the bruise on the left side of Jack Roberts' jaw.

"Good heavens, Mr Roberts! Don't tell me you've been fighting as well!"

"There's no one in the world to whom I could feel enough anger to make me fight." He rubbed his chin ruefully. "This happened when I trod on the cord of my dressing gown and fell down the last three stairs. Poor Kath, she thought the house was falling down!" he laughed.

"So," Joe said as they set off for Mill House, "Jack Roberts isn't going to change his mind. I wonder just how serious the situation is?"

Charlotte didn't reply and when Joe looked at her she seemed to be in a daze.

"Charlotte?"

"I'm wondering if I could persuade Mam to let me help and eventually take over Russell's Bookbinders and Restorers," Charlotte said slowly, her eyes shining.

"You don't really want to work all your life, do you?" Joe said. "What about me? Us? I want you, Charlotte. I want you in our home, minding our children and – "

"Cooking your meals?"

"What's wrong with that?"

"Nothing's wrong with that. What *is* wrong, is you thinking we can't achieve both!"

They were silent as they made their way through the town, cycling over the road bridge and dismounting as the hill steepened. At her gate, Joe pulled her towards him. "I love you Charlotte, I always have. Whatever happens; I always will."

They kissed passionately and her body cried out for him as strongly as ever, but when they parted at her door, she said quietly, "Do you love me enough to allow me to be myself, Joe? To share in all our decisions? Or is your love the convenient sort that wants my love to be submissive, that will mould me into the character that suits you best?"

"I love *you*. Everything else can be sorted. Trust me."

Thoughts of running the family firm excited her. She knew now without any doubt that it was what she wanted to do. And parallel to that revelation, loud and firm, came the knowledge that she didn't want to lose Joe to achieve it. He was as important to her as becoming a businesswoman in her own right. Under her breath she whispered: I hope I can trust you with my life, Joe Llewellyn, I hope I can.

Chapter Three

Snow began to fall in the village and was added to over several days. A wind increased the difficulties of travel by creating mountains of snow against every possible object. The hills were invisible under the heavy opaque air for most of the day and when glimpses were seen nothing looked the same. Blizzards had created caverns where there were none and great monoliths that looked solid but which melted and changed their shape in the first increase in temperature.

To Charlotte it was a beautiful sight and as soon as she was able, she walked up the hill and looked down on the town. Patchwork buildings, half hidden by the white covering, looked like ruins, their shape distorted by the snow and the blue shadows. The roads, made safe with the addition of sand and gravel, were arteries of drabness. Waste ground and the school sports field were still white and unmarked and the river glistened like an exotic bejewelled snake.

Refreshed and strangely excited, Charlotte didn't go home. She went instead along the lane, half filled with the now discoloured snow, and went to the factory. She was greeted by Jack, who arranged for tea and settled her in front of the electric fire.

"It was too good to miss," she said when he had heard about her walk. "And I wasn't ready to go home."

"While you're here why don't you look at some of the jobs we're setting up?"

He led her into the noisy workroom where hammers knocked the backs of books to "round" them, before finishing the job on the Starr Backer that had been working there for almost a hundred years. The Johnie Perfecta guillotine chuntered away and several other machines added to the din. She stopped for a moment and watched a machine clanging its rhythmic beat as it sewed sections of a book. The operator threw the sections onto the saddle, then waited while it was stitched before throwing on the next section. When the book was completed, the girl pulled the saddle forward to separate it before beginning another book.

Charlotte felt the usual excitement as she stood amid the activity and absorbed the percussion of the place, almost getting a hint of a melody from the heavy machines and the lighter banging of the hammers. Her own heart joined in the music and she knew that this was truly where she belonged. Jack looked at her and smiled, understanding the excitement she felt.

In various parts of the same room, people were doing quiet jobs, like folding and creasing pages with the bone-folder, glueing the end papers, putting muslin on the spines and shoulders, unperturbed by the noise. They didn't try to talk but occasionally mouthed a few words and laughter lit their faces. The workers were a team. If only she could become one of them.

In spite of the impression given by the noise of heavy machines, much of the work was done by hand. In one corner, experienced women placed boards on the leather-cloth covers, evenly and accurately each time, cutting the corners and turning in the cover so that the overlap was even, with never a mistake. Charlotte watched for a while in fascination.

A new job that Jack wanted her to see was the book of flower prints her uncle had shown her. Jack turned the book for her to see. It was a collection of water-colours, each page having its own semitransparent protective leaf. Some of the protective paper had become stuck to the painting, leaving a number of small fluffy patches. Gaynor Edwards, who was working on it, smiled and moved so that Charlotte could see the beautiful flower prints.

Jack explained that the painting had been enhanced with gum arabic and left closed for many years and this had caused the damage, which the young woman was carefully removing.

"But I don't understand," Charlotte frowned. "This job was underway weeks ago. Long before Uncle Peter was taken ill. I saw him working on it myself."

"We've only just found it. Packed away in a drawer instead of being with the 'work in hand'. If I hadn't been searching for some fresh rolls of Crompton Tissue for page repairs on a new job I wouldn't have found it," Jack said. "I didn't know you'd seen them. Don't be upset about your uncle, my dear," Jack said gently. "He's unwell and a bit absent-minded, that's all. Nothing for you to worry about. I just thought you'd enjoy looking at the paintings and seeing how well Mrs Gaynor Edwards is dealing with them." He went on to describe how they would be rebound and the cover replaced.

"Thank you for showing me. I do think they're beautiful. But when was the work promised? A month ago?"

"Probably longer," Jack admitted.

"I'll work on in the evenings if you like, Miss Russell, get it finished a few days earlier then," Gaynor Edwards offered. "All right?"

"Thank you. That would be a help."

"Anything for Mr Peter, isn't it, Jack?"

"Miss Charlotte knows that," Jack smiled.

Charlotte's mood was changed. The delight of the walk on the hill was ruined by the reminder that all was far from well in the business. Jack was an accountant yet he was having to arrange the work, search out jobs that had been abandoned or forgotten, keep the orders moving and deal with the replacement of fresh stock. It was crazy that she was unable to help. Gaynor Edwards had been with the firm since she was fourteen and at thirty-nine was a valued employee, but even she needed to be told what to do and when. How much longer could things continue like this without the whole thing grinding to a halt?

"Oh, Miss!" Gaynor called, as Charlotte was putting on her coat. "There's sorry I am, but I've just remembered. We can't work on tonight. Jack and I run the Wednesday meeting at the church. Youth Choir it is. The youngsters won't be very pleased if Jack isn't there to put them through their paces and I'm not there to see to the refreshments. Tomorrow will be all right though."

"Thank you, Mrs Edwards. I appreciate how much you do for us."

Charlotte had the feeling that there was more between the two people than just assisting at the church meeting. Nothing said, just something in the way they looked at each other, a signal, a secret smile. But she was so wrapped in her worries about the firm that the feeling slipped away and didn't take root in her memory.

Instead, she thought about Jack's thoughtfulness, and his secret generosity in wanting to spend his money giving a destitute family a better life. Good deeds done in secret were the finest of all, she decided. He wanted no one told. It was sufficient for him to know he was helping someone. He didn't need the glory of publicity, the flattery of people's admiration. How fortunate they were that he was there to help them.

The snow cleared, Peter returned to work and things settled into an uneasy peace at Mill House. It seemed a good time for Joe and Charlotte to make their plans. But every time Charlotte tried to discuss her marriage, the response was the same.

"How can you think of yourself now, while your father is still missing and your uncle so ill?"

Ashamed of her selfishness, Charlotte reported back to Joe that, "Now isn't a good time."

The sale of Joe's shop was underway and whenever she could, Charlotte went to help him prepare for his move into the old butcher's shop. Legally the shop was not his but the owner, old Maldwyn Prosser, had no objection to his going in and working there. Joe did some decorating but made little effort to furnish the flat.

"I want us to do that together," he said, on one of their rare moments alone. He was papering the walls of the living room a bright yellow, and Charlotte had been washing the drips of paste from the fresh brown woodwork.

"I'll make covers for the chairs to match the curtains," she promised.

While he packed away his brushes, she stood on a rickety old chair to check the measurements. As she was getting down he held her, turned her to face him and kissed her with an urgency that both thrilled and half frightened her. He wasn't going to force her, was he? Men did sometimes lose restraint, she knew that much.

"Joe, you're hurting me," she protested, but she didn't attempt to move from his arms.

He pushed her away then and spoke angrily. "Charlotte, this is madness. Utter madness that we're allowing ourselves to put up with this! I want you. I can't wait for ever. How much longer are you going to give her before you defy her and marry me without her permission? We will marry, we both know that, so why put ourselves through this? Fuss there'll be if we defy her now or in ten years' time, so there's no point in waiting, is there? Get it over and done with. Legally she can't stop us anyway. Twenty-three you are, not sixteen."

"Pity we didn't marry when I was sixteen, Joe." She sighed. "Mam's so changed since Dad's disappearance and Uncle Peter's accident."

"But don't you see? That's *her* life! This is ours,

52

here, making our own way in the world. You're allowing her to live your life as well as her own. That can't be right, now can it? Selfish ol' cat that she is."

She wanted to say yes, she'd ignore the needs of her mother and do what he wanted; that it was what she wanted too. But her sense of duty was strong and she knew that once away from his hypnotic kisses she would have to refuse. It was a sacrifice she had to make or she would regret it all her life.

"It's only until Mam accepts that Dad won't ever come back."

"Charlotte, my pretty," he said more calmly, "it's been seven years!"

"Just a bit longer, please Joe."

Bessie Philpot was leaving the post office, next door to Kath Thomas's boarding house, when she saw a new notice pinned on the wall. She was so finely attuned to what was going on, she recognised a fresh notice immediately.

"What's this then?" she asked the postmistress, tapping the handwritten poster. "A trip to Barry Island is it? When is it for? Your writing is getting worse, Phoebe."

"I didn't write it and the date is April the ninth, Easter Saturday. The seats are mostly booked so you'll have to say quick if you're wanting to go!"

"Of course I'm wanting to go. Don't I always go?" She dug into her handbag and took out the five shillings. "I hope that includes supper," she grumbled.

"Of course it does. Doesn't it always include

53

supper?" retaliated the postmistress. She wrote the name in a small notebook and whispered to her next customer, "One of these days we'll manage to get off on a day trip without having clecking Bessie Philpot to pester us."

"What a hope!" was the response.

Charlotte and Joe were waiting to buy some stamps. Charlotte chuckled with the rest at the long-running feud between Joe's aunt and the postmistress and when she had been served turned to Joe, her eyes sparkling.

"What about our going on a trip to the seaside?" she said.

"Oh yes? And what do we tell your Mam?"

"Ah well, it was a nice thought."

It was a Monday and when Bessie arrived at Mill House to do the week's washing she told Harriet about the trip.

"Why don't you go," she suggested. "There'll be plenty of people you know. Do you good it will to get a bit of sea air in your lungs."

"No thank you. I don't need doing good!"

Charlotte, and even Rhoda, added their voices to the suggestion but it wasn't until Bessie reported that Kath Thomas was going and had a spare ticket that Harriet changed her mind."

"I'm not spending the day with Kath, mind," she warned. "Nor anyone else. I couldn't stand their company for more than the bus ride, common gossipy lot that they are."

"What will you do?" Charlotte asked, afraid to argue.

"Walk around the town. Revive a few memories. We had some lovely holidays there when you were

54

children. All those exciting rides, bracing walks, and the beach is a perfect one for children." Her voice had softened and her eyes had a faraway look, and Charlotte and Rhoda guessed she was thinking of their father.

The weather relented and spring arrived with its display of celandines, snowdrops, wild violets and primroses. Overlapping their display came the miniature wild daffodils that grew in abundance on the hills, waving bravely in the strong winds.

Charlotte watched the seasons unfold through the return of her favourite flowers. In the small copse in a protected part of the hill of windmills, the rich green shoots of bluebells began to appear and blackthorn bushes gave their bridal display of blossoms on their bare branches. For Charlotte, it was a sad reminder that 1950 was well underway and she was still without a sign of her own bridal finery.

Joe had still not moved into the new premises. He ran the bicycle shop with his usual efficiency while he waited for the legal difficulties to be dealt with. Peter was back to his daily stint at the factory and, with Rhoda keeping her mother amused, Charlotte gradually created the habit of spending part of every day with him at the factory. She loved it, and the regular visits had the effect of making her want more and more involvement. In the few hours she could spare, she succeeded in reducing the long list of overdue jobs and pacifying many irate customers.

Her mother going on the bus trip to Barry Island was a longed-for free day and although her first instinct was to spend the day at Russell's Bookbinders

55

and Restorers with Uncle Peter, she accepted Joe's invitation to spend the precious day with him.

The bus load of trippers set off for Barry Island at eight o'clock. Stopping for passengers who lived on the more isolated areas around Bryn Melinau meant that they didn't actually leave the town until almost nine. For the first part of the journey Bessie, sitting in the back with Bertha and Lillian, complained loudly about the few who hadn't been ready on time and who had inconsiderately made them all late.

Kath Thomas tried to bring Harriet into the discussion on the best way to organise an outing, but Harriet turned away from her and stared unseeing out of the window. With only an hour of the trip gone she was already regretting her decision to come. Really, it had been madness to agree. She had nothing in common with these people. She began to make her plans for escaping from them as soon as they reached their destination.

When they alighted from the bus, most of the party headed for the seafront in the hope of finding a café open for a reviving cup of tea. Harriet ignored calls to join several groups, hurried to the railway station and bought a return ticket to the centre of the town. The weather was chilly and there was the threat of rain. Best to get near the shops where there was shelter, she had decided. It was sure to rain.

The wind channelled by the buildings blew, bitingly cold, against her back and she hurried up towards Holton Road where most of the larger shops were situated. She turned into a side road and it was then that she saw him.

A man walked in front of her, some fifty yards away, and when she took a second glance she stopped and held her breath. It was Eric, her husband.

She hesitated. She had see him – or thought she had – so many times in the seven years since he had left. Each time a more careful look had led to disappointment. But this time she was certain. Or almost. There was something about the walk, the way he threw one foot out slightly. But then, she reminded herself sadly, she had often thought that too.

Slowly she followed him, her heart beating fiercely. Gradually, when she reached the busier streets of the town centre, she drew closer to him. At one point he stopped to cross the road and as he turned his head to check on the traffic she saw him quite clearly. Her face gained heat, her blood began to race. This time there was no mistake, Eric Russell was close enough to hear if she called his name, close enough for her to reach out and touch. She followed him across the road but did neither.

Heart thumping so she was afraid it would burst from her body, she followed, dropping back more and more as the crowds thinned, moving forwards again when pedestrians allowed. She just kept him in view. She didn't lose sight of him.

He stopped to buy bread and with two large loaves tucked under his arm, wrapped in tissue that fluttered like a collection of small flags, he returned the way he had come. Feeling a bit silly, Harriet darted in and out of the crowds filling the pavements and set off in pursuit, wandering idly one minute and trotting like a long-distance runner another, as Eric paused to look in shop windows or hurriedly overtook dawdlers.

At a greengrocery there had been a delivery of cucumbers, lumpy ridge cues, Harriet saw, like Bertha Evans grew later in the year in her cold frame, probably bitter and certainly unattractive, but a rare treat all the same. A queue of people stretched past two other shops and around the corner, blocking the pavement to passers-by. Harriet hesitated as Eric stopped.

He went to the front of the queue to see what was on offer then joined the end of the line. In a dreamlike trance, all sounds around her part of another, faraway world, she watched him. Her feelings were mixed, changing direction like an out-of-control switchback ride. One part of her wanted to go and scream at him, hit him, release all the hurt and humiliation he had brought her. Another side of her felt a resurgence of fierce love. Why, why, why had he left her?

Now at the front of the queue, he was served by the lady behind the counter. Waving goodbye to his friend he moved away. Harriet followed as before, keeping wide distances when the roads were empty and closing up when they were full.

In this way she walked for about ten minutes before she saw him take out a key and let himself into a small, stone-terraced house not far from the docks. Daring to walk past after watching for a few minutes, she started with alarm as the door opened and two small children tumbled out.

"Don't be long, your dinner will be ready in a minute, mind," she heard Eric's voice call, and the children tore at her senses by answering:

58

"All right, Dadda."

Dadda? They couldn't be Eric's children! She felt faint. That, on top of the rest, was more than she could bear. She hurried away from the door, sobs escaping in spite of her efforts to remain calm. She followed the little girls, who were aged about four and two. The elder child held a ration book and some money as, hand in hand, they went to the corner shop.

Peeking in, Harriet saw them choosing sweets, debating on the best value for their small ration. Impulsively she took out her own ration book and offered to buy an extra two ounces for them. She wanted to question them but in the end she couldn't. She watched them go back down the road, skipping with excitement, and into the house.

"Nice little girls," she said to the shop assistant. "Russell? Is that their name?"

"Yes, Louise and Petula Russell. Their mother is not too well at present, poor thing. Gloria has been sickly these past months. But Eric copes marvellous. Wonderful dad he is, and Gloria will soon be on her feet again. It's the new baby, see, she's had a bad time carrying this one. Strange really, mind, she's carried the others no fuss."

Every word the woman uttered was like a fresh blow to Harriet's heart. It was hard to take in. Eric, with a wife and children. No, not a wife, just a woman he was carrying on with. They weren't divorced. He'd never asked for one. Not that she'd have agreed if he had! But imagine! Eric with a woman called Gloria and, according to this chatterbox, a houseful of children!

It was cruel. How would she ever live with it now she knew? Ignorance certainly was bliss. That Thomas Grey was right about that; where ignorance is bliss, " 'Tis folly to be wise".

She had become almost convinced that the story she had invented about Eric's breakdown and subsequent loss of memory was true. Now her protection against continuing hurt, the cocoon of sympathy she had enjoyed these past seven years, was smashed. Whatever she had imagined about Eric during the time they had been apart, it was never this.

She sat on the promenade after the train journey back to the beach and stared over the heads of the few people left on the beach and on out over the sea. Waves lulled and eased her pain. Her thoughts slowed to a dull confusion that made her head ache and her body numb.

As she made her way back to where the trippers were to meet for the return journey, her thoughts returned to Bryn Melinau. They must never find out the truth about Eric. She would learn to accept his secret life, say it aloud until it no longer hurt, but she couldn't face the ridicule of her friends and neighbours learning the truth; that he had left her willingly and oh, so easily, for another woman.

The coach was waiting, several of the passengers were waving to hurry her on.

"Hurry up," Bessie called, "Phoebe has almost blown a fuse wondering where you've got to!"

"Last one you are, Harriet Russell, and after all we said about the others this morning!" Phoebe the postmistress scolded. "What on earth have you been doing all this time?"

Harriet realised with a shock that she had kept them waiting almost two hours.

Chapter Four

Charlotte could see there was something wrong when her mother returned from the day out subdued instead of full of chatter. After such occasions she happily shared the rumours and gossip she had been privy to and made them all laugh with her explanations of some of the group's behaviour. A day out, although she had to be persuaded to take it, usually succeeded in cheering her, albeit temporarily. Today there was none of it.

"Is something wrong, Mam?" Charlotte asked as she handed her mother a cup of tea. "Come on, drink this and tell me what's worrying you. Quarrelled with Kath Thomas, did you? Or was Bessie forgetting she was your cleaner and presuming friendship?"

"No need to be pert, Charlotte!"

"But something *is* wrong, isn't it?"

Rhoda and her husband Brian were there to welcome her back after her day trip and they stared at the almost tearful face of Harriet with concern, noticing the way her hands trembled when she took the proffered tea.

"It's Barry Island, isn't it?" Rhoda said emphatically. "I said, didn't I, Brian? Said you shouldn't go.

It brought back too many memories of the time when Dadda was with us. I knew!"

Harriet looked at her daughters, her pale blue eyes heavy with sadness. "I shouldn't have gone. You shouldn't have persuaded me."

"Bringing back memories," Rhoda went on, looking at Brian, tight-lipped, waiting for him to say how right she had been.

"I saw your father," Harriet whispered.

"Mam," Charlotte said gently, "we've had this talk before. You've seen Dad a dozen times and each time you've been mistaken."

"Not this time. I followed him for an hour or more, saw him go into that house and heard the children call him Dadda. I spoke to the woman in the shop and she said they were called Russell." Her voice broke as she went on. "*My* name he's given the woman, mind. My name. *I'm* Mrs Eric Russell, not her, whoever she is. It just isn't fair."

"What else did you find out?"

"That his wife – so called! – this Gloria woman, has been ill since the latest baby was born. *Latest* baby mind! Not the first." She shook her head solemnly. "This wasn't a mistake. I feel more cheated now than when he first left us. Fancy going off and getting mixed up with some woman and having children, and all the time leaving me, his lawful wife, wondering and bewildered by his disappearance. How could he do it?"

"You need to talk to someone, Mammy," Rhoda said. "Brian agrees, don't you, Bri?" Brian gave a cursory nod. "Someone who'll know the best thing to do."

"No! I couldn't bear anyone to know. You're the only ones who know the truth. You won't say, will you? I'd be so shamed for anyone else to know."

"Joe will be told," Charlotte said firmly. "He has a right to know what goes on in the family that will be his one day."

"No! Not Joe Llewellyn. I don't want Bessie Philpot to know! I'd die of embarrassment!"

"*Twp* you are, Mam. What shame is there in all this for you? It's Dadda who should be shamed! What have *you* done? It's Dadda who ran off, and him who's living over the brush with some woman, pretending to be her husband!"

"Not Joe," Harriet said firmly. Charlotte noticed that her mother's hands were shaking again with shock.

"At least talk to Jack Roberts. He's trustworthy and he won't tell anyone. You have to have help in this."

"Uncle Peter will have to be told," Harriet sobbed. "It's his own brother who's done this to us."

"I agree with Charlotte, Mam, don't you Bri?" Rhoda said to her husband who sat there swallowing his adam's apple, afraid to say a word. "I think you should tell Jack Roberts and ask for his help. Church Elder he is, mind. Surely you can trust him?"

It was late when they finally persuaded Harriet to have a few sips of brandy – for the shock – and go to bed. She was so exhausted by the day's events that she slept almost immediately. Rhoda and Brian left a few minutes later and Charlotte looked at the clock, wondering if ten past ten on an April evening was too late to call on Joe. She

65

had to tell him: there had never been any secrets between them.

A few moments later, Charlotte was cycling down the hill towards the town. She was practically running when she passed through the gate and up the path to the front door where, mercifully, a light still showed.

Joe listened to Charlotte's story, his arms around her to comfort her. He guessed that while Harriet talked, Charlotte would have remained calm and strong, now, with no one to support, she could let her feelings show. It was her father they were talking about, someone on whom she should have been able to depend. Harriet seemed not to realise how this affected her daughters as well as herself, Joe thought grimly. Typical of the woman.

"How could he do it?" Charlotte whispered. "There isn't any reason for his behaviour."

"How can anyone ever know what goes on in another's head? He and your mother might not have been as happy as she pretends. She's hard work to live with, you must know that. Like your sister Rhoda."

"I'm sure Rhoda and I would have known if they were so unhappy that he had to leave."

"Your mother was probably right, had a breakdown he did, then couldn't face coming back," he soothed.

Then Charlotte pulled herself out of his embrace and said angrily, "You don't believe that! Don't talk to me as if I were a baby, Joe Llewellyn!"

"All right. I'm sorry. He must have been very miserable at home."

"He and Mam were perfectly content!"

66

"Perfectly content? Were they?"

"Well, there were plenty of rows. But we thought that was just the way they were, we never considered it was serious."

"Didn't you?" Joe asked gently.

Charlotte looked away. Of course the rows had been serious. She remembered lying in bed listening to them when they returned from some party or other, marvelling that the plaster didn't fall off the walls.

"They were deeply unhappy and you know it," he chided.

Hurt and angry with him for making her see how things really were, something she had covered with pretence, Charlotte stormed out, half running back along the lane to where she had left her cycle. Joe called after her but she ignored him and ran on, tripping, almost falling, tears blinding her, not stopping until she reached the road.

Harriet was persuaded, after hours of tears, to allow Jack Roberts to know that the missing Eric had been located. Peter was already there when they walked up the following morning and met in his office. Harriet held her temples against the noise of the machines, and ran a disapproving finger along the dusty desk. "What a noisy, filthy place to bring me to to discuss such a predicament," she scolded Charlotte. "I don't know why we had to come *here*."

"It's Bessie's morning for cleaning, the gardener will be there this morning too and the window cleaner comes after twelve. Too many ears altogether. If we cancelled them all, Auntie Bessie Philpot's nose would vibrate and almost fall off as she ferreted around for secrets!"

"She isn't your auntie, she's a servant . . . and I wish you wouldn't call her that!"

Jack listened to Harriet's story with spurious anger. He doubted very much if Harriet had really discovered Eric's whereabouts. Surely the man would have had the sense to move further away from Bryn Melinau than Barry? But he knew from past incidents that, with Harriet, it was better to appear to agree. "If you think it best," he said finally, "we'll drive to Barry so we can check on the address." In her misery, Harriet had failed to take note of it. "Then," he went on, apologetically hushing her protests, "you and I will prepare a letter asking for him to meet you and discuss a divorce."

"I couldn't." Harriet meant she couldn't divorce Eric. Jack thought she couldn't face meeting the man.

"We'll be with you, Charlotte, Rhoda and me. I promise you'll have our full support."

"I'm not afraid of meeting him, the scoundrel," Harriet confided to Charlotte when they returned home that evening. "It's the divorce. Couldn't Eric and that woman take my home? It was my mother's and now it's mine, but I could lose it, couldn't I?"

"Don't worry," Charlotte said confidently. "I'm sure we'll find a way around it. Relax and leave it to Jack and Uncle Peter." But she was dreadfully afraid her mother was right. Mill House could be sold and the proceeds used to support her father's second family, half-brothers and -sisters she hadn't known about just twenty-four hours ago.

68

The consequences of a divorce were mind numbing as she thought them through. One of them being the postponement of her marriage to Joe for as far into the future as she dared to look. Blown like a seed before the wind, you are, Charlotte Russell, she told herself, blown by the wayward wind. When are you going to make a stand and choose your own route?

Not yet, she thought sadly, not yet.

The drive to Barry was almost silent, each of the occupants of the Ford Prefect wrapped in their own thoughts. Jack parked Peter's car in the street a few doors away from the house pointed out by a trembling Harriet. Several times the door opened and small children wandered in and out, and a few young women, including a nurse. Charlotte presumed they were friends of the woman her father lived with.

At five o'clock Eric turned the corner, wearing a neat suit and carrying a raincoat over his arm. His hands held two carrier bags, from which vegetables and bread protruded. He obviously dealt with the family shopping. That the man really was her father she had doubted until this moment. Now, seeing him pause, look down the road and smile at a neighbour, her doubts faded. It left her with a sick feeling of half joy, half hurt and bewilderment.

"It's Dadda," she blurted out.

"I knew you didn't believe me," Harriet sobbed.

Charlotte wanted to go and hug him, feel his arms around her, breathe in that special, well-remembered smell . . . the factory, pipe smoke, laundered shirt, tweed suiting and soap. They watched for a while longer and drove home more subdued than on the outward journey. There was no discussion concerning what they would do next. Jack drove without even looking at his passengers; Harriet sobbed quietly. Charlotte was eaten with regret that after seven years she had seen her father and had not been able to talk to him.

The following morning, Charlotte enjoyed a few hours alone. Uncle Peter was at the factory, her mother and sister had pushed aside their worries, put on forced smiles, dressed up in their most glamourous clothes and sallied forth to wander around the shops, stopping for coffee at Vi and Willie's café and meeting friends. Charlotte ignored the dusting and tidying and went up onto the hill.

She sat on a fallen tree. Distorted by the wind, it had finally succumbed to the winds and lay on its side, already colonised by lichens and mosses and with a frill of dead grass along its edge. It moved as she relaxed her weight. The voice startled her so, she almost lost her balance on the precarious seat.

"Hello. I hope I'm not disturbing you, miss."

Charlotte turned and saw a tall figure smiling down at her from beside a nearby hawthorn tree.

"No, er, of course not. Good morning." She looked at the tall stranger. He was young, about her own age, she guessed, and obviously a walker. He wore a weatherproof jacket, and corduroy trousers tucked into heavy boots. He had a rucksack carried casually across one shoulder; a woollen hat was pushed back from his forehead revealing curly brown hair. Uneasy, self-conscious, she moved away from him.

"I can't stop," she said, rising and brushing her skirt

70

with a nervous hand, "but if you want to know where you are, this is Bryn Melinau below us."

"Yes, I know. I'm walking up towards Breconshire, but I had to detour and look at this place. It's in my guide book, see. Hill with the remains of seven mills. That right, is it?"

She looked at the grinning face, the hint of mischief in his eyes and smiled. Something about him made a smile inevitable.

"Don't you believe the guide books then?"

"I don't believe anything until I check for myself. I do believe in luck, though. How else could I explain our meeting? Who'd believe I'd find someone like you on a lonely hill at this time of the day. Will you direct me to the nearest café and have a coffee with me?"

Reluctantly, Charlotte shook her head. "You'll find Vi and Willie Walters' café next to the clothes shop, but I can't go with you. I'm on my way to do a few hours work. My uncle's factory is just down the lane."

"All right, but at least meet me later and show me where these windmills and watermills are. Please?"

"I live in a house that was once a windmill," she said, looking at him, trying to make up her mind. "All right, come for me at two and I'll show you the ruins." She explained where Mill House was situated and watched as he walked away.

She didn't go to the factory but went home instead. What had got into her? Inviting a complete stranger to call. Agreeing to show him the hill. She wondered if there was time to go down and ask Joe to go with them, suddenly afraid of where the afternoon might lead. But she didn't.

71

Explaining to her mother that she had offered to show some tourists around the area, she stood by the gate at five minutes to two, not wanting the man to knock on her door and meet her mother. She wanted this afternoon to be hers alone. She would tell Joe of course. Later.

He strolled up in a leisurely way and waved when he saw her waiting. She had brushed her hair and added an alice band to keep it out of her eyes. Her clothes hadn't changed from the morning, sensible skirt and jumper, strong shoes and short socks.

"Where do we start then?" he asked, his eyes looking deeply into her own. He looked so pleased to see her she felt herself blushing under his stare.

"We'll walk to the top and work our way down."

She led the way, up paths that grew narrower and more overgrown, until they were threading their way through heather and gorse on what were little more than animal tracks.

"The hill was home to a number of sheep before the war," she explained to him, "but since we have more visitors, many of them with unruly dogs, the farmers no longer let them wander. So the heather and gorse have taken over. Doesn't take long for a place to change, does it?"

"No, but it's fascinating to imagine the hill's history."

She waved towards Mill House then showed him the ruins of the other mills. Clouds had gathered over the hills, dressing them in deep purple gauze, and it was already dark by the time they were back at the gates of her home.

"Thank you for sharing the afternoon with me," he

said, offering her his hand. "I must go now, I have a night's lodging booked with a Mrs Kath Thomas, just near the road bridge."

As she waved away his thanks, he took hold of her hand again and drew her towards him. He kissed her lightly, then walked quickly away, arm raised, hand waggling in salute, disappearing into the gathering gloom of the evening. It was as if a light had been extinguished somewhere inside her.

She realised she was still holding his guide book. As if she had been given a gift of a few more seconds in his company, she shouted and ran after him to return it. As she reached him, Joe appeared, pushing his bicycle.

"Charlotte? Where are you off to? Just coming to see you I am."

"Oh, Joe, this is, er – " She looked at the stranger, embarrassed to realise she didn't know his name. "– a tourist. I've been showing him the ruins on the hill."

"Hi," Joe said. "Staying long?" Then he frowned, something about the man's appearance and voice suddenly familiar. "Say, weren't you here a week or so ago? I seem to remember you asking me how to get to Barry."

"Not me, mate. I haven't been here before and I know where Barry is. Just come from there on the train, haven't I?"

"Funny. I could have sworn – " Joe shrugged.

"Got to be off. Nice meeting you both." A wave and he was gone, his long legs taking him out of their sight in moments.

"What did you want to see me about, Joe?" Charlotte asked.

"Oh, it's nothing really, my pretty. Just to tell you the sale of the shop seems to be going through and I wondered if I dare ask you to help me do a stocktake. Boring ol' job it is, mind, counting all the thousand and one things I sell. D'you think the Dragon will let you give a hand, say, on Sunday?"

"Let's ask her when Uncle Peter's there. Better chance of her saying yes, then." Disturbed by her few hours with the fascinating stranger, she hugged Joe to reassure herself that he was real, the visitor only a passing fantasy.

On Jack and Peter's advice, Harriet wrote to Eric, marking the letter private and confidential. A response was immediate. To her chagrin there was no apology, no remorse, just a few sentences saying how surprised he was to hear from her and suggesting they meet at a fourteenth-century public house in the Vale of Glamorgan, this being what he called neutral ground. He promised to telephone and arrange a date.

Eric intended to see his brother Peter before the reunion with his wife and daughters. He telephoned the factory and arranged to meet Peter there one morning.

Peter wheeled his chair away from the desk that had been Eric's and waited, watching the door for his brother's arrival with some agitation. Eric slipped in through a side door without walking through the workroom and startled Peter with his unexpected appearance. Peter thought he was thinner and less well dressed than he remembered. His hair was greyer but still the same as it had always been, untidy and overlong. But the look in the dark eyes was one of contentment.

"Eric, you old sod. How are you?" Peter said opening his arms for a hug.

"Hello, long-lost brother," Eric said, putting his arms around the thin shoulders, glad of the excuse to hold Peter and hide the shock he'd had at the man's sickly appearance.

"This is a bit cloak-and-dagger, boy, creeping through the goods entrance," Peter laughed. "Why aren't you in disguise? Someone will recognise you for sure and news of your visit will be round the town faster than Ianto's bus!" Ianto's bus was a local joke. The old man, long dead, had owned a bus that rarely travelled between one stop and the next without breaking down.

"I hope I won't be recognised. I wouldn't like news of my sudden recovery from amnesia to get out before I've talked to Harriet and the girls."

"You know about that, then? Your Harriet pretending you had suffered memory loss, to save face?"

"Yes, I know," Eric said sadly. "Sorry I am that it was necessary." He pulled a chair around and sat facing his brother. "Heard about your accident too, Peter. But I couldn't come back. I was well past the point of no return." He seemed about to explain but changed his mind. "I just had to hope that you'd be able to keep things running here to support Harriet. That Jack Roberts is a good man, from what I've heard of him."

"Why did you leave so suddenly and without explanation?" Peter asked.

75

The look in Eric's eyes sharpened and he glared at his brother. "You know better than most!" He lowered his gaze and said more quietly, "I had to get away. It seemed pointless to stay. Harriet and I had nothing to say to each other. It was as if I were a fly on the wall watching two strangers prattling on, neither listening to the other.

"Unperturbed about my grief she was, sucking the tragic situation for all it was worth, making sure everything fitted into place for her as if it was her right. Complacent, comfortable, demanding everything, giving nothing. And there was Gloria cheerfully struggling. Dealing with the death of her husband, coping with her children, losing her home after someone cheated her, then making a happy home out of the two small rooms she rented. She was so pretty, and so bright. Never complaining, always ready to smile. I thought she needed me more than Harriet did and I certainly needed her. I was miserable, Harriet was miserable. I didn't think I could do anything about Harriet's happiness but I knew that with Gloria I would be happy. Cruel I know, but – " He smiled then and his pale face lit up as he added, "– I was right about being happy."

"What will you do now Harriet knows where you are?"

"I hope to persuade her to divorce me. Then Gloria and I can legitimize the children."

"Children? How many for God's sake?"

"A houseful. Beautiful they are." He grinned again and in the smile his happiness clearly showed. "Two are Gloria's and the rest are ours." He opened his hands in a gesture of, what else can I do? "We owe it to them."

"What if Harriet refuses?"

"Then I'll divorce her. Somehow." Again he stared coldly at his brother. "It'll take time, but I can wait. I want to be free to marry the woman I've found happiness with."

Jack recognised Eric Russell the moment he saw him. He had been curious about Peter's visitor, who had crept in via the goods deliveries entrance, and so he made an excuse and pushed open the office door.

Sensing rather than seeing his presence in the doorway, Eric looked up and gave a half smile. "Hello, you must be Jack. How are you then?"

"Startled at seeing you! Does your wife know you're here?"

"No, and I don't want her to. Not until I've had a chance to talk with her, right?"

"She saw you in Barry. I drove her back to check on the address. We all saw you; Harriet, Charlotte, Rhoda, Brian and me."

Eric jumped up, startled. "Charlotte and Rhoda know? I wish I could have explained before they found out."

"Damn it all," Peter said, exasperated, "you've had seven years to explain!"

"Not a word about me being here though. Not yet."

"That was a terrible thing to do to your family," Jack said quietly. "You haven't the look of a lothario, but two women. *Duw*! If you had to, you could at least have been honest."

77

"What's it to do with you?" Eric demanded.

"I've seen what it's done to young Charlotte."

"Yes, I suppose it affected her badly."

"I can't say I'm glad to meet you," Jack added coldly. "You're a cheating coward, Eric Russell."

"I am that. And a very happy one. And," he emphasized, "I intend things to stay that way, no messing." Eric's lips tightened determinedly as he stood to leave. He was a small man, only a little over five feet tall. His grey, absent-minded hair fell in all directions, undecided about where it belonged. He had on a suit that was far from new and his shoes were worn, but well polished. His shirt was snowy and neatly ironed. He looked well cared for, even if a bit shabby.

Eric walked down the hill, glancing only briefly at Mill House. He hurried through the town, trilby hat pulled well down over his face, the collar of his mac pulled up. He didn't want anyone to stop and speak to him. They might remember, even though seven years was a long time. His heart was racing as he sat on the train taking him back to his home, away from the place he had once thought he would never leave.

On Sunday morning, once the vegetables were prepared for dinner, and Peter was comfortably settled, Charlotte walked down the hill and along Main Street to Joe's shop. He was already there, the contents of drawers tipped out into cardboard boxes, lists and pencils on every shelf. Stocktaking was underway.

After greeting her with undisguised relief, Joe explained.

"Put the total in the first column, the price in the second. I'll do the additions and fill in the end column later."

"Joe Llewellyn, are you suggesting I can't add up?" she teased and with the light bantering setting the mood, they worked steadily and contentedly for the rest of the morning. Charlotte had been invited to have dinner with Joe's Auntie Bessie Philpot and at one o'clock they walked along the quiet footpath; arm in arm when it was wide enough, Joe's hand resting on her shoulder when it was not. The man they saw coming towards them had obviously been in a fight. It took a few seconds for Joe to recognise him.

"Jack Roberts! What on earth happened, man? You look like you've been hit by a train!"

"It's nothing. It's all right. Just a misunderstanding, that's all."

"It wasn't Eric, was it?" Joe whispered.

"No, not Eric. It was no one I know," Jack replied emphatically.

Joe insisted he came into his aunt's house to be cleaned up and Jack agreed. "I don't want to go back to Kath's like this."

"Very thoughtful of you," Joe said grimly. "But you aren't going anywhere until you've spoken to the police."

"No, no," Jack protested. "I tell you, it's all right. I was mistaken for someone else, that's all."

"Then that 'someone else' will be more than glad if we can get the bloke before he catches up with him, won't he!"

Auntie Bessie didn't fuss or try to get explanations; she presumed it was the same 'madman' who had attacked her. Bustling about her kitchen, she gathered cloths and hot water and ointment and quickly sorted out the worst of Jack's injuries, which turned out to be less serious than they looked – most of the mess being mud – then went back to getting the dinner.

"Did you see the man who hit you?" Joe asked, persisting with his questions. "Was he tall? Young? Brown hair, dark eyes? Heavily built?"

"I didn't see a hair of him," Jack insisted.

Charlotte was silent. Joe was describing the stranger, with whom she had spent the afternoon on the hill.

Bessie's next-door neighbour, Bertha Evans, came to see what had happened, and stayed to listen to Jack's very brief explanation. Bertha was small, very slim, her grey-green eyes gentle and slow. She was a quiet person who rarely spoke unnecessarily, and her movements were restricted to the minimum. When she sat, she was utterly still and when she listened to someone she flattered them by giving them her whole attention. There was about her an air of calmness and peace and Charlotte always loved to see her.

Bertha seemed to survive on what she could grow or make herself. She had never worked, and how she managed was a mystery that even Bessie had been unable to untangle. She grew vegetables in the large garden behind the cottage, and the remains of an orchard gave her fruit for bottling and jam-making, some of which she sold. Chickens and ducks, which ran free on the grass near the river, and goats for milk both for use and to sell, gave her sufficient money to buy flour for the bread she baked in her oven twice a week.

There had to be more money, Bessie reasoned, and she grew more and more discontented when her relentless questioning and devious investigations failed to satisfy her curiosity.

Bertha's daughter Lillian, now eighteen, but with the mind of a child more than ten years younger, had tried on countless occasions to get a job. But although the kindly people of Bryn Melinau sympathised with the amiable girl and tried to help, it was soon found to be impossible to employ her, even for the simplest tasks. Very overweight, Lillian enjoyed eating to the exclusion of everything else. When not so employed, she could sit for hours and stare into space, oblivious to boiling pans, crying babies and unwashed floors, and no matter what type of work she tried, she rarely lasted more than three days.

After listening to Jack's story, Bertha nodded and said, "Well, Jack, it's up to you, perhaps you'd be wasting Constable Hardy's time, but I think he should be told. The same man might have hit Bessie and if you're the second, well, he must be caught."

Jack was adamant and the matter remained a secret between the few people involved. Bessie was most upset, believing the assailant was the same man who had attacked her.

A further disappointment for Bessie was the news of Eric Russell's return. In the way of all small communities, Bryn Melinau had ways of rapidly spreading news. Bessie was usually the first to put her expert skills to work but for once she was second in the race to tell everyone. It fanned out via the Russells' bookbinding factory.

Jack told Gaynor Edwards who the visitor to Peter's office that morning had been; Gaynor confided the interesting tidbit of gossip to one of the others in the workroom and before Eric's train had left the station, a dozen people knew. It only needed a few knocks on doors, a few shared cups of tea, to make it common knowledge that Eric had recovered from his 'amnesia'. He was back.

No one mentioned him to Harriet, although conversations ceased on her approach, there were gigggles stifled behind gloved hands and Harriet guessed that her secret was out. She wanted to jump off the nearest cliff, she confided to Rhoda and Brian. "But be sure that if I do I'll push him off first!"

They were sitting in the lounge of Mill House while Bessie washed the kitchen floor. They were unaware that the scrubbing brush had ceased its rasping until Bessie came in with a tray of tea.

"Best you tell him to clear off. You're happier without him," Rhoda was saying tearfully, "isn't she, Bri? We don't want him coming back and upsetting our lives. Hurt us terribly he did and I for one will never forgive him. No, Mammy, leave things be."

"Your Rhoda's right," Bessie said, undisguisedly eavesdropping.

"You wouldn't say that if he was yours!" Harriet snapped.

"Wouldn't I?" Bessie hauled herself to her full height and said, "What makes you think I wouldn't send him packing?"

"Because you've never had a husband!"

"And that's a crime? Look at you then. What an advert for wedded bliss!" She plonked the tray of tea down and pulled off her apron.

With a haughty expression on her face, Harriet turned to Rhoda. "Pay the woman and ask her to leave, will you?"

"Don't worry, I'm going!"

Rhoda looked at Brian and smiled. These spats were a regular occurrence and always forgotten by the next time Bessie was due. Harriet knew she wouldn't get anyone else to do what Bessie did, and certainly not for the money she paid her.

Charlotte and Joe were finishing counting the stock one evening when someone tapped on the shop window. It was after six-thirty at night and the windows had been shuttered to show that the place was closed for the day.

"Can't they read!" Joe grumbled, getting down from the ladder where he had been checking the contents of boxes on the top shelf. "Shuttered windows, a notice big as a double-decker bus and still they knock."

"Sorry I am to disturb you, boy, but is Charlotte there?"

"Come in Bertha. She's in the office going through the lists. Can't miss anything out, not when it's my last chance to add to the price," he joked, nodding towards the corner partition.

"Wondered how poor Mrs Russell is today," Bertha said. "Got over her terrible shock, has she? Fancy

Eric – I mean Mr Russell – turning up like that after all this time."

"Eric has never turned up! Well I never!" Joe grinned, feigning ignorance. "Rubbish, woman! Nothing but a lot of ol' rumour."

"Indeed he has," Bertha said confidentially, "and I'm so worried for Mrs Russell, she doesn't deserve that, does she, poor dab?" Cupping her mouth to hide her words from Charlotte on the corner, she added, "She found him with a woman calling herself Mrs Eric Russell, and them with a houseful of kids, would you believe?"

Charlotte didn't show herself; she didn't want to discuss the family's predicament with anyone.

"I'm surprised at Bertha, coming here for a few more items of gossip," Charlotte said when the woman had gone. "She doesn't usually involve herself in tittle-tattle. But there, I suppose this is second only to the election results in national importance; Eric Russell and his notorious vanishing trick! But I wonder why *she's* so excited?"

"Come to make sure it's true, I expect. But it can't make any difference to her, can it? He can hardly make her an 'honest woman', can he? Him with a wife and daughters plus another woman and a houseful of kids!"

"What d'you mean, make Bertha an honest woman? What's Dadda's reappearance to do with her?"

"Some say he's Lillian's lost father."

"Joe!"

"Well, someone's been keeping them for the last eighteen years."

"Well it isn't my father! Worse than your Auntie Bessie Philpot you are, Joe Llewellyn! How dare you even think it!"

"I'm only saying what I've heard," he protested.

"From your Auntie Bessie Philpot no doubt!"

Joe saw from Charlotte's face that a row was imminent and he sighed with relief as Constable Hardy knocked on the door and entered to make sure all was well.

Chapter Five

Shocked by Joe's accusations about her father and Bertha's slow-witted daughter, Lillian, Charlotte avoided seeing him for several days. How could Joe have told her so casually? He was smiling as he said the hated words, as if the whole thing was a joke.

She wanted to talk to her father, hear him say it wasn't true. She hardly left the house, waiting for the phone to ring, hoping to be able to talk to him, hear him explain, tell her it was nothing more than a malicious rumour. But although Charlotte spent a lot of time wandering around the house, waiting for her father's call, it was Uncle Peter who actually picked up the phone and arranged with Eric the time and day on which he was to meet Harriet and discuss a divorce. Peter passed the message on to his sister-in-law when she and Rhoda returned from the shops.

Charlotte watched her mother's face, hoping to see a sign that she was coping, that this wouldn't mean her leaning more heavily on her daughters. But the white face, upturned eyes, the gradual falling back onto the couch all suggested that as usual, Harriet was going to make as much out of the situation as she possibly could. Ashamed of her coldness with her mother's genuine difficulties, Charlotte nevertheless thought more about how events would affect herself and Joe.

"I don't think I can go," Harriet said after Rhoda had passed sal volatile under her nose several times. Charlotte sighed inwardly. The arrangement was for three days' time and Charlotte guessed that those three days would be filled with sobs and recriminations and appeals for support. She knew she would have to listen while her mother went over and over what had happened, giving her version of the events and making sure that no kind thought was spared for her father.

Charlotte was exhausted by the evening before the proposed meeting. She couldn't sleep although she was very tired. She still hadn't seen Joe, deliberately staying away from town and slipping out of the back door when he called. Once the meeting of her estranged parents had taken place, then she could talk to Joe and decide on their future.

She lay on the bed thinking that the outcome of the following day would affect her as much, if not more, than her mother. If the matter was dealt with calmly and amicably she and Joe might stand a chance of a future together. She sighed. Amicability and her mother couldn't be considered in the same breath.

At three in the morning she gave up trying to sleep and got dressed. She spent the next three hours polishing brass and copper, then finished off the last of the silent hours polishing the furniture. When everything was as shiny as it possibly could be, she washed the kitchen flags and put the coconut matting out on the line and beat it until it was practically threadbare.

The morning was still and beautiful. Below her the town was gradually waking, its outlines bathed in mist, the river a silver streak, curled around the town. The hills in the distance were newly washed as the mist had cleared from them, an amphitheatre waiting for the curtains to rise on the performance of the new day.

The sun came up suddenly, bursting out from the hills. Surely an omen of good fortune? Whatever happened to her, whatever disappointments she faced, she would always be glad she lived here, in this beautiful place among such contented, caring people.

Her next task was breakfast. Charlotte dealt with the meals and organised the running of the house, and had done so since she left school. She fed her family well considering the fiddling portions of food they had on ration, she knew that. Four ounces of margarine and five of butter, four ounces of bacon to last a week. You needed to be a magician these days, not a cook! Being helped by Bertha's off-ration duck eggs helped. Plus her own skills of course. Her meatless pies and fatless sponges were better than most. Didn't she tease Joe that her cooking was his main reason for wanting to marry her?

Her mind drifted off from her problems of the day but kept returning with a shock. Her father was meeting them like some businessman with a proposition to their mutual advantage. She forced herself to think of dinner. Potatoes mashed with an oxo and a tin of Woppa peas mixed in. Fried in a little bacon fat they'd be pretend rissoles. Everything in my life is pretend, she sighed. Pretend engagement, pretend meals, and now I'm expected to pretend not to mind that my father has an illegitimate daughter, has founded a second family and threatens to throw Mam out of her home!

At ten-thirty they went to the car and Charlotte saw that her mother was literally shaking with anxiety. Charlotte tucked her arm in hers and said brightly, "Let's pretend it's an outing, shall we? Going to the seaside for the day we are, a picnic in the bag, dippers in there too in case the sea's warm enough for a bathe, the promise of fish and chips on the way home. Right?"

Harriet forced a smile. "Right. Seaside, here we come."

The inn where they had arranged to meet was a thatched building, situated on the road close to the sea, dating back to the early fourteenth century. Although modernised to create a comfortable and pleasant ambience, it still retained the air of timelessness and calm beauty that only very old buildings can have. The inside was dark after the strong sunlight and for a moment, the low-ceilinged room seemed empty. Then Eric stood up from a chair near the fire and said:

"Hello, Harriet my dear. Charlotte, how lovely you've grown, and Rhoda, a married woman now, and is this your husband?" He hugged his daughters and shook hands with Brian but to Harriet he only smiled. She had taken a step back, afraid he might be going to hug her as well. She would

90

hit him if he tried but was disappointed when he did not.

Eric calmly handed drinks around and gestured for them to sit down. "I hope you still like a port and lemon, Harriet. A beer for you, Brian, and soft drinks for you girls as I no longer know your preferences."

There seemed no trivialities to discuss to break the stiffness of the gathering. Brian slurped his drink and began to cough. He scurried from the room with undisguised relief.

Rhoda called after him, "Don't forget you've got something to say, Brian."

Harriet sipped her drink, put the glass down with a hand that shook and demanded, "Well? What d'you want to do, then?"

"I want a divorce," Eric said quietly. "It's the only honest thing to do."

"No." Harriet's voice was equally quiet. But her mouth was a straight line of defensive determination.

"It's the children, you see," Eric said, still in his modulated voice. "I can understand your anger, I'm not denying that I've behaved shamefully. But there are the children, who are innocent of any guilt. I'd like to give them my name."

"It's *my* name! *I'm* Mrs Eric Russell. That Gloria woman is using *my name*."

"I'm sorry Harriet, but I want it to be hers."

Harriet's lips tightened further and she turned her head away from him. Brian intervened then, walking back into the room and nervously interrupting. The silence had seemed set to continue all day, both parties looking away from each other, staring unseeing at the woodsmoke-stained walls.

"If you do agree to a divorce – " Brian began, swallowing nervously, and Harriet's head turned sharply and she glared at him. "– I'm not saying she should, mind. But if she does, what will happen to Mill House?"

"Nothing at all," Eric said, looking at Harriet. "It's yours, Harriet, and always will be. I don't want the house or anything in it, all that is yours by right, if not by law. Gloria and I have a home, rented and without much in the way of luxury, but we don't want to take your home from you." They all saw the lowering of Harriet's face as the tension of that particular worry eased. "Sorry I am, Harriet, if you've been worried. That has never been my, or indeed Gloria's, intention."

"Will you give that assurance now, in writing?" Brian suggested. Eric looked surprised at this apparent doubting of his word, but he nodded agreement.

Harriet gave an audible sigh of relief as Eric wrote the words dictated by Brian, promising that the divorce settlement would not include the house or its contents, which would remain in the complete ownership of Harriet. "We'll go to a solicitor as soon as possible and get this made legal," Brian said with his own sigh of relief that his part in the proceeding was over. He put the piece of paper in his pocket then stood up. "Come on Rhoda my dear, and you, Charlotte. I think we should leave your parents alone to discuss what needs to be done. We'll be outside when you're ready to leave, all right, Mother-in-law?"

Harriet looked more anxious than before as Charlotte stood with her sister and prepared to leave, but she nodded her agreement in repetition of Eric's.

Charlotte squeezed her mother's shoulder briefly before going out into the warm sunshine. Rhoda and Brian went for a walk along the road to look down on the beach but she didn't go with them. She sat and leaned against the ancient, sun-warmed walls of the public house, where many hundreds of people must have sat in the years of the building's existence. She half closed her eyes, imagining generations of men sitting there wearing stout trousers and Welsh flannel shirts, clay pipes in their mouths, looking at the same scene that was before her, which could hardly have changed.

"You're looking well, Harriet," Eric said, his voice low and gentle. "Your hair is still fair, not much sign of grey. Your skin is as smooth as when you were a girl."

"You haven't worn so good!" was Harriet's reply. He was unnerving her with his mild flattery and the urge to hurt him was not softened by it. "Your hair looks like something I've used to scour the sink. And your neck's all scraggy!"

Eric laughed. "I was never a beauty!"

"Good cook is she, this Gloria?"

"Not as good as you."

He seems determined to be nice, she thought. "All those children. The place must be a tip. You always liked things orderly."

"Marvellous housewife you were."

She wanted to ask, why did you leave me then? Why did you put me through seven years of hurt and humiliation? Instead she stood up, dragging the chair noisily over the slate floor and called the others.

"No," she said, as she pulled on her gloves and hat and prepared to leave. "No, I won't divorce you. You and that woman will have to live in the mess you've created. None of it is my making. Remember that, Eric Russell. None of it is down to me!"

"Sure about that, are you, Harriet?" For the first time there was a hint of censure in his voice. "Sure of that, are you?"

She was not inclined to speak on the return journey. Apart from thanking Brian for getting the agreement with Eric not to claim half of her house, she said nothing.

Charlotte saw that her mother's eyes were overbright and staring and guessed she longed for privacy so she could howl. She looked out of the window at the burgeoning countryside and the occasional glimpses of the blue, sparkling sea, calm in the bright sun, and allowed herself to dwell on her private thoughts. When her mother was ready to talk she would be there, willing to listen.

Rhoda invited Charlotte to meet her in town at the café run by Vi and Willie Walters. When their coffee had been served with a plateful of cakes from which to choose, Rhoda told her sister of her plan to throw a house-warming party.

"I'll do the food if you like," Vi, carefully listening to the conversation, called from the counter.

"Thank you Mrs Walters, but I think I can manage," Rhoda replied in her careful, clipped voice.

94

"Catering's extra to the rations, remember," Vi coaxed.

"All right, I'll let you know," Rhoda promised. She whispered to Charlotte, "It might be an idea, Brian can afford it and if I can wheedle the extra cash out of him it will leave me free to get my hair done and all that. Perhaps you'll come early and help me set out all the food?"

Charlotte was not keen to attend: she and her sister spent little time together without disagreeing.

"I'm not sure how I'll be fixed for Saturday. It's Joe," she extemporised. "He's very busy now, with the shop sale almost ready to complete."

"Joe? You can't bring Joe," Rhoda said. "Mam would be most upset!"

"What?"

"Charlotte, Mam's had enough upsets recently. You know how she feels about Joe. It would ruin my evening. Don't make a fuss, please."

"I won't make a fuss," Charlotte said coldly. "I simply won't come."

"But you must, Charlotte! What will Mam say?" Rhoda wailed, but her sister was standing, gathering her shopping and preparing to leave.

"Please, Charlotte."

"Not without Joe."

Before Charlotte left the town, she called to see Joe.

"Dad wants a divorce and Mam won't agree," she told him. "I'm sorry I haven't seen you but – "

"But your Mam comes first, I know that," he said quietly.

"Joe, it isn't like that. I've had so many shocks

lately, and well, it isn't easy you know." Her voice sharpened with anger. He ought to understand, not stand there disapproving.

"If I'd had shocks or problems I'd have run to you, not away from you," he said, sadness in his eyes.

She told him about the party, between serving customers, and explained that she did not want to go. He closed the shop door, put a "back in ten minutes" notice on the door and took her back to Vi and Willie's café for a teacake.

"When is this party?" he asked.

"It's on Saturday, April the twenty-second," she told Joe. "So I want us to be doing something that prevents us from attending."

"They didn't invite me, did they?"

"Of course," she lied, "but I really would hate it. Can we book to go to the theatre or something?"

"They invited you but not me and you aren't able to tell them you're angry. Instead you want me to pretend we have an unbreakable arrangement. When are you going to stand up for us?" he added. "Don't you think we're important enough to make a stand for?"

"I do, Joe, of course I do, I told Rhoda I wouldn't go without you. But you know what Mam's like. She's so easily upset. She is trying to cope with Dad's reappearance, a threat of divorce as well as Uncle Peter's illness. It's hard for her."

"Duty I can understand. I even approve. But martyrdom is for someone else, not me."

"What d'you mean?"

"Come back to the shop. We have to talk." Leaving the "back in ten minutes" notice pinned to the door he pulled her into the partition and kissed her fiercely, then he stopped her protests with another kiss. A third was gentler, his lips moving slowly on hers, his body moulded against her own, a kiss which reached the deepest parts of her and which she didn't want to end.

He turned away then and talked gruffly as if in anger.

"You know how much I want you. You know I've loved you since we were kids being cared for by my Auntie Bessie while your mother had a full and happy social life. She ignored you then. Had no time for you in her hectic round of parties and dances and theatre visits. Now, when that life has ended, she clings to you, demands your loyalty, uses you as her crutch. Well, my need of you is greater, and less selfish than hers. But the choice is yours, my pretty." He turned then to face her, staring into her rather startled eyes, but he didn't touch her. "I'm not waiting until I'm an old man to marry you," he said quietly. "It's now or not at all. We postponed when your uncle was taken to hospital, we didn't cancel. There's no problem that can't be overcome if the will is there. There's no need to wait any longer, unless you've changed your mind."

"Joe, I'll marry you as soon as it's possible. But – with Uncle Peter and the divorce and – "

"Middle of June. That's possible. The shop will be mine, the flat above will be habitable and we can work on the rest of it once we're in."

"Middle of June – " She looked away from his intense gaze. A sigh made her glance at him. Something in his expression made her realise that for all his amiability, he was determined to get a firm answer. "All right, Joe, let's make it June."

Joe took out his pocket diary and said, "The tenth."

"Twenty-fourth, gives us more time."

"The tenth, there's no more time to waste."

"All right." She smiled up at him and moved into his arms. "We'll start making arrangements very soon."

"Now, Charlotte. We'll go this minute and tell the Dragon."

Her protests were ignored and she found it very exciting to have him so resolute.

A customer knocking on the door broke them from their final kiss. Joe went to open it and found Kath Thomas demanding a screwdriver to fit a screw she had brought with her. She looked up as Charlotte came from behind the partition, then looked at Joe.

"So that's what you've been doing. No wonder ten minutes became almost half an hour!"

When Charlotte arrived home a few hours later she found her mother waiting for her at the gate, a sure sign that all was not well.

"Get in that house," Harriet said.

"Mam! There's no need to talk to me as if I were a child! What on earth is the matter?"

"You! That's what's the matter. Locking yourself in that shop with that repair man! That's what's the matter. Haven't you any pride? Everyone is talking about you. Locking yourself away with that bicycle man so everyone knows you're there but not answering the door. And in that flat above that slaughter house. Don't think I haven't heard."

98

"A butcher's shop, Mam."

"In there for hours you are, just you and that Joe. He shows no regard for your reputation. But there, what d'you expect from the likes of him!"

Charlotte stared at her mother but declined to argue. She guessed that frustration over her father caused her mother to welcome an excuse to explode over something. Pity it isn't Rhoda once in a while though, she thought irritably.

"I couldn't tell her, she was in such a state," Charlotte explained to Joe that evening. "Please, Joe, don't be angry. I want us to wait just a few more days and announce it at Rhoda and Brian's party."

"Clever trick that'll be. I'm not invited, or had you forgotten?"

"Rhoda can hardly refuse to allow us in!"

The following day, Charlotte asked Joe to go with her to see if there was anything that needed attention at Russell's Bookbinders and Restorers.

Joe agreed but insisted they went to confirm their wedding date first. Carrying all the necessary papers, they went on their bicycles to the registry office. They cycled home with the date firmly booked. At ten o'clock on the morning of Saturday the tenth of June, she would become Mrs Joseph Llewellyn.

She was filled with a sense of excitement and utter happiness, unable to resist smiling at everyone she saw. They pushed their bikes up the steep hill, remounted at Mill House and rode along the quiet lane to the factory.

While she checked the work book trying to ensure

that all the jobs were flowing easily through the various stages, Joe idly glanced through the accounts. It was one of Jack's rare days off or he would have felt unable to pry. Something puzzled him and he asked Charlotte if he could take the books home for a proper examination.

"Why?" she asked. "Surely they are impeccably kept. Only Jack Roberts deals with them. Uncle Peter can hardly have messed them up the way he messes up everything else." She did not notice that he gave no reply.

Recent correspondence was revealing. An order for two hundred booklets had ended up as two thousand. A request for supplies of tape and muslin had been wrongly sent to a firm they no longer dealt with and they had to pay more than they expected. A customer had asked for a book to be restored and instead of replacing the original cover, the work had been given a new one. Not surprisingly, the customer was refusing to pay. How could her uncle be so careless? She could hardly blame the staff. They only did what Uncle Peter told them to do.

The joyful mood was lost. She was so upset by the neglectful way the work was being done she was hardly aware of Joe carrying out the ledgers with their beautifully marbled edges, and strapping them to his bicycle carrier. She only nodded vaguely when he promised to get them back before morning, so Jack wouldn't know they had been examined.

On Saturday morning, Charlotte woke early. Her first thoughts were of Joe. Warm thoughts. Tender, loving thoughts that made her body ache for him. Today they

100

would tell the world they were to marry. She had the usual attack of guilt at the way she was announcing it without discussing the details with her mother but she knew it was the only way. Telling everyone, making it official without prior warning, might prevent her mother from attempting to dissuade her as she had so many times in the past.

The dawn broke with sunshine so bright that Charlotte felt the warmth of it before she opened her eyes. She bathed, dressed in the new dress she had bought specially for the day, and went downstairs to begin preparing breakfast. Everything about the day seemed perfect.

"Look outside, Mam, isn't it a perfect morning?" she said when Harriet came down and accepted the cup of tea Charlotte had ready.

Her mother looked at the sun-washed garden with bees already drunk with an excess of pollen. "With such a start it can't possibly last all day." But even Harriet's doomladen forecast couldn't deaden Charlotte's happiness. The secret added spice to the morning. She hugged her mother and laughed.

Charlotte quickly realised that Uncle Peter was far from well. The doctor had called the previous day and advised him to stay away from the office for at least another week. Charlotte attended to his morning needs then phoned and requested another visit. Harriet went into a panic. She knew Peter was seriously ill; Charlotte had told her the poor man hadn't passed water for an alarmingly long time, and besides, you only had to look at him to know he was very sick. But she just couldn't bring herself to listen to the doctor's words. She couldn't face anything more. It was all too much for her.

If Peter were to die, what would happen to her? Charlotte would have to give up any idea of marrying for the foreseeable future, that much she was certain. Thank goodness it was Rhoda who had married and moved out and not the sensible Charlotte. It was a huge relief when Charlotte phoned and told her that the doctor had declared him well enough to go to the Saturday evening party at Rhoda and Brian's. Now she could forget it: if he was well enough to go to a party it couldn't be serious, could it?

Charlotte had been pleaded with, and bullied, but had refused to tell Rhoda or her mother that she would attend the party. So when she walked in with Joe there was a sudden silence. Uncle Peter, in his wheelchair, sat beside Jack. Harriet sat on the other side of the room with an elegantly dressed Rhoda and her young friends. It was Uncle Peter who first greeted them.

"Charlotte! Joe! We thought you weren't coming. Change your mind about the theatre, did you? We're so glad, aren't we, Harriet?"

"Lovely," Harriet said, with as much grace as she could manage.

Bessie, who had invited herself to the party by offering to help, shouted, "Not gone to the theatre then?" Lowering her voice she added, "Now there's a waste of good money. But then, what do you expect of a girl who rides a bike in high heels," and she gave them a huge wink.

"We aren't stopping," Charlotte said, as she took a drink handed to her by Brian. "We have a bit

102

of news ourselves." Charlotte touched Joe's cheek with a kiss and said, "Congratulate us, won't you? Joe and I are getting married on June the tenth at ten o'clock. We hope you'll all come and wish us well."

Again it was Peter who spoke first. "My lovely girl, I'm so pleased. I've been feeling very guilty, responsible for delaying your wedding like that. We're thrilled, aren't we, Harriet? To see you both ready to settle down and start a life of your own."

"Lovely." This time Harriet found it impossible to smile. She turned away and went into the kitchen, followed quickly by Rhoda.

"Well done, Joe." Brian stepped over, kissed his sister-in-law and shook Joe's hand. Jack was next and soon the room was filled with wedding talk. Harriet came out of the kitchen, eyes reddened by tears.

Joe and Charlotte stayed about an hour and by that time it was apparent that Peter was still far from well. His face was puffy and hot; he looked very tired, and he admitted to some lower back pain and a headache.

Joe pointed this out to Harriet, who had not spoken a word to him since his arrival.

"Peter is all right," she insisted.

"I do feel ready for my bed," Peter admitted, and Jack stood up to drive him home.

"We'll go as well," Charlotte said.

"But you haven't looked at the new lounge suite," Rhoda wailed.

Charlotte ignored her and she and Joe left with some relief. The forced gaiety, the undercurrent of her mother's disapproval, had spoilt the evening.

"It should have been a wonderful evening," Charlotte said sadly. "I'm so sorry, Joe."

"At least it's over, my pretty. And we both knew that however we spread the news it wouldn't have been cheerfully received. Not by the Dragon at least. Your Uncle Peter seemed genuinely pleased."

"It should have been a celebration, but Mam spoilt it as I knew she would."

"I'll make it up to you, I promise." Joe grinned at her then. "Tomorrow we're going out for the day. Our own engagement party it'll be. I've booked us seats on a trip to Clifton Zoo."

"I'll have to ask Mam – "

"No you don't! We'll sneak off early in the morning without telling her where we're going. Knowing she disapproves has got to be part of the fun. Like two naughty kids *mitching* from school we'll be. Now, what say you get a cup of tea made; I have to talk to your uncle before he goes to bed, about business.

"Business, today? Just got ourselves officially engaged we have and you want to talk business? Joe Llewellyn, I'm surprised at you." She smiled at him then and added, "Wait till I'm there, mind, I don't want to miss anything!"

"Just got officially engaged and you want to listen to business talk?" he teased. "No, my pretty, make us a nice cup of tea and I'll tell you all about it later."

What Joe said was serious, but he had a feeling that Peter was hardly aware of his words. The man seemed vague, lost in other thoughts, yet uneasy, looking at him intently as if trying to concentrate at times, and staring into space like a sleepwalker at others.

"There's money missing from the firm's accounts,

Mr Russell," Joe began. "A lot of money I suspect. There's a charge for twelve pounds I noticed first, for materials that are being ordered for a second time. The stock cupboards and stock lists show no sign of the first lot arriving. You've been charged for stuff you haven't received."

"Twelve pounds you say?" Peter's voice was low and Joe could hardly hear him. He thought it must be because the man was shocked. He said nothing for a while, his eyes were restless as if he were trying to gather his thoughts. "It's a simple mix-up, Joe," he said at last. "Nothing more than that. It will be in the reckoning further down the column, cancelled and allowed for."

"I looked and it isn't."

"Still, twelve pounds, it isn't that terrible," Peter said, his voice still strained. "An oversight. That'll be it. Ring the suppliers, perhaps they are late delivering."

"I have and they aren't." Joe spoke slowly, allowing for the man to take it all in. "The trouble is, Mr Russell, that's only one instant. I kept the books overnight and found several. What I found in a few hours amounts to almost two hundred pounds."

Joe looked at Peter, as there seemed to be no response to his words. Peter was sweating and Joe noticed suddenly how swollen the man's face had become recently. Flushed now, it was more apparent. "Are you all right?" he asked. Alarm grew as Peter groaned, held his head. The man was obviously very ill.

"Charlotte! Come quick. I'll phone for the doctor, you wait with your uncle."

An hour later, Peter was on his way to hospital with the siren urging other motorists to make way. Having been told the news by Joe, Rhoda was alarmed, concerned, but wailing most loudly at the premature ending of her party. Charlotte was comforting her mother and agreeing with her that the wedding must be delayed once again, that she couldn't possibly leave her mother at such a time. Joe protested but was sent on his way by Harriet, who made it clear that it was he who had caused Peter to be ill.

"Worrying him about weddings and troubles at work when he was so tired. Cruel and thoughtless that Joe Llewellyn is for sure. Haven't I always said so? But will you listen to me? No!"

Trying to console her distraught mother, Charlotte held back her own tears. She had hoped that in making the announcement so publicly her mother would have to accept it. She knew now that it was a hopeless dream.

There was a time to fight and a time to submit. This was a time to submit, to accept what fate so clearly had planned for her. Her life was unfolding before her, a long, straight road caring for her mother without any deviations to find a life of her own. Acceptance was the only way. To fight it would only bring resentment and bitterness.

She didn't know when, or even *if*, she would marry Joe, but she knew it would not be on June the tenth. Not unless her mother dropped dead. She cried then, shamed at the wicked thought. Tomorrow she would go and tell Joe that the wedding was off, indefinitely.

Chapter Six

"What d'you mean, the wedding is off? Honestly, Charlotte, dealing with you is like coping with a petulant child!" The normally placid Joe shocked Charlotte by reacting in serious anger when she called into the shop to tell him that the wedding had to be cancelled.

"But Joe, you don't understand – "

"I understand that when there's a problem you push me away. Won't you ever think of us as a team? A partnership? Sensible, dependable Charlotte! That's how people see you, isn't it? Well I think you're simply afraid."

"Joe, that's ridiculous." She backed away from him, startled at the unexpected rage.

"Is it? The truth is that you seek the easy way out. Rather than confront your difficulties you fall over backwards to avoid dealing with them. You're a coward, Charlotte Russell, and you haven't the guts to become one of a couple. You haven't the guts to stand up for me, for us. Always on your own you'll be, unless you change, and pretty damned quick!" He walked out of the shop, slamming the door behind him and after the shock of his explosive anger had faded, she wondered what to do.

107

She'd never had anyone walk away from her in a huff before and she didn't like the feeling. She looked around the neat, orderly shop and felt trapped. She didn't want to be there when Joe finally returned, yet how she could leave the shop open and unattended? She sat on a chair in the small office, trembling, frightened, his words stabbing into her brain like knives. He was so unfair. She couldn't help her mother being the way she was. How could he expect her to walk away and leave her to face her father's return, her uncle's illness and the possibility of a divorce?

Two hours later she was still there, worrying about getting the dinner, but still unwilling to leave Joe's shop unlocked. She decided that the dinner was unimportant on this occasion; Joe did come first. She felt guilty, but less so than she would have if she failed to look after Joe's property. Mam wouldn't die without dinner, she might even get something for herself, although that she doubted.

She sold a few small items, demonstrated a bicycle to someone considering moving up from an old sit-up-and-beg bicycle to one with three-speed gears and drop-handlebars, and between times she sat and stared into space. There was a phone but she didn't telephone home. What was there to say? No sympathy from her mother over having quarrelled with Joe, that was certain!

The door opened and Joe stood there, the anger still in his eyes and her instinct was to push past him and run out, but she didn't.

"Oh, Joe," she said softly and he came towards

her, his expression softening, his arms opening to enfold her.

"Charlotte, I'm sorry. But we really do have to deal with it, together."

"I'll try, Joe."

"At least everything is out in the open now, she knows what she has to face. The worst is over."

"Unless she finds out about Lillian. If she were told about Dad and Bertha – "

"*If* it's true, mind, you know what this place is for rumours. Besides, a secret kept for eighteen years isn't likely to break now, is it?"

"I hope not, Joe, I hope not."

"Remember" – the steel was back in his voice as he touched her cheeks and made her look at him – "remember, my pretty, if it does, we'll help her but it's something for *us* to cope with, to face together. Right?"

Together. It had a lovely sound.

Charlotte went to the hospital frequently. On the third day of her uncle's stay she found him improved and able to talk to her. For two days he had been semiconscious and it was with relief that she looked around the doorway and saw him propped up on his pillows and looking towards her. He waved a greeting and she ran to hug him.

"Uncle Peter! What a relief to see you're on the mend."

"I'm certainly better than yesterday. Did you come?"

"Of course I did."

"What about your mother?"

"She's well," she said, deliberately misunderstanding him.

"I meant, did she come?"

"I know you did." She busied herself packing away the clean clothes she had brought and taking out items for washing. The speed of her actions revealed her anger. "I've tried to persuade her, Uncle Peter. She won't consider it."

"Don't be angry with her."

"Even Rhoda came in to sit with you yesterday with her patient and adoring Brian. She sat holding your hand being terribly brave, as if *she* were the patient and about to have surgery. But Mam went to the pictures."

"I've never told you about your mother's childhood, have I, Charlotte? I'm sure she hasn't told you either. It was an empty and sad one. Everyone she began to care for left her. Your grandparents lived abroad and your mother was left here. From a cruelly early age she attended a boarding school. During the holidays she came home to an empty house with only indifferent servants to look after her, and mostly they were servants who were new to her, they never stayed long. And I suspect that her parents found it cheaper to close the house and employ someone just for the holiday then close it again."

Charlotte said nothing, she only half listened, closing her mind to sympathy. Hadn't it been similar with herself and Rhoda? Left with Joe's Auntie Bessie Philpot night after night? If it had been so terrible for her mother without parents constantly near, why had she treated her own children in the same way?

110

"There was no Auntie Bessie Philpot for her," Peter added, cutting across her thoughts.

Again Charlotte didn't respond. She admitted to herself that Joe's Auntie Bessie had been a loving, caring, deputy mother. How could that sort of childhood make her mother so unfeeling? How could that explain her non-appearance at the hospital to comfort Uncle Peter when he was so ill?

"But why doesn't she come to see how you are?" she asked finally. "I don't see how a lonely childhood could stop her wanting to make sure you're all right. You've never left her alone for a day since Dadda went away. Not even during the war. She was one of the lucky ones."

"She was sent to nursery school as soon as it was possible and during the holidays, stayed with a succession of friends. Many of whom didn't really want her. She sensed this and was bewildered and sad. At seven she went to boarding school and, because they were so far away, her parents couldn't even visit on open days. When all her friends had their families with them she stood in the background utterly alone. Imagine how she must have felt."

Peter closed his eyes for a few moments and Charlotte wanted him to stop talking, to stop trying to make her understand. Why should she understand a mother who allowed an unhappy childhood to ruin her own daughter's life? She's trying to prevent me marrying Joe simply for her own reasons, not out of concern for me, Charlotte thought. Resentment, not pity, filled her heart.

"At term's ending," Peter went on, after another, longer pause, "when all the other children were being collected by their parents, swept up, kissed, hugged, she had to wait until the person who was paid to mind her turned up. Always the last. A stranger every time."

Charlotte saw that Peter was tired and she said nothing while he closed his eyes and rested again, dozing intermittently. Lost in her own thoughts, she began to imagine that lonely little girl and it became impossible not to feel sympathy for her. Yet it didn't really explain her mother's non-appearance at the hospital. She depended on Uncle Peter so much, some affection must have grown between them? Even if there was no affection, normal behaviour must deem it proper for her to pretend some? To put on an act?

The loneliness of which Uncle Peter spoke was of long ago. She had been married more than twenty years. Since her father's disappearance she'd had Uncle Peter for support. Surely it was time to forget her hollow childhood? She saw Peter's eyes reopen and she prepared to listen with exaggerated interest. It seemed important for him to tell her. Perhaps once he had, he would rest. He looked so dreadfully tired, his eyes bright and feverish.

"Then," he went on, as if he hadn't paused, "when the immiment return of her mother and father promised a life filled with love, attention and security, her parents died. They caught a fever during their last weeks in Malaya and in days they were dead."

"She couldn't have missed them. She didn't know them."

"Their most recent letters had been full of what they would do on their return. It all sounded like a wonderful dream. Holidays together, picnics, visits to friends, everything she had imagined, and everything she had seen other children enjoying." Again his eyes closed and she sat patiently, trying to imagine the little girl that her mother had been.

"She had a calendar on her bedside table on which she was marking the days. With only two weeks to go they let her down, finally and irrevocably, by dying and leaving her practically peniless."

"But then she had Dadda and now she has you," Charlotte insisted. "And Rhoda and me."

Peter seemed not to hear. "She was engaged to marry and he let her down too, abandoning her only days before the wedding. The banns were called, then he told her he was marrying someone else. She married your father on the rebound and all the years they were together she constantly reminded him he was second choice.

"Poor Eric, he tried so hard to do everything she asked, to compensate for being the wrong man. Her guardians refused permission for her to marry your father, you know. They considered him far below her socially, even though all the money her family once had was lost in some financial swindle." He smiled at her and went on. "They married anyway and I think were happy, for a time. At least until the disappointment of not having the large family they both wanted so much. Then your father gave her the social life she craved, for as long as he could stand it, then – well, you know what happened then."

"So why is she so against Joe? Didn't she learn from her own experience of others deciding for her?"

"Joe was – but no, that's another story for another

113

time. She has never lost the fear of losing those she loves. She's afraid of losing you, I suppose."

"She won't lose me if I marry Joe. In Main Street I'll be, not Malaya! She'd only have to shout and I'd hear her!" She sighed with impatience. "Really Uncle Peter, you'd think she'd sympathize, not stand in our way, having been in the same position with a guardian disapproving of the man she loved." Peter seemed not to hear.

"Your mother and father desperately wanted children. There were three babies which failed to survive before you arrived healthy and yelling your head off," he went on, his weary eyes staring into space as if seeing again those sad events. "Losing three babies after a childhood like she had had would be enough to send many women out of their minds. The fear is constantly there. She was very anxious about you and Rhoda when you were small. If you and Rhoda weren't home from school on the stroke of three-thirty she was in tears."

"I don't remember such concern," Charlotte whispered rebelliously.

"When your father went away, she transferred her anxieties onto me, heaped the reasons for panic onto my shoulders," Peter said. "It's as if she has to have someone to worry about, someone on whom she utterly depends."

His voice was low now and Charlotte had to bend close to him to hear. "If I'm five minute late home she imagines me crushed under the wheels of some enormous lorry. I let her down you see. Like all the rest. I'd promised her she could rely on me forever. I swore I'd always be strong. By getting

114

myself injured and stuck in a wheelchair, I let her down too."

Charlotte sat unmoving, silently digesting her uncle's words. She tried to see how such experiences could make it impossible to overcome fear with love, and she failed.

As she saw it her mother had let Uncle Peter down by her reaction to his disability. Surely she could have taken over and cared for him? Surely she owed him that much?

She wouldn't let Joe down, whatever happened to them, and why, if childhood without attention was so damaging, why had her mother left her and Rhoda so much? Going on holidays without them, spending evening after evening entertaining and being entertained, leaving them with Joe's Auntie Bessie Philpot? She couldn't make sense of it.

The only time she and Rhoda were included was when they were dressed up prettily and brought into a room filled with people they hardly knew and were made to sing for them, an embarrassing and painful experience for herself. Although, she remembered, Rhoda had seemed not to mind being paraded and admired. What her uncle had told her only added to her belief that her mother was a selfish woman. That she was repeating the follies of her childhood without a thought for what her own children were suffering, simply made it worse.

She wondered if she dare discuss her mutinous thoughts with her uncle but when she turned to him, he was sleeping. Not a peaceful, replenishing sleep but one that appeared agitated and unrestful. He began moving his arms about, thrashing the covers as if locked in a nightmare. His swollen face and his unhealthy, moist, red skin alarmed her. Anxious now, she ran to fetch a nurse.

Bertha walked down the lane leading to her home and saw her daughter walking up to meet her.

"Thought you'd got lost, Mam," Lillian said, smiling as if she had told a brilliant joke. Bertha laughed and hugged her.

"Never. Fat chance I have of getting lost when I never leave the town."

"I cleaned out the chicken's coop and put the straw and shit in a bag for the allotments."

"Hush that talk! Call it manure, Lillian."

"That isn't what they call it over the allotments, Mam."

"You must call it manure."

"Why?" Lillian wore her stubborn look and Bertha resigned herself to a hour of sulks.

"Go and talk to Auntie Bessie while I get dinner," she told Lillian. Talking to Bessie always restored Lillian's normal good temper. Perhaps she would be able to have an hour's lie down. She pushed a couple of potatoes into the oven. They'd be nice for tea with a bit of sauce to hide the lack of butter.

Lillian hauled herself up from the chair she had flopped into and watched her mother climb the stairs, and heard the creaking as she lay on the bed. Knocking on next door's window brought a smiling Bessie to the door.

"It's my birthday soon, Auntie Bessie."

"Yes, darlin'. Eighteen you'll be, quite grown up now, you are."

"Perhaps he'll come with a present, my father. Some people have lots of presents for their birthdays, don't they?"

"Some," Bessie said. "But not all." Dropping her voice she added sadly, "Never have a present, I wouldn't, if it wasn't for my Joe."

"My Dadda coming home, that would be a present, wouldn't it?"

"A wonderful gift." Bessie handed her the glass of home-made lemonade and a small Welsh cake. "Eat up now then we'll go for a walk along the riverbank." Lillian picked up the flat, spicy cake with a nod of thanks.

"Do you think he'll be like Ronald Coleman?"

"Who, my darlin'?" Bessie asked, although she knew who Lillian was thinking of.

"My Dadda. Tall he'll be because I'm tall. But not fat. I won't be fat when he comes, or shy. Mam says I'm shy because I haven't got a father. But I have and he'll come and he'll make everything better."

Bertha called to tell Bessie where she would be, and walked up the hill to Mill House. The door was opened by Charlotte, for which she gave silent thanks. If Harriet had answered her knock she might not have said what she came for. Snooty beyond was Harriet Russell.

"Called for a word with your uncle I have," she explained. "Home from hospital, isn't he?"

"Home but far from well. Come in and I'll see if he's awake." Charlotte led her into the back room overlooking the garden and left them to talk. It had

117

been apparent from Bertha's tightened lips that she wanted to talk to her uncle privately.

"I'll make us some tea," she said, closing the kitchen door behind her.

Peter smiled at his visitor. "Bertha, nice to see you. How are you managing. All right?"

"That Jack Roberts of yours has been fighting again," she said. "Funny mind, considering how well he's thought of, but I've never trusted Jack Roberts. He lives in one of Kath's cheapest rooms, yet he's got money. I was behind him in the bank once, changing five shillings worth of pennies that I'd saved, I was, and he was drawing out a lot of money. All them white fivers like I've never seen more than twice in my whole life. What could he be wanting to draw such a large sum for? What did he do with it? He's never left the town so far as I can discover. And more's to the point, where did he get it?"

"As you say, he doesn't spend much of his wages, living in one room, with Kath doing his cooking and his laundry. What he does with his savings is his concern. We mustn't pry."

"So long as he doesn't cheat Kath." The small woman looked so fierce that Peter was reminded of a ferret he used to keep when he was young. Small, intelligent and looking rather cuddly and harmless, but with a bite that could kill a rabbit in seconds.

"I'm sure he wouldn't do that. Not Jack."

Peter was thoughtful as they sat and sipped their tea and Bertha talked to Charlotte. It was intriguing to wonder what Jack was doing with a bunch of fivers. Then he smiled in relief. Of course, it would have been the business account. Jack went to the bank and took out money to pay the wages every week. He explained this to Bertha.

After Bertha had gone he frowned. The wages paid to the small work force didn't really explain why Jack had a load of five pound notes. One pound notes, and ten shilling notes and lots of silver and copper, but there weren't many who earned more than five pounds.

He mentioned it to Charlotte then put the puzzle from his mind. Whatever the explanation, Jack had the right to do as he pleased with his own money.

Harriet overheard some of the conversation and repeated it to Kath some days later.

"Bertha says he's taking you for a fool, living cheap while he has a lot of money."

"My lodgers are *my* business and no one takes me for a fool. I decide who should live in my house. I don't want the likes of you discussing my boarders."

"How dare you speak to me like that?" Harriet said angrily.

"Dare, is it? Why shouldn't I *dare* talk to you like that? Because you think yourself above the likes of the rest of us? Damned cheek telling my private business to all and sundry. For all your fancy pretentions you've got a mouth bigger than the Severn Tunnel, you have."

"I don't spread – "

"– You aren't going to say you don't spread gossip? Harriet Russell, may my tongue come loose and fall out if you aren't the biggest gossip this side of Offa's Dyke!"

"I've never seen you blocking your ears so you can't hear!"

"Bertha was concerned, and talked to Peter for reassurance. You're passing it on for the joy of it, there's a difference!"

"You support Bertha Evans, a woman with an illegitimate child, and not *me*!"

"Your life isn't so pure that you could afford for people to talk about you, mind!"

"At least I haven't got a child with no known father!" Harriet said haughtily.

"No known father, is it?" Kath was furious now. "No known father? Well then, Mrs High and Mighty, what if I tell you what I should have told you years ago. Your Eric! That's who's been paying for Lillian's keep. Why would he do that if he wasn't responsible? No known father indeed! Paying her a couple of pound every week he's been ever since she was born, to help feed the poor girl. There, how's that for a juicy bit of gossip then? Like it do you, when you're the victim? Mrs-superior-sodding-Russell?"

Harriet ran from her, stumbled along the pavement, stepping out onto the road, running for Rhoda's house to hide her shame. She ran blindly, oblivious of traffic. Bicycles swerved, horses pulled up, cars squealed their brakes and irate drivers shouted and called her names. She was aware of none of it, hardly caring if she were knocked down or not.

Eric, with Bertha. It couldn't be true. He wouldn't. Not with Bertha. And all this time Bertha hadn't said a word. She wouldn't have kept it to herself. Not for more than eighteen years. Lying Kath was, for sure.

She reached Rhoda's house, then remembered with

a wail of dismay that Rhoda and Brian were still in Aberystwyth. In a daze, she walked home. Her shoes, unsuitable for walking, cut into her feet. She puffed as she hurried away from the town where she imagined everyone was laughing at her. Sobs wracked her body. Life was too cruel. How could she live through this? Nothing, nothing could ever be worse than this.

Charlotte was out. She didn't go in to see Peter, she had almost forgotten he was there.

What she needed was to be alone to consider this latest punch in the face from a cruel fate. First Eric turning up to make her story about a mental aberration a lie, and now this. How could it be true? How could the slow, overweight Lillian be half-sister to her lovely Rhoda and Charlotte? Going to her bedroom, she lay on the bed, eyes dry now, but the ache in her heart was like a stone.

Eric had been such a catch. A neat, attractive man, mannerly and quiet, hard working and helpful in the house. He had been earning a good wage up at the factory and he had saved money to buy into the firm. The previous owner had died and he and Peter had taken over the business and made a success of it. He had restored the neglected Mill House and refurnished it and they had planned to fill it with children. Even during the war, when he had been exceptionally busy and had been called to do extra duties like fire watching, he found spare moments to work on the house. She had believed he was content with her and their life together. It had all been a lie.

She had boasted to everyone that her husband was generous and kind, comparing him with her friends' husbands and making them discontented. And all the time he'd been straying, and, she realised with a shock of pain and grief, others must have known. In the bleakness of this latest discovery, others knowing about the affair seemed the worst of his cruelty. She wouldn't divorce him though. That way she could prevent that Gloria woman from winning everything. No, she'd make him pay by refusing to let him marry the woman and legalize her children.

A few days later, a letter came from a solicitor in Barry, explaining that Eric was beginning proceedings to divorce her. She didn't reply to the letter.

Charlotte and Joe knew nothing about the newest revelation that had given Harriet so much grief. Her depression was put down to her worries over Peter, who was still terribly unwell.

"Mam," Charlotte said one day in early June. "I want to marry Joe."

"Don't be ridiculous, it's impossible at present, surely you can see that!"

"I can see my twenty-fourth birthday approaching. How much longer do you want me to wait, Mam?"

"Until you find someone suitable."

"Joe is my choice. Surely you can understand. I love him, like you loved Dad, in spite of others trying to persuade you different."

"Who's been talking to you? Uncle Peter, I expect. Well, when you think of how your father has treated me, I might have been wiser to listen to those dissenting voices!"

"You had twenty happy years. I'd settle for that while hoping for more."

"Happy? You don't know the half of it!"

Surprised at the vehemence in her mother's tone, Charlotte raised her own voice and said, "Uncle Peter tried to make me understand your unreasonableness but all I understand is your selfishness!"

She stood angrily, wanting to say more but afraid to. She had so rarely answered her mother back, and even now, at her age, when so much was at stake, she couldn't continue. They glared at each other and the air prickled around them as if filled with electricity. The knock at the door startled them.

"I'll go," Charlotte said, but her mother pushed her aside.

"Go to your room until you've calmed down!"

Irritated by the interruption, she pulled open the door.

Eric stood there, his hand raised to give a second knock. Standing beside him was a girl of about eighteen, whose hands were held by two small girls.

The toddlers were holding on to Eric's trouser legs and peering up at her with curiosity. Eric had a small baby in his arms, wrapped tightly in a woollen shawl.

"Can we come in, Harriet?" Eric asked.

Bewildered, not knowing what or how she should feel about such an invasion, Harriet stepped back and watched like someone in a dream, as Eric ushered his brood through the passageway and into her living room.

The children stood in a row while he introduced them.

"Miranda, who is eighteen, then Ellie, six. Isabelle, five. Louise is four, Petula is just two and this," hugging the infant in his arms, "this is Matthew.

He's only three months old and missing his mother very much, as we all are."

"Missing her?" Harriet stuttered. This was her home, yet these people were making her the odd one out. Where was Charlotte? She looked around, desperate for her daughter to appear and help sort this out.

"Gloria died three weeks ago. I was wondering if you could see your way to taking us in here."

"What?" Harriet shouted the word and Matthew jumped in Eric's arms and began to cry, a snuffling, dry sound that ate straight into Harriet's heart. For some obscure reason, memories of her own lost babies flooded back and the once familiar ache of bereavement returned with an intensity that was an acute pain.

"But – I don't have room for all of you," she said, trying to think clearly. Where was Charlotte? She should be here. How could she manage anything like this without Charlotte?

Eric was jiggling the baby and saying soothing words to comfort him. "I realise you'd have arrangements to make. If we gave you a week?"

"Give him to me, Dad," the eighteen-year-old Miranda said, and she took the baby, sat down and began to give him a feed from a bottle taken from Eric's coat pocket.

"Dad?" Harriet faltered.

"He isn't really my father," Miranda smiled. "Our father, mine and Danny's that is, was killed at the battle for Tobruk."

"Danny? How many are you for heaven's sake?"

"Seven," Eric replied, sitting and taking the two

124

youngest girls on his knees. "Lucky seven we used to say, while Gloria was carrying little Matthew here. Sadly, he didn't bring us luck. Gloria didn't recover from the birth." He looked at Miranda and they shared a look that brought a tightness to Harriet's throat. It seemed so long since anyone had looked at her with love or even genuine affection.

"You won't turn us away, will you, Harriet?" Eric said. "I don't know how I'll manage if you refuse to help us."

"Why should *I* help?"

"No reason at all, except your basic goodness."

Eric watched her as fleeting thoughts and changing emotions flashed across her face. A small, untidy figure, in a creased suit and less than pristine shirt and tie, his grey hair awry, a gentle, patient smile on his tired, pale face.

"What would I tell people?"

"The truth is always the simplest. The people of Bryn Melinau are kind folk; they'll welcome us all for sure. Shocked they'll be, but they'll soon forget."

"Forget? You waltzing in here after seven years with a family I knew nothing about and expecting me to welcome them like they were my own?" She shook her head. "Shamed I'd be. I couldn't, Eric. You're mad to even ask. My friends, all the people in the town, they'd all know."

"Gossip is always popular here, but people are good deep down, they wouldn't make us feel unwanted. Time will see us settled and accepted."

"Damn what they think of you! What about *me*?" Harriet shouted and again baby Matthew started and began to cry.

"What's most important, your hurt feelings or the happiness of these beautiful children?"

"I don't know how to care for children. We always had servants to cope. I couldn't have any more after Rhoda or I might have learnt. Not that that stopped *you*. Because your wife didn't oblige, you found plenty of others who did. Bertha Evans and that soppy Lillian. That's down to you, isn't it!" She couldn't stop the words coming out, even though she knew it wasn't the right time. She was thrown into utter confusion by this unexpected and unbelievable situation. The need to hurt him was a pain that wouldn't go away. "I think I hate you, Eric. I couldn't bear to sleep under the same roof."

"Then take the children. Miranda will care for them, just give them a home to grow up in together. Please Harriet, I'm begging you not to turn them away. They'll go into a home if I can't find us a safe place to live. Separated, growing up not knowing their brothers and sisters. Remember how we planned to fill this house with children?"

"Don't talk about what we planned," she said sharply, memories stabbing her heart. "This is something you did that was wicked, Eric. Truly wicked to do this and come back here to taunt me with it."

"The blame is mine and I readily accept it, but how can you refuse them? Innocent they are, and so beautiful."

Harriet looked around the room filled with strangers. Where was Charlotte when she needed her?

"Please," Eric said again, softly.

She turned away from his pleading eyes, tried not to look at the drawn and frightened faces of the children and looked instead at Miranda. The girl was sitting feeding baby Matthew, her head bent watching his face, long lashes on her soft, rosy cheeks, dark hair falling around her shoulders in natural waves.

She's a very pretty girl, Harriet thought, this stranger who calls my husband "Dad". There's a gentleness about her, a trusting look in the dark eyes. She looked away. Although she was the one wronged and being asked the favour, she found she was unable to look any of them in the eyes. She had to stay unemotional, hard, tell them to go, forget they ever came.

"What do you think of all this?" she demanded, looking towards Miranda but focusing her gaze above the girl's head.

"Eric and Gloria were so happy, it's a tragedy."

"I don't mean how do you feel about your mother stealing someone else's husband and being happy with him! I mean this," she waved her arms, encompassing the children and the now silent Eric. "You, expecting me – the wronged wife – to come to your aid."

"Dad has always told us how much you love children. I think the children would be safe with you."

"And me? What d'you feel for me?"

"I think your friends will be impressed by your loving and noble act and think very highly of you."

"You do, do you?"

"I do."

"Why can't *you* look after them? They're more yours than mine."

"Dad thinks living with you would benefit us all. Even my brother Danny, who goes to sea, will want a place to come home to. You're the one. We need

127

you desperately. After your own sad childhood and your desire for a large family, I – "

"I do not want my private affairs discussed!" Harriet, overcome, fled from the room. An hour later, Harriet was clearing the dishes after feeding her guests with soup and a salad.

Eric smiled at Harriet as he stacked the dishes preparatory to washing them. His smile was still capable of weakening her resolve. There was a beat of excitement in her heart. Telling others was going to be a challenge but the idea of a ready-made family was beginning to appeal. Time in her life for a change. Lucky seven indeed! Well perhaps it might be just that – if it meant Eric was back! She'd made him promise to go along with the story about amnesia though. He owed her that much.

Chapter Seven

Charlotte had walked out of the back door when her mother had sent her to her room like a naughty child and ran down the hill to find Joe. When they walked into Mill House a couple of hours later they thought they had become involved in a dream. The place was filled with children. One was sitting on the stairs picking bits of wallpaper loose, one sat cross-legged on the hall carpet runner, being pulled along by an older child, and from the kitchen, voices were raised in anger. Uncle Peter could be heard laughing and on investigation was discovered reading a story, with actions, to a solemn little girl aged about five.

"You're back," he said unnecessarily. "This is Isabelle, she's five and already at school. Isn't she beautiful?"

"Uncle Peter, what's going on?" Charlotte demanded. "Where's Mam and who are these children?"

"Best I let your mother explain," he smiled. He turned back to the little girl, who sat waiting patiently for her story. "Now, Isabelle, where were we? Father rabbit was just bringing home a bag filled with carrots from Farmer Thomas's field . . ."

Charlotte stared at Joe and he took her hand.

They went to the kitchen door and, pushing it open, saw her mother and her father having a row.

"Dad!" She couldn't hide the pleasure she felt at seeing him.

"I know this is a shock for you all, my dear," Eric said. "But these children, and Miranda here, are my new family."

"Miranda?" She looked at the young woman standing in the doorway, a baby on her arms.

"A sort of adopted daughter. These beautiful children are mine and Gloria's. He said the names and added their ages and Charlotte and Joe listened in disbelief. "Miranda here, and her brother Danny, belong to a previous marriage. Their father was killed and – "

"Wait a minute, Dadda. You mean these are yours? They are my half-sisters?"

"And brother," he said proudly, pointing to baby Matthew in Miranda's arms.

It seemed to Charlotte that the four most active children, Ellie, Isabelle, who had tired of Peter's stories, Louise and Petula, multiplied in number as she watched. Miranda nursed the baby but the other four ran amok without a word of stricture from the bemused Harriet, who seemed unaware of her carpets and rugs being used for sleighs, her polished floors for skating rinks.

Later, when they had departed by taxi, the silence trembled around the house for a long time.

"What are you going to do, Mam?" Charlotte asked, into the hollow silence.

"Emigrate!" Harriet said with a weak laugh.

"Mam," Charlotte said in disbelief, "you're going to take them in!"

"Good on you, Mrs Russell," Joe whispered in awe. "Bloody good on you."

Once Harriet had formally agreed to Eric's family moving into Mill House, Eric began to order beds and, with Charlotte and Joe's assistance, turned two of Harriet's five bedrooms into dormitories with three beds in each, plus a cot for baby Matthew. He also arranged for Bessie to do an extra morning to deal with the ironing, and bought a washing machine, "Because," he said to Charlotte, with his gentle smile, "I don't want our arrival to completely exhaust you and your mother!" He hugged her and added, "Besides, you and Joe will be marrying soon from what I hear, and then your mother will be glad of any machinery that will reduce her burden. Glad I am for you, Charlotte. Joe seems to be a very decent and caring man. I'm sure you'll be happy."

Charlotte thanked him but wondered if this new chapter in the saga of Mill House would allow her marriage to take place as planned.

Once the news broke, there were many offers of help. People struggled up the hill to bring an assortment of furniture and china to help Harriet cope with the influx of the extra family. Cutlery and china appeared on the porch, brought by women who gave gladly. They talked about the event almost with pride. Even from those who liked Harriet the least, there wasn't a single malicious word. Everyone was glad to help, and almost every household provided something to add to the comfort of Eric's new brood.

Outsized saucepans no longer needed by families who had grown up and dispersed, bedding, extra chairs and even a table, came up from Kath's boarding house, carried by two of her boarders.

"The house is no longer ours, Mam," Charlotte said one evening when, exhausted after pulling up a worn carpet and helping Joe to cover the floor of the bedroom with linoleum, they sat drinking a cup of cocoa.

"It's worse than I imagined," Harriet admitted. "I'd thought of all the extra persons but not their possessions, nor the furniture and bedding and the dozens of other things needed to accommodate them all. Their clothes alone need a small room! The house is so full I don't think Bessie will be able to clean it."

Charlotte was preparing to sympathise with her mother but to her surprise she saw that, far from needing comforting words, Harriet looked happy.

"What about Dad, Mam?" she asked.

"*What* about your father?" The response was sharp and Charlotte realised, too late, that Eric was a subject best avoided. Her mother would sort out how she felt about having her wayward husband sleeping under the same roof but it wouldn't be solved as easily as fitting an extra seven people into Mill House. Eight, when Miranda's seaman brother came home.

On June the tenth, the day on which they had planned to be married, Charlotte and Joe sat at the top of the hill above Mill House looking down at the town below. Neither was inclined to talk. They watched

132

the early afternoon traffic below, both thinking about the flat above the ex-butcher's shop that was to have been their new home; Joe remembering how he and Charlotte had hurriedly decorated the rooms so they would be ready for today, and Charlotte sifting through in her mind all she had collected in her "bottom drawer", wondering if she would ever use them.

It was a dull day, the sun refusing to shine, the hills around them holding clouds around their peaks like scarves to ward off the chill.

"Come on, Joe, my thoughts are becoming melancholy," she said. "Let's go and have a cup of tea. Mam is probably out with Rhoda and Dad has taken Uncle Peter and the children to see a cricket match."

In the living room sat her mother, Rhoda and Brian. Rhoda was in a frilly hat and summer dress, nylons on her shapely legs, slim feet in a pair of Joyce sandals. Brian was smartly dressed in a grey Hector Powe suit, blue shirt and soberly matching tie. His expensive shoes were polished, socks a perfect match with his tie. A man, Charlotte thought, who would never answer the door before looking in a mirror and tidying his hair. Brian and Rhoda were a couple so alike in their attitude and behaviour she couldn't imagine them apart. Of all the couples she knew, Rhoda and Brian were the most perfectly matched. Harriet ignored the couple's arrival. Brian had just announced that he was moving into larger premises owing to the rapid increase in his business.

"Very clever, my Bri," Rhoda said proudly, greeting her sister and Joe with a wave.

"My move has been postponed again, would you believe," Joe said. "It should have been all settled. There's some trouble with the buyer getting the loan, although it was approved some time ago."

"You took a chance doing all that work in a shop that isn't yet yours, then," Brian said. "I hope the sale doesn't fall through."

"No chance of that. I suspect that the couple who're buying the bicycle shop are delaying so they don't have to start paying until next month," Joe said. "Another couple of weeks and it should be all settled."

"Bri said he shouldn't have done all that work on the meat shop until it was his," Rhoda confided in her mother. Harriet said nothing.

"The new shop is in a good spot." Brian and Joe began to talk about stocking the new premises.

"Charlotte, can't you see something different about me?" Rhoda said petulantly.

"No," Charlotte frowned. "New hat? New sandals?"

"Not my clothes, silly. *Me!*"

"You look the same as always, dressed up for a wedding and you only going to the shops."

"I'm a mother-to-be. Charlotte, I'm going to have a baby!"

"Rhoda! That's marvellous! Oh what a thrill. That means I'm going to be an auntie!"

Joe smiled and winked at Brian. "Well done! Well done!"

"What d'you mean, well done?" Harriet asked. "What a thing to say in response to such news."

"Congratulations to you both," Joe said.

"So that's why you didn't go shopping today,"

134

Charlotte said. "You came to tell us the good news."

"My Bri took the afternoon off," Rhoda said, "he's coming to the shops with me. I can't carry much you see, not now. He says I've got to be spoilt for the next seven months. And there's so much to buy, isn't there, Bri?"

"You should see the lists she made," Brian groaned. "I didn't dream babies could be so expensive."

"With Rhoda everything's expensive!" Charlotte laughed. "You should know that by now. Let's all have a celebratory cup of tea."

For the next few weeks Rhoda spent her time in a flurry of frantic shopping. She bought everything a child could need up to two years of age. She would have gone further in her desire for her child to "have everything" but, not knowing whether it would be a boy or girl, she had to stop at two.

"But we won't need to make the garden fence higher until next summer," Brian sighed one morning when she was looking through her lists and demanding that a sandpit must be prepared, and a play area cemented ready for the tricycle – which her mother had insisted on buying so Joe couldn't. "We'll have to slow down, Rhoda, the money is pouring out faster than I'm earning it. I can't break into the money set aside for the second shop; it has to be fully stocked or we won't attract customers. You know that the business is more important for the baby's future than a sandpit and a new fence."

His voice held a hint of irritation, and Rhoda was surprised. She had never known him to be angry with anyone and certainly not herself. It didn't persuade

135

her to ease up on her demands though. Instead she was more determined to get what she so resolutely believed to be the essentials for her child. He had to know straight away that their child was going to have all the necessary toys and activities he needed for growing into a healthy, happy and clever person. She knew he would be clever, and he was certain to be handsome, you only had to look at herself and Brian to know that.

The irritation grew and by the time Brian left for work his patience was sorely ruffled. When she gave him a grocery list to hand in for delivery later that day he threw it back at her.

"I can't see to this today," he said as he pulled on his coat and reached for his hat. "I have an important meeting with a new supplier from whom I want delayed payments. I want to concentrate on that. It's our livelihood for God's sake. You'll have to attend to your own shopping, you've plenty of time after all; with the people I pay to do work here there's nothing much left for you to do!"

Rhoda put on what she considered her pretty pout. "Oh, I see, so now our child is on the way I'm no longer important! Now you have shown yourself in your true colours, Brian Carpenter! Ignored I'm to be from now on! Nothing but a childbearing drudge!"

The door slammed. Her petulant expression vanished in alarm. Unbelievably, he had gone out without saying he was sorry. Their first quarrel and he'd gone without putting it right. She dressed herself, tearfully reliving every word of their disagreement, called a taxi and went to talk to her mother.

*   *   *

Brian was seethingly angry. He loved Rhoda and enjoyed the comfortable home and the loving atmosphere she provided.

A car came out of a side street and made him slow down. Irritably he pressed the horn, tooting repeatedly to show the inconsiderate fool behind the wheel how stupidly he had behaved. His tension tightened as two boys cycling to school wavered and made him stop to allow them to recover. His mind drifted from his driving, the gear changes, the overtaking became automatic. He overtook a bus and didn't remember doing it. If he didn't persuade this supplier to give two months' credit the new shop was in danger of overstretching his resources. He wished he had listened to the advice of his accountant. He could be heading for disaster. For the first time, he blamed Rhoda.

There was a third incident in the short drive through Main Street. A little girl ran out of a shop and straight out into the road. Why hadn't he gone the other way, through the small quiet streets like he usually did? It was Rhoda, getting him all ruffled. Today of all days he needed to be calm, cool, in control.

He accelerated once she had crossed the road and his speed increased in a snarl of acceleration. Leaving the town and its irritations behind him, he headed out towards Swansea where he had arranged to meet his new supplier. He wasn't in the mood to talk business. This simply wasn't the day.

A huge brewer's dray was in front of him a few miles out of town and he tapped his fingers irritably as he followed, waiting for a chance to overtake.

Surrendering to his impatience he overtook on a bend, wildly swinging the car around the dray, through the sharp corner and saw, to his alarm and disbelief, a lorry directly ahead of him. The vehicle appeared before he had straightened out from turning the corner and overtaking the dray. Before he could attempt to swerve from its path, with only time to scream "Rhoda . . .!" his car was half under the lorry's bonnet and Brian was dead.

In Kath Thomas's boarding house near the road bridge, Jack Roberts stared in disbelief as Kath's words slowly sank in.

"You want me to leave? Find other accommodation?" he said. "But why?"

"I've decided to let my rooms to summer visitors."

"But surely, one little room? I don't mind changing. What if I used one of the attic rooms?"

"Best for you to go anyway, Jack," Kath said. "Imagine, school holidays, all them kids charging about. This won't be the quiet place you've known much longer."

"No, I hadn't thought of that. You're right." He shuddered dramatically. "I'll start looking straight away. How long do I have before you want me to go, say, a month?"

"I've said the first lot can come next weekend."

Kath was not telling Jack the truth. Bertha's warning that Jack had been in possession of a lot of money had worried her. That, and the fact that he had obviously been fighting on at least two occasions and had told her some story about falling down the stairs.

138

He could be a burglar, or a blackmailer. The things you read in the papers these days made a woman fear for her safety when she allowed strangers into her home.

Her other three boarders were harmless enough, she was certain of that. Emrys Walker was a teacher in the local school. The other two worked on the roads, filling potholes, tidying the verges and maintaining road signs. Called Eb and Tad, they were very little trouble, spending much of their time out of the house. Work took them off at six-thirty in the summer and all three of them returned at four-thirty. But Jack had to leave.

While cleaning his room the previous Saturday, she had dishonestly searched through his belongings. The amount of money she found was more than she had ever seen in her life. Fivers, one pound notes, all piled together by elastic bands in hundreds. Her hands shook as she lifted them from the battered toffee tin which was filled with them.

It must be illegal, or they would be in a bank, she reasoned. Putting them back with care, she went downstairs and took a rare sip of brandy to steady her nerves.

Jack set off for work, disturbed at the prospect of finding fresh accommodation, but with an idea already growing in his mind. If he could persuade Gaynor Edwards of the advantages of having a lodger, things might be changing for the better. Her husband was a soft old thing, too lazy to get out of his own way, and he wouldn't see the harm.

Peter wasn't there when he got to work, so he went straight to find Gaynor.

"I'll ask," Gaynor said doubtfully, "but he doesn't like too many people about."

"Just till I find something. Like a mouse I'll be. I won't be any trouble, well – not trouble-trouble, but I might be a bit demanding of the right sort of attention." Jack grinned.

"You'll pay, for the room?"

"The same as I'm paying Kath Thomas, how's that?" He mentally reduced the amount by three shillings, promised her an afternoon out in Swansea to celebrate, and Gaynor finally agreed.

Peter hadn't appeared by lunchtime and Jack walked down the country lane to Mill House to see him. Sometimes there were things Peter wanted him to attend to. If not, he was usually glad for someone to talk to for half an hour. Jack smiled. He'd be able to tell him about his plans to move in with Gaynor and her idle husband. Peter was the only one who knew about his affair with Gaynor.

He could see something was wrong as soon as he reached the gates. His first thought was that Peter was being rushed into hospital again, as the doctor's car stood near the front door, which stood wide open.

He hesitated, wondering whether to leave and come back later, but decided to knock in case Harriet was alone. He tapped on the heavy front door and saw Charlotte hurrying to answer.

"Is it your uncle?" he asked.

"No, although he's in a terrible state of course. It's Brian, Rhoda's husband. Killed this morning in an accident."

140

"What?" Jack stepped back, involuntarily moving away from such unbelievable news. "Oh Charlotte, what awful news. I'm so very sorry. Can I help? Shall I go and find the vicar? Or sit with Peter perhaps? I can ring the factory and tell them I won't be back." He walked into the house which already seemed to have accepted the hush of a funeral.

"Stay with Uncle Peter, will you?" Charlotte said. "Mam is prostrate on the bed, the doctor's with her. I have to go to Rhoda. It happened this morning but she's only just phoned us."

Jack went to the phone and made three calls, one to the factory and one to the vicarage. Then he phoned Joe.

"Brian dead, Harriet unconscious and Peter quite ill. Miranda is managing the little ones but I think you should come and keep an eye on your Charlotte," Jack advised. "You know what this family is for leaning on her."

Harriet spent the rest of the day in blissful unconsciousness, Jack stayed with Peter, and Charlotte, with Joe for support, went to stay with a distraught Rhoda.

"We'd quarrelled," was all Rhoda would say. She repeated it over and over again. "We'd quarrelled. For the first time ever. I know I'm to blame for him driving too fast. I nagged him, you see, demanded so much. I've just been sitting here since the police came and told me, thinking about how horrid I've been and how I killed him."

"Rhoda, love, you can't think that."

"There was plenty of time to get everything ready for the baby. Months we had. But I kept on and on,

141

and we quarrelled. He left the house still angry with me. Oh, Charlotte, what will I do?"

Charlotte made soothing sounds, Joe made tea. Charlotte did some telephoning to let people know and it was Joe who attended to the undertakers when they called. Somehow the terrible day was lived through and Charlotte went home to Mill House to see what she could do for her parents. Joe stayed with Rhoda, who refused to leave her home until the following day.

"I have to stop here tonight, I feel that Brian is around and he needs to know I'm here," she said. "Have to stay here and try to let him know I'm sorry."

The following day an almost continuous stream of people walked to Rhoda's house near the river to offer their condolences. Finding the house empty they went across the road bridge and up the hill to find her with her mother. Charlotte made tea for them all, glad of something to do, using the ritual to evade thoughts of what would happen to her sister without Brian to look after her.

Forebodings in which she saw herself looking after Rhoda as well as her mother grew over the days approaching the funeral when Rhoda admitted that she knew nothing about Brian's business affairs, had no idea even how their bank balance stood and didn't even know how to write out a cheque.

It was Joe who went with her to see the bank manager and a solicitor. Joe who guided her through the difficulties of probate. He even lent her money to see her through the first weeks until money became available to her. Charlotte was grateful but found that

142

jealousy crept into her heart when Joe no longer came each day to see her, and was sometimes absent when she popped into the bicycle shop to see him.

Her jealously was increased by Auntie Bessie Philpot's remarks when she came to clean one morning.

"There's lucky that sister of yours is," she said, her beady-bright eyes watching Charlotte's reaction. "All the help she's getting from Joe. Such a kind boy, my Joe. Stays there for hours he does so she isn't frightened being in that big ol' house on her own."

"Joe is very thoughtful," Charlotte agreed. Bessie rolled her eyes then stared contemplatively at the ceiling. "Thoughtful? Well, I dare say that is one way of putting it."

"What d'you mean?"

"Nothing. Thoughtful, yes, that's what he is, your pretty sister widowed and missing all her husband's – care."

"Where have you been all day?" Charlotte asked Joe when she met him as he was closing the shop. "Twice I called this morning but your famous 'Back in Ten Minutes' notice was on the door. My sister bothering you again?"

"No. This time it's the estate agent. That bloke who's supposed to be buying the shop. Another delay now. He says there's some trouble with the buyer of his house. Damn it all, I could have been in the new place for the start of summer. I'm losing some of the best months. He's looking for a new buyer now and I'm hoping we don't lose the butcher's shop.' Specially after all the work we've done there."

"We haven't seen Rhoda all day," Charlotte told

him. "She's accepting what's happened and starting to get used to living alone, at least until the baby's due. She's slept in her own place for three nights now. That's good, isn't it?"

"Not exactly alone," Joe said. "I expect you'll be told soon enough by Kath Thomas or one of her cronies. I've been sleeping there. On the couch mind! Just to help her get used to the empty house."

"Is that wise, Joe?" she asked. "You're right about my being told, but it was your Auntie Bessie who gave me the news, a bit unhappy she was and understandably too. Can you imagine what people will say?"

"Sorry you didn't hear it from me."

"She told me this morning that you've been helping Rhoda. Just giving me the hint that my pretty sister would be lonely."

"Sorry Charlotte. You're 'my pretty' and always will be. And I should have told you before."

"Doesn't matter," she lied. As casually as she could she asked, "Will you be staying tonight too? I wouldn't mind going out somewhere. I've been tied to the house listening to the same old thing from dozens of lips. I could do with a break." She tried to keep the petulant tone from her voice, but failed. Why, she wondered, did she always come so low down in order of importance?

"We'll go out. I'll call for you at seven and we'll walk over the hill and along the river. We could stop in The Swan and have a drink. Right?"

"Right." She smiled, and went home reasonably content. But the contentment faded when she saw the

144

apologetic expression on Joe's face when he arrived at seven with an elegantly dressed Rhoda.

"Sorry my pretty, but I couldn't leave her on her own, not with the funeral tomorrow. We'll go for a walk then I'll take her back home. Tomorrow will be a terrible day for her."

"Terrible for us all," Charlotte reminded him. "Look, I'm busy getting food ready for tomorrow so why don't we leave it and go tomorrow instead. Glad of a breath of air we'll be then." She watched as the couple walked back down the hill, Joe's hand ready in case Rhoda faltered. Charlotte had the feeling that she was watching Joe step out of her life and regret, not anger, was her strongest emotion. She was filled with the belief that somehow, she and Joe had missed their moment, that it wouldn't ever come right for them again.

The evening was warm, the light far from fading and she stood at the gate for a while, unwilling to go back inside the over-full house; there she would have to deal patiently with her father's silent regrets and her mother's tears.

Watching Joe and her sister walking down the hill made her feel unimportant and alone. Her patience was teetering on the edge of an explosion. Ashamed of her anger, only hours before her brother-in-law's funeral, she nevertheless felt it was high time that life gave her more than the job of picking up other people's pieces.

A man crossed the bridge and paused for a moment to talk to Joe and Rhoda before continuing up the hill. She waited, curious to know who it was this time, bringing talk of deaths past and present, and Rhoda's bravery. Some friend of Brian's probably, everyone who called at Rhoda's house was redirected here.

The man looked familiar and she frowned, wondering where they had previously met. Then she remembered. He had been the walker who had asked about the mills and with whom she had spent a pleasant afternoon.

"Hi yer," he said. "Glad to see you again. I want some information, but not about windmills this time."

"How can I help?" she asked, taking in the corduroys and the thick "cowboy" shirt and the heavy walking boots. His eyes were brighter than she remembered, blue like the sky and sparkling with pleasure so she felt herself blushing under his gaze.

"I'm looking for someone called Eric. He has some children with him I believe."

"He's moved in with us," she explained. "Their mother died and we are giving them a home until something can be decided about their future."

"They're my half-brother and -sisters. Gloria was my Mam," he said. "Me and Miranda, we lost our father during the war. This – Eric, is father to the rest, including baby Matthew, whose birth killed her."

"You must be Danny, Miranda's brother?" Charlotte said. "I am sorry about your mother. Eric is my father."

He held out his hand. "Danny Saunders."

"Charlotte Russell. Next week," she said, bold suddenly, "I'd love to show you more of the countryside. It's very beautiful."

"So are you," he said. He spoke factually with no hint of artificial flattery.

He turned to wave several times as he walked back

down the hill and she stood, leaning on the gate, looking down the road long after he had disappeared from her sight.

After the funeral, Charlotte cycled back down the hill and let herself into Rhoda's house. Her sister needed looking after that evening. No lights showed and she stood in the dark hallway and listened. One of the relatives from the funeral was staying the night; where would the cousin be sleeping? She didn't want to wake either of them if they were sleeping. She opened the bedroom door and was about to call her sister's name when she heard a sound which she realised was muffled sobbing. Sighing with the thought of a long, sleepless night, she went into the bedroom and saw Rhoda lying on the floor. She had no medical knowledge but as she touched the switch and light flooded the room she knew that her sister was losing her baby.

Joe arrived at the same time as the doctor.

"Joe, what are you doing here?"

"I was worried."

"I said I'd come," she said.

"I thought the Dragon might have changed your mind for you. I had to be sure she was all right."

Joe and Charlotte sat with Rhoda all night. Joe gathered up the toys, baby clothes and the newly purchased cot and with Charlotte's help packed them away in the loft.

"You're a lovely, caring person, Joe," Charlotte whispered as the loft door was closed.

"Let me care for you, my pretty."

Charlotte felt a slight resentment. She didn't want

147

caring for, she wanted to be treated like an equal partner. When he kissed her the magic wasn't there. They had missed their moment all right and, from the look in Joe's eyes, he knew it too. Their parting the following morning was tender but without the tightly reined passion of recent weeks.

Chapter Eight

Lillian Evans knew she was slow. She had heard people say it often enough but she couldn't understand how the word related to her. She knew she wasn't fast. Everything she did took a long time, but she always finished what she began, and what was so terrible about taking a long time? So why did people shake their heads and sigh and say she was "slow, poor dab", as if being slow was some awful disease?

And why didn't anyone stop and talk to her? A nod was the most she ever had. Old Ebenezer Daniels was slow, he walked with two sticks and took forever to cross the road, but people stopped and talked to him. So why didn't they ever talk to her?

It was the day after Brian's funeral and she was walking along the bank of the river towards town. In her hand was a florin, worth two shillings and something she had to hold very tight, her mother told her. A florin was enough to buy potatoes and cabbage for a week and too much to lose.

Bertha had sent her to buy the week's sugar ration in advance of Friday, making her chant the message, repeating it until Lillian was word perfect. "Mammy says, can we have a bit of sugar, from Friday's ration, for to make a bit of cake," she muttered, her lips moving exaggeratedly as she concentrated on the words.

She stopped and looked down into the water, sluggish now, as the tide, flowing in a few miles away, held it back. Catching sight of some small, brown, speckled fish, she knelt down to look at them. Fascinated and with her errand forgotten, she stretched out on the fresh grass and gazed with admiration at their movements as, to her contented eye, they seemed just to enjoy themselves in the warm, shallow water near the bank.

When she eventually walked on, her dress spotted with mud from the water's edge, she left the florin in the grass. She was frowning as she went into the grocer's shop and the frown deepened as she waited amid the other shoppers for her turn to be served.

"I want some off Friday's ration," she said, stuttering in her anxiety. "Mammy says – can she have – for Friday."

"What is it she wants? Can you remember?" Betty Beynon asked, a slight edge of irritability in her voice.

"I think it was cake," Lillian frowned.

"Cake isn't on ration!" Betty tutted. Other shoppers laughed, good-naturedly, but it was enough to throw Lillian into complete panic.

"It was for tea," she said, meaning the cake her mother was making was for their tea.

"A packet of tea? Right then, here you are, I'll put it on her bill but you'll have to tell her she's started on next week's tea ration with this mind! There's none left for Friday." Pushing a bag containing the silver-foil packet into Lillian's hands,

150

she noted the purchase in her book and turned to the next customer.

Bertha was angry when Lillian returned with tea instead of sugar and without the change from the two shilling piece. When the girl admitted she had lost it, she punished her.

"For being so careless you won't feed the hens tonight," she said. "You've got to learn, Lillian. If you do what you're asked straight away you manage fine. It's when you dawdle you get forgetful. If only you'll learn not to linger and daydream, you wouldn't lose the money or forget messages."

Tearfully, Lillian went to her room and gave a tea party for her dolls. If only her father would come home. She just knew everything would be all right if only he'd come back. He'd talk to her, she was sure of that. Perhaps tomorrow he'd come. She looked out of her window and saw her mother walking down with the bucket of mash for the hens and wished she could feed them. It was one of her favourite tasks.

Harriet was unnerved by the presence of Eric. She had expected him to be apologetic and after his first regrets he was not. She had presumed he would creep around the house trying not to intrude too greatly into her life but he walked around the house that had been his home with as much ease as she herself did. She behaved in a haughty manner but he seemed not to notice and when he spoke to her to ask for yet another favour there was not the slightest hint of humility.

Mill House, being large, had been easily separated into "hers" and "theirs" and apart from the kitchen, which they used by rota, they hardly needed to cross

151

paths. The hall was the dividing line, rooms on the town side were for Eric and his "waifs and strays", as Harriet referred to them, the rest for herself, Peter and Charlotte. There was even a spare room, which Harriet insisted Eric's brood did not invade.

"It's as if I'm a landlady with paying guests," she said to Kath one morning when they sat in Vi and Willie's café. "He doesn't consider himself a part of our family, yet he treats me like a wife in some ways."

"Not in *that* way?" Kath queried with a grin.

"Indeed not!" Harriet was outraged. "Not that he hasn't tried, mind," she lied. "I've had to make it quite clear on several occasions that there was no return to that sort of relationship! Good heavens, the nerve of the man!"

The truth was that Eric had treated her with kindness and utter politeness, nothing more. And although she knew that after his cruel treatment of her she couldn't ever allow him back into her life to that extent, there was an insult implied in his lack of trying.

She had been startled by her reaction to his presence in the house. In spite of all the hurt she still loved him. She waited for some overture to a new beginning but there was none. Brushing past him in the kitchen when he helped Miranda prepare food, she expected a touch, or a look of returning interest, but he was never more than polite and friendly. Seeing him playing with the children in the garden made her ache with regret and a loneliness she thought time had healed.

She had been so desperate to forget the ending of

152

their plans for a large family. A frantic social life seemed the only way to drown out the heartbreak and the emptiness of the house on the hill. She had been unaware she had ignored the children; she had grieved for those she would never see. She was unaware, too, of Eric's equally painful grief, his need to stand still, resign himself to his loss. In her unhappy mind she was the only sufferer.

Now he was back and she grieved anew, for the babies they had longed for, and for Eric himself. She waited for a sign that one day they might return to what had been for her a happy marriage. The nights were the worst. When she lay awake thinking about the peculiar situation, she had longings that alarmed her. How could her body be so treacherous? She fought off the yearning for a while but gradually succumbed to wallowing in them. She thought about the feel of his cheek, the way he used to kiss her. She pictured him in his pyjama bottoms – he never wore the top – sleeping so near to her. She wanted him, and wondered if he were thinking about her.

The erotic thoughts tormented her. Because of her longings, she was sharper and more unkind to him during the day.

Two weeks after Rhoda's miscarriage, Joe and Charlotte spent an afternoon with her trying to sort out how best to deal with the business. They met at Mill House. Harriet criticized everything Joe said; Peter offered advice and Rhoda cried . . . Charlotte felt exhausted. They all quickly realised that whatever state the business was in, Rhoda was unable to cope without a great deal of help. The manager Brian had employed since the end of the war had made it clear he was unwilling to take on more responsibility.

"Sack him," was Peter's advice. "Sack the man and find someone better. You have to have staff you can rely on."

"I agree," Joe said, which made Harriet disagree. They discussed the possibilities and Joe was asked by Rhoda and Peter to go and see Brian's accountant the following morning.

When he reported back it was with the news that the business was on the brink of insolvency.

"What d'you mean?" Harriet demanded. "I knew we shouldn't have sent you! What d'you know about high class trade? Brian was about to open a second shop. How can the business be in difficulties!"

"What he hadn't told you," Joe explained patiently, "was that the accountant advised against a second shop. He wanted Brian to wait at least another year before committing so much of his capital to this venture. He recommended that Brian bought another shop, a smaller, cheaper shop, but in place of the large one, not in addition to it. He saw it as an attempt to cut costs and keep the business afloat. He was strongly against Brian borrowing money he couldn't afford to involve himself in grandiose schemes."

"Let me see the figures again," Peter asked, and Joe handed him the papers given to him by the accountant.

"Talking rubbish, isn't he?" Harriet said, but her voice held less conviction.

"What do you think Rhoda should do, Joe?" Peter asked.

"Sell. The longer she leaves it the less she'll come out with. Debts multiply in a frightening way. If she could get a buyer now, this month, there might be something left, but she won't be able to save the house."

"What d'you mean, save the house?" Charlotte asked in alarm. "Surely Rhoda's home is secure?"

"It was, until last year. Brian took out a second mortgage then, and I doubt if the sale of the shop will repay the business debts and allow her to continue to live there."

"The normal precautions would have prevented it being sold to pay the creditors of the shop but, unfortunately, Brian didn't make them," Peter said, sadly.

"What will I do?" Rhoda whispered.

"We'll sort something out, won't we, Joe?" Charlotte said. For once her mother didn't protest at Joe's proposed intervention.

Rhoda went home and Charlotte helped her mother wash the dishes, and leave the kitchen tidy for Miranda to deal with her family's needs. Peter and Joe discussed how to proceed to sort out the mess Brian had left. Charlotte saw the raw anguish on her mother's face when laughter was heard coming from the kitchen, where her father's "other family" were enjoying their meal. She felt a surge of aching sympathy for her.

"Why don't you go and help them, Mam?" she suggested, guessing from her mother's expression that she would love to become involved.

"Don't be ridiculous, Charlotte. Your father's illegitimate children are nothing to do with me."

155

"Don't call them that, Mam. They might hear you."

"That's what they are. And I think I've done more than most, allowing them to live here. Help them indeed!"

"I just thought – "

"Then don't think!"

When Harriet and Peter settled down to listen to the radio, hoping to be distracted from their worries, Charlotte and Joe went for a walk.

It had clouded over during the afternoon and by nine o'clock the sky had lowered and a chill, damp air filled the quiet streets. They walked through the town, wandering without purpose until they found themselves heading downstream almost level with Rhoda's large house with its gardens stretching to the river bank.

"Shall we go and see if she's all right?" Joe said. Charlotte hesitated, she had really had enough of her sister for one day. Sensing her reluctance, Joe smiled and said, "No, let's forget Rhoda and her problems for a while and sit in the cricket pavilion instead. It's ages since you and I had a proper cuddle!" Laughing, he led her to the sports field alongside the school and there, in the dark of the abandoned building, with its smell of dust and rubber "daps" – the local name for plimsoles – and amid the discarded oddments of school children, they put their arms around each other and kissed, and held each other tight.

Charlotte enjoyed the closeness, was excited by his kisses and wondered if, perhaps, there was a hope of a future together after all. But they didn't discuss

156

marriage. Charlotte was thinking about her parents. Joe was thinking of Rhoda.

Joe walked Charlotte home after she had combed her hair and replenished her lipstick.

"The Dragon will still know what we've been doing," he teased. "The eyes give it away, my pretty."

He didn't go in with her, he just stood at the gate while she walked down the drive and slipped in through the door with a final blown kiss. Walking back down the hill and over the road bridge, he was about to turn left and head for his Auntie Bessie's cottage, but decided to check once more on Rhoda. She had been dealt another devastating blow, learning of the instability of Brian's business, the likelihood of losing her home.

The death of her husband – for which she still blamed herself – losing her child and now this. For someone strong it would be hard but for someone like Rhoda, who had leaned so much on Brian, it was even more so. Some people seemed to have an inner reservoir of strength, but not Rhoda. She needed help, she wanted someone strong beside her. He warmed towards the unhappy widow. He loved Charlotte but could see how Rhoda's helplessness would flatter a man.

Perhaps she'd be glad of a chat. It was half past ten, but he knew she was awake by the lights illuminating the house.

There was no response to his knock and gradually he became alarmed. He couldn't explain it later, but he just knew something was wrong. Without wasting time trying to find the police constable, he banged loudly for a minute then smashed a window and climbed inside, calling her name, reassuring her it was "– only Joe, come to see you're all right".

Lights were blazing everywhere it was as if she were expecting visitors to arrive any moment, waiting for friends to burst in with laughter, chatter and loud music to chase away the shadows. But the silence was absolute, no sounds apart from those made by himself, each step, each breath, loud and intrusive.

He pushed each door wide and finding no one in any of the downstairs rooms, ran up the stairs. The bedrooms were lit, bulbs sparkling from ceilings and from table lamps, repeated in reflections from windows and mirrors, but there was no one there. The atmosphere was eerie. He was calling all the time but heard nothing but his own voice, hearing the panic, the breathlessness, as if it were that of a stranger.

He seemed to have been in the house for a long time but it could only have been a minute before he pushed at the bathroom door. There was no sound, and the door was locked. Without stopping to consider, he put all his weight behind it and snapped it open.

Rhoda was in the bath. The water was a sickening red.

He hauled her out, wrapped towels and Brian's thick dressing gown around her and ran downstairs to the telephone in the hall. After phoning the doctor, he wrapped the wounds on her wrists tightly, hoped he was doing the right thing, promised himself he would join the Red Cross and learn for future incidents, and made her drink hot, sweet tea.

When she seemed safe to leave for a few moments,

he telephoned Charlotte and, trying to keep his voice calm, told her what had happened.

"No, don't come down," he advised, when she said she was on her way. "I'll go with her to the hospital. Don't tell your parents until tomorrow, there's no point in them being told now."

"But what if she – " Charlotte couldn't bring herself to say the word.

"I don't think she will. But I'll telephone you from the hospital."

"Promise?"

"I promise. Now, rest if you can and I'll talk to you as soon as the doctor's seen her."

Constable Hardy was Rhoda's first visitor. He didn't discuss her attempted suicide; that was for others to consider. Instead, he talked about Brian. Stories of when he and Brian were at school together, funny stories and embarrassing ones. He kept his tone light, making sure the conversation didn't end in a maudlin display of sympathy. He wouldn't allow her to change the subject, although she tried, guessing that she had not been allowed to mention Brian's name in her mother's presence, and in the weeks since his death she had seen almost no one else. He was upset when tears filled her eyes but didn't try to discourage them.

He held her hand and when she had calmed down and was sleepy he stood to leave. "When you are recovered, we'll go the the seaside for the day," he said. "A few breaths of a sea breeze will be such a benefit."

She nodded sleepily and smiled. "That would be nice, Ned."

Yes, Ned Hardy thought as he left the hospital grounds, it would be nice. Very nice indeed.

Over the following weeks, Joe spent a lot of time with Rhoda. Besides helping Peter and the accountant to deal with the selling of the business, he often called and spent an hour with her in the late evening. Sometimes Ned Hardy was there and he didn't stop more than a few minutes. Twice, when he was aware of the danger of another suicide attempt, he stayed for the whole night.

He was conscious of that fact that he had little time for Charlotte. Besides the time given to Rhoda, his own business affairs were taking a lot of his time. The sale of the bicycle shop was constantly being held up, by the purchaser of the shop delaying for one reason then another. The most recent problem was not the fault of the purchaser but a flood. Heavy rain plus a sudden and exceptionally high rise in the flood waters of the river, had reached the lane behind the premises, and the back wall of the shop had to be replastered.

He was cycling away from the factory one lunchtime, having talked to Jack Roberts about the need for someone to take over the day-to-day running of the business, when he saw Charlotte leaning over the gate of Mill House talking to a tall young man. From the way Charlotte was laughing, they seemed to be friends. The man was unknown to him. He saw he had a kitbag at his feet and he wondered what he could be doing wandering so far out of town on a road that led nowhere except for the hills, and the small bookbinding factory.

He stopped and watched them, and instead of

calling and waving a greeting to Charlotte, he waited until the man had set off back down the hill and Charlotte had gone back inside Mill House.

When he knocked at the door a few moments later he waited for her to tell him who she had been talking to. When she did not, he was unwilling to ask. Their meeting, the first for a week, was strained and he went back and opened the bicycle shop, putting the kettle on for tea and refilling the heater that was drying out the walls; automatic tasks to mask his agitated state of mind. Seeing Charlotte with the stranger had left him feeling uneasy and more than a little frightened. So much was against him and his plans for the future.

Danny visited Eric and the children at Mill House but there was not room for him to stay. Harriet was adamant about the small spare room. He was glad. It wouldn't be wise to spend a lot of time around Eric. He was still angry over the death of his young mother. In her short life she had produced seven children, been bombed out of one home and, due to the dishonesty of someone she believed to be her friend, had lost the house her husband had bought for her just before he was killed at Tobruk. Unreasonably, he blamed Eric for all her disasters and her death. Best he stayed away.

But he wanted to be close enough to see his sister and half-sisters and baby brother whenever he was home.

"Try Bertha Evans," Willie Walters suggested. So he found accommodation with Bertha and her daughter Lillian, next door to Joe and his Auntie Bessie.

161

At once Lillian was fascinated by the tall, pleasant young man. He talked to her, listened to what she replied, never rushing her. He seemed unworried by her hesitant pronunciation of words and smiled encouragement as she struggled to complete a sentence. Usually she gave up, aware of the listener's impatience. With Danny Saunders, her confidence grew.

When she made him laugh with one of her tales about her forgetfulness she thought she could never be happier. He would sit on the grass outside the cottage and blow smoke rings, and tell her she was "cute" and she adored him.

Joe saw them there one evening when he had finished work and stopped to speak to Danny, recognising him as the young man whom he had seen talking to Charlotte.

"Hello, you must be Joe the bicycle man," Danny said, standing up and offering a hand. "I'm Danny, brother or half-brother to that brood of Eric's."

"Glad to meet you," Joe said. "Staying at Mill House with the rest of them, are you? Bit of a crush, isn't it? How many kids are there?"

"Seven of us altogether, including me and my sister Miranda, but no, I'm not stopping there with that mob, thank you very much! Got a room for my week's leave with your neighbour, Bertha Evans and her lovely daughter here." He winked at Lillian, who giggled, backed away, then turned and ran indoors.

The two young men chatted for a while, each sizing up the other. Joe wondered if the arrival of this personable young man would change things between him and Charlotte. He decided to spend less time with

162

Rhoda and remind Charlotte that their wedding date had still to be confirmed. Too much time had been allowed to pass already and if he didn't get things on a firm footing he could see her slipping away from him forever.

After he had eaten the meal of fish and boiled potatoes with parsley sauce his Auntie Bessie had ready for him, he changed and went to see Charlotte.

"She's gone out," a smug Harriet told him. "Out with a handsome sailor boy. She can do better than you, Joe Llewellyn, and best if you don't bother her any more."

The words burned into him but he refused to let Harriet see his emotion. He left a note inviting Charlotte to go with him to the pictures the following evening. He signed it, "Your loving Joe" and left it with Peter, to be sure she received it. With the Dragon he could never be sure.

Vi and Willie looked up when Harriet walked into the café. They looked around for Rhoda, who was recovered enough to meet her mother there sometimes. But to their surprise Harriet was followed in by three little girls.

"What's this then?" Willie chuckled. "That Eric got you looking after his by-blows, has he?"

"Cheek of the man, isn't it?" Vi added, with a shake of her head.

"Miranda had to take the baby to the clinic, and, as Eric is working, I said I'd bring them here for a drink of lemonade, but if you're going to make personal remarks then I'll take them elsewhere!" Harriet said sharply.

"Lemonade and a cup of tea coming up," Willie said with mock humility.

"Coffee. I'll have coffee."

"Have them on me, God love 'em," Willie said. "Earache, pass the lady a coffee and I'll get the kids their pop!"

"I'll give you Earache – " The couple went into their usual arguments but Harriet didn't hear. She was busy taking the cruet and the sugar bowl away from Louise and trying to stop Petula from slipping off her chair.

This was the third time Eric had asked her to mind some of the children. She had agreed each time, tight-lipped and declaring it would be for the last time.

Joe met her coming out of the café, hat askew, make-up less than perfect and, heavens above, wearing stockings that had a great long ladder at the back.

"If she knew that, she'd be devastated," he chuckled to Willie.

"Nothing like kids for sorting out the snobs, eh, Joe?"

Lillian began to feel confident for the first time in her life. It was almost a physical thing, growing and swelling inside her and threatening to burst as her happiness increased. She no longer thought Danny was being kind like Auntie Bessie Philpot and Joe; he really liked her. When he asked her to go for a walk down the river bank and into town to buy some fish and chips she put on her best hat, the one she only wore to church. It was made of green felt and had a brim that wavered a little with age and was decorated with flowers and ribbons which hung over the edge, half hiding her eyes. Danny laughed when he saw it.

"God 'elp, there's daft you look in that! You aren't daft, Lillian, far from it, so why let them scrag your hair back and dress you up in funny hats?" He picked it off her head and threw it in the river.

At first she was alarmed, imagining what her mother would say when she went home without it. Damn it all, she wouldn't be allowed to feed the hens for a week! Then, as it floated slowly downriver like an abandoned bird's nest, she joined in his laughter. Hands to her face, fingertips in her mouth she laughed until tears flowed.

Danny pulled gently at the alice band that held back her hair and pulled the long strands around her face. Then he smiled, and said, "Now that's more like it. You don't have to let them dress you as if you're half-baked."

They bought their fish and chips and decided to eat them out of the paper, something Bertha did not allow, down by the river. Although it was summer, the clouds were heavy over the hills, obliterating them in a grey shroud. The peculiar light and the humidity gave a hint of thunder. The first crack came at the same time as the rain began, quietly at first, then in a hissing curtain.

"I should have saved my hat!" Lillian wailed.

"Yes, it would have sheltered us both!" Danny tucked the newspaper-wrapped parcels in his coat and grabbed her arm, pulling her towards the back of the Main Street shops. The gate of Joe's yard was open and they went in. The storage shed was padlocked but the back door of the shop only needed a push for them to get inside and shelter from the heavy downpour.

"We'll get a terrible row for this," Lillian said, but she was laughing.

When they had eaten their supper, Danny pulled out a cigarette packet and lit two Woodbines. He offered one to Lillian, and amid more merriment, she took her first puffs. Danny watched her innocent young face in the light of the small match-flame, shiny from the cold and the rain, but with eyes as large as a child's at Christmas.

His evening had been well spent. The memory of the adventure would keep Lillian in happy dreams for weeks. The thunder rumbled around them for ten minutes, while Lillian puffed her way through the cigarette and asked for a second. As the rain slowed to a trickle, he stood to leave. Disappointedly, she stood beside him. Pulling the door shut he took her home.

Two hours later the rain had eased and Constable Hardy stepped out of his parents' house, where he had sheltered during the worst of the storm. No one would know he hadn't cycled around his route for a few hours, there wouldn't be many bent on mischief on a night like this.

He saw the light flickering and at first thought it must be a bonfire. People were always burning rubbish in their back gardens, although after so much rain they hadn't chosen a very good time.

He walked down the street, leaving his cycle against

a lamppost, trying the doors, warning two young lovers that they ought to be home, and turned to walk back to his cycle along the back lane. Then he realised that the bonfire was in fact one of the shops on fire. He ran to his bicycle, and peddled as fast as he could to the phone box.

The fire engine arrived quickly but by then the interior of the shop was already well ablaze. Hoses sent streams of water glistening down the roofs of the adjoining properties as others flooded the inside of the shop.

When Joe arrived he saw that the plans to move into his and Charlotte's "marble hall" had suffered another setback, one which might never be overcome.

It was five o'clock in the morning when, smoke-stained, red-eyed and weary he went to tell her.

"But it can't be burnt!" she gasped. "Have you seen it? Are you sure it was your shop? Joe, how could it happen in the middle of the night? You say it was after six when you left there. No one else could possibly have got in and done this. Oh, Joe, what an awful thing to happen."

"I won't be able to move into our Marble Hall for months – if ever," he said. "Charlotte, you will wait for me to get this sorted, won't you?"

"Oh what a disaster."

But the worst disaster was yet to come. Ned Hardy and an inspector asked Joe to explain how his shop, which he was desperately anxious to get rid of, had been set alight, and Joe realised they suspected him of arson.

Chapter Nine

The suspicions that Joe had deliberately set fire to the bicycle shop were unpleasant while they lasted. It began when Willie Walters repeated Joe's words about the shop being like a bloody albatross around his neck and wishing something would happen to release him from its problems.

"But I didn't mean something like this!" Joe insisted. "How can burning the property help me sell it, for God's sake? Tell me how?" He explained about the cancelled wedding to reinforce his argument, but the investigators just looked at him stony-faced, then continued with their questions.

The police had found the burnt-out remnants of a box of matches and some burnt newspaper near the seat of the fire and Joe insisted he had not left them there.

"I use a lighter," he said, showing it to them. "I don't smoke but I carry a lighter. Whoever left matches there it wasn't me!"

Charlotte cried with dismay when she saw the results of the fire. She told the police that Joe had been with her at Mill House earlier that day.

Harriet didn't help, insisting that, as far as she knew, there were no immediate plans for them to

169

marry, hinting that Charlotte had changed her mind anyway.

"Why did you leave a heater on, Mr Llewellyn?" the investigator asked with quiet insistence. "Midsummer it is and the night was very warm, wasn't it? Thunder if I remember right."

"There was a patch of plaster that the purchaser insisted needed doing. I didn't fancy paying for such a small job so soon after having the back wall replastered, so I did it myself."

"The heater?" the man persisted.

"I put the heater on low to help dry it quickly so I could get the painting done and sell the bloody place!" Joe snapped. "That's the seventh time I've explained all this. The man who is buying the property – "

"*Was*, buying the property," the man smilingly corrected.

"Was buying the property, then. He kept finding things he wanted done before he would sign the contract. I agreed to the small repair in the vain hope of getting the matter settled. I have a shop all ready to move into. He's kept me waiting for months with one stupid thing after another. This fire has ruined everything for me!" He felt his anger rising.

The questions and veiled accusations went on and when Joe was about to explode and hit someone, the man nodded, snapped his notebook shut and said, "Well, Mr Llewellyn, I think I can clear you of the suspicion of arson. As you say, there was more to lose than gain from such an accident. Now," he went on, as Joe stuttered his thanks. "Now, do you have any idea how the fire could have been caused?"

"Someone might have gone in to shelter from the

rain. That's all I can think of. It's happened before, see. I once found the back door open and evidence of someone having slept there."

"And you didn't change the lock? Reinforce the door? Really, Mr Llewellyn, I'll have to look with greater care at your policy. Carelessness is not to be condoned. I wouldn't be doing my job if I ignored such an admission!"

The man went at last, the police declared themselves satisfied and Joe began the messy job of clearing out the burnt building. Charlotte came to help.

Danny knew he had left a box of matches in Joe's shop. He and Lillian had crouched close to the heater, and he remembered watching with amusement as Lillian's fumbling hands took out a red-tipped match and struck it, her face screwed up with the concentration of lighting her second cigarette.

The box of matches had been there, close to the heater, but he did not have it when he reached home. His final cigarette of the day had been lit with a paper spill from the dying fire in Bertha's living room. The heat must have caused the matches to blaze up and with plenty of oily cloths and combustible material, it would not have taken very long for the fire to take hold. He knew he was responsible for the blaze but did not own up. Best they were left thinking it was some poor old tramp.

He was confident that Lillian wouldn't tell anyone they had been there. The evening was a secret and one she would enjoy keeping. Besides, she wouldn't risk losing the occasional outing with him by letting anyone know. Poor kid, he sighed. She hadn't had much fun in her life. Being taught to behave, to be quiet, and to keep out of sight as much as possible.

When he left at the end of his leave he gave her a bag full of pennies, twenty-four all together, two shillings worth and enough for some more fish and chips or a few ice creams. He felt adequately paid just seeing her childish face bubbling with unacustomed pleasure.

She was on the verge of tears the morning he left to return to his ship. She helped him to heave his kitbag onto his shoulder and watched sadly as he set off to walk to the station. He was sorry to leave her, guilty almost, after adding a small amount of fun to her drab life. But forgetting Lillian, poor dab, the real regret was leaving Charlotte behind. He had that special feeling about her, knowing that they might have a future together.

It wouldn't be hard to oust Joe Llewellyn from Charlotte's life altogether! The man was a bumbling fool, messing about trying to please a buyer who was nothing but a time-waster. Joe should have found someone else to take on the shop and because he hadn't, he, Danny Saunders, was in with a chance. The fire might not have helped Joe Llewellyn but Danny Saunders could benefit greatly!

Lillian spent hours daydreaming of Danny's return. Everyone knew that he had been kind to her but no one had learned about the evening of the storm and how they had sheltered in Joe's shop, eaten fish and chips and shared a packet of cigarettes.

Danny had explained that it was their secret, a

private moment not to be shared. She sighed, her child-woman's face intense with happiness. Her jaw dropped, the wet lips parted, the blue eyes stared into space as she saw again the events of that evening. Hers and Danny's, a secret to be kept and enjoyed.

Rhoda gradually came out of her deep depression, helped by Joe as well as by Harriet. With her mother down helping Rhoda with the sale of her home and Joe spending his time between Rhoda's affairs and his own, Charlotte was free to go to the factory.

Not knowing the routines thoroughly, she hovered around doing very little but gradually understanding the stages of the bookbinding processes. She couldn't match the skills of the work force no matter how she tried. She persevered for a while but then gave up.

Besides the practical knowledge, she used Jack Roberts' occasional absences to find her way around her uncle's peculiar book-keeping system. Her father would be able to help, the accounts had been his special responsibility. But when he was home, at weekends, he refused to even allow her to talk about what went on at the factory.

"It has been in your uncle's capable hands all the time I was away," he said with his gentle smile. "I wouldn't insult him by daring to interfere."

That all was not well had been apparent for some time. Now, with her slowly increasing comprehension, she was able to at least stop some of the gaps. She wished Jack would allow her to work with him for a while so that she could understand at least the basics of his book-keeping. If she were even to consider running the firm one day, she needed to be fully conversant with the accounts, but Jack insisted that she had enough to do dealing with the factory floor.

"It's marvellous having you see the work through and making sure there aren't any hiccups causing delays," he smiled. "It leaves me free to concentrate on what I do best, getting the bills out and the money in. Your father must be proud of you; your Uncle Peter sings your praises every day."

Uncle Peter gave her a hug. "Valuable you are, Charlotte." He gave a sigh. "And it seems no time since you were a little girl coming up here and having a ride on one of the trolleys."

She looked around the empty workshop. It was after six on a Friday evening and everyone had gone home. With Joe doing some work on the damaged bicycle shop, Harriet and Rhoda at the cinema, her uncle settled next to the radio, her father enjoying his evening with his other family, she had taken the opportunity to spend a few more hours sorting the work and making notes for a few simple changes to the layout of the place for when she was able to do things her way.

She wanted so much to be in charge, to be able to tell the employees what she wanted done and when. She knew she could ensure that promises were kept, rebuild the factory's reputation for first class work and reliable delivery dates. The dream filled her with excitement.

She was examining a discarded batch of booklets, dismay and frustration at the waste showing on her face. They had been ordered for a local train spotters club, intended to be offered for sale at their annual general meeting, to which many out-of-town members regularly came. They had failed to complete in time and now the order, both this year and future years, was lost to them.

She was about to drop them in the rubbish bin to clear the table for fresh work, when she heard a sound. The outside door was unlocked, footsteps were coming through the small entrance hall and the doors of the workroom were pushed open. Frightened, aware of the emptiness of the building, she instinctively ducked down behind the large guillotine.

She sighed with relief when she saw it was Jack. But something made her stay hidden and she watched from the safety of the heavy machine as he walked through the workshops to the office.

She was concentrating so completely on Jack, who was standing at the safe, turning the lock and heaving open the door, she was unaware of the main door reopening and Gaynor Edwards coming in. Jack slipped something into his inside pocket and when Gaynor reached the office door the couple embraced and Jack kicked the safe door shut with his foot. As the kiss continued, he bent down and gave the knob a couple of turns before lowering Gaynor to the floor and their combined breathing echoed loudly through the quiet room.

In a state of panic, afraid of being seen, Charlotte crawled between the tables and machines until she was only a few yards from the door. Taking a chance she ran, scuttling, almost on her knees. She went out of the door and around to the back of the building where she had left her bicycle.

Joe was sitting on the grass kerb, leaning on the gate when she reached the gate of Mill House.

"I've been waiting for you for an hour," he said, kissing her damp cheek. "Where have you been, ghost hunting? You look as if you've been running for miles."

Breathlessly and with some embarrassment, she told him what she had seen.

"He was meeting her, not going to do some work," she explained.

Joe was beginning to wonder about Jack Roberts, who had been twice involved in a fight and who kept appointments with other men's wives. Stalwart member of the community perhaps, but the man was beginning to show a dark side. He would love to know what had been taken from Peter Russell's safe.

They went in and Charlotte prepared supper for when Harriet and Rhoda returned, mashed potatoes with some cheese and marmite added, browned under the grill. While she worked, Joe talked to Peter. She hoped Joe wouldn't stay long. She wanted to think about a new order that she had found casually placed on one of the tables. Like so many others it would probably be lost amid the chaos. If she could be there every day, neglected orders simply wouldn't happen. She decided to try again to get permission from her mother to spend regular hours there. It should be she running the business, not Jack, who was using his keys for other things!

Eric was helping Miranda with the Friday evening meal. This had become a ritual, a welcome home to Eric after five days at work, a celebration of the weekend just beginning. As usual, the sounds from the kitchen were reminiscent of a party.

They heard a long drawn out crash as plates and saucers and cups slid to the floor. Harriet stood up.

"Now what have they done!"

"Go and see, Mam," Charlotte suggested. Her mother went towards the kitchen, wrenching open the door, and then stopped. Charlotte stared at Joe and her sister as Harriet's rarely heard full-throated laughter rang out.

Petula, Harriet's undoubted favourite, had slipped from her chair and pulled the table cloth with her; the resulting chaos, with the table contents spread across the room, the solemn little girl sitting in the middle of it, seemed so funny that Harriet forgot her resentment and her uneasy relationship with Eric and ran in to help.

Surreptitiously, Charlotte crossed her fingers, unaware that Joe was doing the same. If Harriet and Eric grew closer together, they might stand a chance of taking control of their own lives. Joe's thoughts were of finally marrying Charlotte; Charlotte was thinking of running the factory.

Joe offered to walk Rhoda home. While Miranda settled the children into bed, Charlotte helped her mother and Eric wash the dishes, in water softened by soda and with a cloth rubbed with soap. Soon, she went to her room.

She found she was unable to think about the factory as she usually did. Besides the almost obsessional desire to run Russell's, there was Danny to dwell on. He was due for another leave soon and she began to think about meeting him, listening while he told exciting stories about his travels. He made her laugh and forget her problems. She was excited at discovering things about him. She and Joe knew everything there was to know about each other. She gave a melancholy sigh. There were no more surprises to be had with Joe.

Harriet's main concern now was that no one learned about her youngest daughter's suicide attempt, but the town's information service worked as efficiently as usual.

Harriet overheard Bessie reporting the details to her friends in the queue for tomatoes at the greengrocers and knew it must have come from Joe. On the following day, when Bessie arrived to clean, Harriet stood tight-lipped and told her she was no longer required.

"Saves me giving notice that does!" was Bessie's reply. "Don't know how I've stood it so long. What with your complaining and the way you neglect that poor dear brother-in-law of yours. No wonder your Eric left you. Miracle is that he was brave enough to return. Desperate he must have been."

"Loyalty and control of your wicked tongue," Harriet said. "Those are the things you lack. You *and* that nephew of yours."

"It wasn't my Joe who let on, so don't think it. No, Bertha told me. She heard it at the doctors. Don't go blaming Joe."

"Bertha Evans is as bad as you. Fine pair you are, no wonder you've never found yourself a man!" she hissed.

"At least I'd look after him if I had one *and* visit

178

his brother if he was in hospital!" Lowering her voice, and turning to the rest of the queue, Bessie said lugubriously, "You can tell a lot from the way a woman treats her in-laws."

"I'll talk to your nephew about this. You're wicked, Bessie Philpot." Unable to wait for a taxi, Harriet walked home, fuming at Bessie and her repair-man nephew and with Charlotte for involving herself with them.

"*Now* what will we do!" Charlotte wailed, when her mother told her Bessie was no longer their cleaner. This was another problem that would increase her burden. "*I'm* not doing it, I want to spend more time at the factory with Uncle Peter, not less!"

"Miranda must help more."

"She's busy with the baby," Charlotte argued.

"I saw that Danny when I was in town with Rhoda," Hariet said to change the subject. "I expect he'll be coming to call, don't you?"

Harriet was pleased when the young seaman began showing an interest in Charlotte; it couldn't be anything but good for someone to push that Joe Llewellyn out of her daughter's life.

She didn't want Charlotte to marry Danny any more than she wanted her to marry Joe. He was just a diversion, a means of getting her free from the bicycle repair man. She would encourage him for a while but not for long. She didn't want a pregnant daughter to cope with . . . everyone knew what sailors got up to.

Bessie was distressed at leaving Mill House, where she had worked for so long. Notice had been given

179

and accepted many times and had been ignored, but this time she knew Harriet, the old screech, had meant it.

She soon found work to replace the hours she had given to Harriet. Kath, who had managed all the work in her small boarding house herself, agreed to Bessie giving a hand with some of the routine cleaning.

Charlotte couldn't persuade her mother to discuss the need for a replacement for Bessie so she and Miranda, and Eric when he was home, shared the work between them. Harriet did nothing extra, but pointed out any areas where their efforts were less than perfect. It was hard though, cleaning several mornings each week, feeding Eric's brood and attending to the endless washing and ironing. Twice a week, the kitchen was filled with steam, as they boiled whites and rubbed the coloureds on the washing board, Eric being the only one able to use the new washing machine.

Harriet accepted the situation without a moment's guilt. Eric was to blame, so Eric should deal with it. She ignored the fact that it was her daughter, and young Miranda, who bore the brunt of the extra work.

One day, she returned from an afternoon shopping trip with Rhoda and flopped in her chair. The house was unusually quiet. The fire was almost out. She wondered where Charlotte was. She relit the fire with sticks, set the kettle to boil and waited, relishing the thought of a good strong cuppa, even if she did have to make it herself.

There was a knock on the door and a delivery van

stood outside, the driver's assistant waving a piece of paper.

"Got a delivery for a Mrs Eric Thomas," the driver announced.

"That's me, but I'm not expecting anything," Harriet frowned.

"There's a cooker by yer, smart white one it is, and electric. My missus would give her eye teeth for one of them – if she had any! And there's a fridge as well. God 'elp missus! Someone loves you all right! Fifty-six pound for the fridge alone! Don't I know! I'm buying my missus one on the never-never, paying six shillings a week I am." Joking, and chattering about how fortune smiled on some, the two men struggled through the passageway and into her kitchen where they set up the machines, connected them, tried them, and left a bemused Harriet stroking them as if they were pets.

Danny's sister Miranda had been born in 1932 while Gloria was married to Geoff Saunders, who had been killed during the war. She was now eighteen and, when her mother died soon after giving birth to baby Matthew, she had given up her job of shop assistant, to look after her half-brother and -sisters. When Eric arranged for the family to move to Harriet's house in Bryn Melinau, she had continued to care for them while Harriet determinedly went on with her own life.

She had been in the park, with baby Matthew in his pram and Petula, aged two sitting on the edge of it. Four-year-old Louise was walking beside her, chattering happily about all she could see. Isabelle

181

and Ellie were at school, and after playing ball with the two little girls, Miranda sat outside the school and waited for them.

She was very like her mother Gloria in appearance, long, wavy hair, a serene expression on her face, a quiet manner that made people warm to her.

She smiled a welcome as the two girls ran out of the school gates to kiss Matthew and hug their sisters. Throwing their bags, cardigans and books onto the pram, they began out-shouting each other, telling her all that had happened in the hours they had been apart.

The move from the small terrace in Barry to the large house in Bryn Melinau had been a happy one. Here there was more room for the children to spread their treasures; a town filled with caring people who took the motherless family to their hearts. The upheaval seemed to have affected the young ones very little and Miranda knew that most of that was because of Harriet's kindness in allowing them to stay. She would always be grateful to her for keeping the family together and perhaps, one day, she would find a way to repay her for her generosity.

Harriet walked up and down with impatience, stopping now and then to listen to the hum of the fridge motor, and give the new cooker an extra wipe, waiting for Eric to return. He came in at five, after the children had had their tea and were out in the garden building dens with the empty boxes.

She wondered if this gift had been intended as the start of a new phase to their relationship. It had been a complete surprise. She had complained about the difficulties of cooking on the small, worn-out stove but never on the lack of a fridge. She was pleased and intended to tell him so. Perhaps her grateful thanks would grow into a closer partnership. She decided she would take out one of her best nightdresses just in case.

Apart from brief moments when the children did something amusing, there had been a formality between them since his return with which it was more and more difficult for her to cope. Eric was polite and he seemed relaxed during the occasional moments they were together, but he had never even attempted to touch her. His thanks, often repeated, were given in the company of others. It was a further humiliation.

To her friends she had pretended that she'd had to fight him off, declaring loudly that she would never take him back into her bed.

"A stranger he is, mind," she told Rhoda and the customers of Vi and Willie's café. "All that time being out of his mind has changed him. I don't want a stranger in bed with me." But still she hoped.

She heard him coming through the door and felt the familiar surge of blood as her heart began to beat faster. She stood near the cooker, a cloth in her hand, giving it yet another rub. Eric smiled at her as he came in, stopping at the kitchen door and nodding approval.

"Pleased then, are you?" he said. He was smiling, looking into her eyes, a warmth in his expression which she read as invitation.

"Delighted." She stepped forward, half expecting him to hug her but sensing the move he turned and said, "Glad I am to be able to help, after all you've done for me and my family. A saint you are, and that's a fact."

Embarrassed by her incipient show of affection that he had neatly fielded, she began to wipe the dishes resting on the draining board.

"Your Miranda told me to tell you it's only corned beef hash for your supper," she said sharply. "We haven't worked out how to use that cooker yet. And I don't know where Charlotte's got to."

"We'll look at it afterwards," he said, his eyes showing guilt and regret. "Sorry, Harriet."

"What for?"

"For landing you with all this."

"I can cope."

"Could you cope with the children for an hour or two tomorrow? I want to take Miranda to buy a new dress for her birthday. She has so little and deserves a treat."

"I can cope," Harriet repeated dully.

Danny went straight from the station to Bertha's cottage near the old bridge. Lillian was feeding the hens and he stood at the door waiting for Bertha to rise from where she was deeply embedded in an armchair and come to answer the door.

"Hi yer, Lillian," he called and the girl spun around. She threw down the rest of the feed and came to greet him.

"Danny! There's lovely," she said in her slow voice. "Shall we go for fish and chips again?"

"Yes, but not tonight," he whispered. "I've got a date, with any luck."

184

"Kissing and all that stuff?" she asked, blushing to the roots of her pulled back hair.

"All that stuff," he laughed.

Bertha gave him the room as before and he unpacked his belongings, drank two cups of tea and went to find Charlotte.

The door of Mill House opened as he was about to knock. "Charlotte. You look stunning!" he smiled. Her slim-fitting dress was of crisp seersucker cotton. It was white with sprigs of flowers over it. She had a pair of lacy gloves on her hands, in which she grasped a shopping basket. "Aw, just going shopping are you? I'd hoped we'd be able to go for a walk," he sighed.

"Hello again." Charlotte was thrown by his unannounced appearance. "I'm only going for a few duck eggs from Bertha."

"I've just come from there. What say I bring some up for you tomorrow? Then you're free to come for a walk up on the hill."

She laughed and put the basket down on the hall table.

"Mam?" she called. "I've changed my mind about the eggs, I'll get them tomorrow. I'm off for a walk, all right?"

Harriet's pained voice pleaded with her not to be too long. Gloves discarded, sandals changed for more comfortable shoes, Charlotte set off.

As they left the main path and began to walk amid the summer display of cornflowers, poppies and lilac-hued scabious, Danny took her hand. The path narrowed and it was almost impossible to walk side by side but he didn't release his grasp. When

185

they reached the shelter of the first ruined windmill, he pulled her to face him, looked down at her with such a loving expression on his face that her heart leapt; then he kissed her. His hands played up and down her spine, pressing her against his body in a way she found utterly thrilling.

"I've dreamt of nothing else but this since we parted," he said.

"But there's Joe – " Her feeble protest was stifled by his lips.

He touched the back of her knee and gently lowered her to the ground and they lay kissing, caressing each other, Danny wriggling until he was half on top of her, Charlotte more daring than she had ever been with Joe. The wonder of it made her want to stay for ever in Danny's arms. Thoughts of Joe and her disloyalty danced like dust motes in a sunbeam, faded and were gone.

He began to slide her skirt up, his hands roving further and further, exploring her thighs. Hypnotised by the sensation, she lay there, knowing she should stop yet wanting him to succeed. Then, as every inch of her began to respond in an alarming, rhythmical way, she pushed him aside and stood up. She was shaking. "No Danny. I'm sorry, I – I shouldn't have led you on like that."

"It's all right, Charlotte. I'd never do anything you didn't want. You must believe that. I wouldn't harm you, you're too precious. Come on, I'll take you home. I was overcome. I've been filled with longing, you see. I've wanted you so much, ever since we first met and you showed me the mills on the hill."

They walked back silently, still holding hands,

Charlotte's heart racing, her body hungry for his loving. Confused and guilty, she was hoping that Joe wouldn't call that evening as he sometimes did. She couldn't face him, not until she had calmed down. He would look into her eyes and he was sure to guess.

Joe worked all day and often long into the night to get the shop ready to sell. Thankfully, soap was no longer rationed. The original purchaser, after messing him about for months, had backed out but a new one had come forward and it seemed to Joe that at last he could make a start on his new business. With petrol off ration – although the price had increased to three shillings a gallon – the future for the British motoring industry looked hopeful.

On the evening of Danny's return, he cycled up to Mill House to invite Charlotte to see what he had done. The last lick of paint had been applied, the shop was spotless, the smell of burning had been vanquished. Shelves were pristine, waiting for the new stocks which were about to arrive.

"Come and see the shop, Charlotte. It looks great. Never think there'd been a fire. Now we can move into our marble hall," he said, as they embraced in the little hall. "Don't let anything stop us this time, Charlotte, my pretty," he said. "I want us to start out new life together at the same time as starting the business. We'll grow together, a proper little empire, you, me, the shop and our family. Sounds perfect, doesn't it?"

"I want that too, Joe, but – "

"Oh, not more 'buts'! What's the old Dragon dreamt up to stop us this time!"

"Nothing. It's just me. I want to work for a while at least in the factory, that's all." She could hardly admit that her thoughts were on Danny, that now she wanted time to decide whether her future lay with him or Joe.

"At least let's go and tell your father. He'll be pleased for us," he pleaded.

"No, not yet."

"But what's there to wait for now?" he asked, exasperated. "Worked damned hard I have so as to get the shops sorted and for us to make our plans. Our home is ready, waiting for us to move in."

"Mam's superstitions have begun to rub off on me, I suppose," she lied. "Each time we announce our wedding plans, Uncle Peter's taken ill."

"You *are* joking! Please tell me you're joking, Charlotte, that is nonsense." He turned away from her, biting his lip in irritation.

They cycled down to admire the replenished bicycle shop and rode past the old butcher's shop with hardly a glance. Joe suggested they cycled out of town and stop somewhere for a drink but she declined and said she wanted to go home. The strain between them was inexplicable to Joe.

They rode in silence through the town, like two people who hardly knew each other. As they dismounted on the hill and began to walk, Joe looked at her face, its expression taut and strained. He wanted to hug her, tell her he loved her and they would work out whatever was worrying her but was afraid to risk even reaching out and touching her; a dread in his heart warning him that the moment was a precarious one, without understanding why.

He wondered if it was the extra work tiring her, now that his Auntie no longer worked at Mill House.

"What if I ask Auntie Bessie to defy the Dragon and go back to doing your cleaning? Won't say no, will she, your Mam? Although," he said stiffly, "I don't suppose any of the extra work has affected her."

"It's the factory, Joe. I want to work there full-time."

"I think it's great, you wanting to get the family business back on course. I do. I really do. I'll support you from my feet to the top of my trilby, but why can't we be supportive of each other at the same time? As man and wife?"

"It won't be easy and – "

"Listen my pretty, now Rhoda is getting over her double loss she'll keep your mother out of your hair and you can spend time working beside your uncle. There's glad he'll be to have your help. Smart girl you are, my pretty. I can spare you for a while, all day, every day, I won't mind. We'll manage the chores between us, how's that? A real partnership, until the babies start coming," he whispered, and laughed at her blushes.

"Can't we leave it until Christmas? That will give me time to satisfy myself that I've done something to help."

"We can marry now, this month. You can cycle up to the factory in about twenty minutes, and freewheel back down the hill in ten!"

"No, Joe, love. I don't want to marry until I can give you my full commitment."

"That sounds ominous! Not going off me are you?"

"How could I? Part of my life you are Joe Lewellyn and always will be."

"It's *what* part that worries me," he said slowly. "You still want to marry me, don't you? After all the hanging about trying to start a new business, your uncle ill, then your father turning up like that, and your Mam acting the dragon and putting every obstacle in our way. It's enough to put anyone off."

They had reached her front door. She didn't reply but pressed herself closer to him. She couldn't answer, not with complete honesty. She was no longer sure whether she wanted him for his love or because he offered a safety net in case she fell from the suddenly discovered charms of Danny Saunders with a bump.

Chapter Ten

Charlotte spent several evenings with Danny during his occasional visits to Bryn Melinau. He seemed to have plenty of money and was generous with his gifts. She said nothing about their meetings to anyone, deliberately avoiding being seen with Danny, although her mother knew and approved.

"Best you see a few others, then you'll see just how unsuitable that bicycle repair man is for you," Harriet said. "You watch yourself mind, everyone knows what sailors are like, experienced with women from other lands. Notorious they are. You avoid trouble by never being alone with him." Charlotte chuckled. That was the nearest her mother had ever come to telling her the facts of life!

She smiled widely and said, "Danny is very much a gentleman, so far at least. And so far, I've been the perfect lady!" She winked, and left the room, wickedly leaving Harriet in a state of some anxiety.

On one occasion she met Danny at the railway station and they went out of town. Each wanted to keep the friendship secret. Danny was not sure if he really wanted to settle for one woman when until now he had enjoyed several. Charlotte's obvious determination not to succumb to his sexual advances was irksome.

Lovemaking with her would be exciting, he knew that from the way she had responded on a number of occasions, but she was strong enough to hold back. He usually managed to persuade a girl after one or two dates and buying a few gifts. It was becoming quite a problem. Celibacy was not for him.

He pondered this walking home after an evening at the pictures and supper at a café, having seen Charlotte home without anything more than a very chaste kiss. On his way along the path leading to Bertha's house where he was again lodging, he saw someone on the river bank. He slowed his steps and called good night without recognising the figure who sat so still.

"Hello Danny. Too hot to sleep," a slow voice replied and he went and sat down beside her. Her feet were bare and she wore a thin dressing gown.

"Lillian, what are you doing out here all alone?"

"Too hot to sleep," she repeated. "You been kissing that Charlotte again?"

"Hush love, it's our secret, for a while, remember?"

"Like when we sneaked into Joe's shop?"

"That's right. Come on, now. Let's get you back into the house."

"Don't want to."

"But it's late."

"Too hot to sleep."

"You'll get a chill sitting there in your dressing gown and nightie."

"No nightie, look." She opened the front of her dressing gown and he saw with a shock that she was naked underneath.

"Lillian, love, you mustn't do that. Someone could take advantage of you."

"I can kiss too." She pushed her face clumsily into his and a moist kiss missed his mouth and pressed against his cheek. He stood up and took her hand. "Come along, young lady. Too pretty you are by half!" He pulled her upright and tied the belt of her dressing gown tightly around her and marched her home.

Danny didn't sleep for a long time. He lay there smoking cigarette after cigarette and thinking about the girl. She was plump, but had a surprisingly attractive figure. Standing there in the darkness, silhouetted against the rippling water and illuminated by a thin sliver of a moon, she had about her the aura of a water nymph. He couldn't get the sight of her out of his mind.

He rose early the next morning and, leaving a note to say he didn't want breakfast, went out and walked on the hills. He returned tired and refreshed and with the decision made. He would persuade Charlotte that love was good when there was a commitment, and he would give that commitment. He would oust Joe and promise to marry her.

The first thing he must do is leave Bertha's comfortable lodgings and the confused Lillian, and look for something nearer to Eric and the children. He smiled, imagining Mrs Russell's face if he asked to stay there. Or with Charlotte's sister Rhoda. Now *she* looked as if a night of love wouldn't be refused!

He must stop thinking such thoughts. If he were to marry Charlotte then all other wanderings must cease. He wondered whether Charlotte would be

193

passionate enough to satisfy him and prevent him straying. He pushed aside his doubts and prepared to find out.

On three separate occasions, Joe had arranged to call and take Charlotte out. Twice for a bicycle ride and once to the cinema. On each occasion he failed to arrive. She later discovered that a phone call from Rhoda, pleading for help with some new crisis, was to blame. Angrily, she had stormed into his new premises where he was still squeezing new additions to his stock on overloaded shelves, and told him he needn't bother to come at all.

"Stay with Rhoda. She's obviously more important than me!" she ranted.

"I promised to help her sort out the sale of the house." Joe was surprised at her outburst. He had phoned and left messages with Harriet. Why was Charlotte so unreasonable? "I did explain, that she wanted some help selling the furniture and dealing with packing and storing her favourite pieces."

"Explain? You left me waiting on three occasions, Joe Llewellyn, and three chances is all you get!"

"But I phoned and you're never in. I left word . . ." She wasn't listening and Joe shrugged. The Dragon had, in spite of her promise, obviously failed to pass on his messages. He took out the last of the Lucas head-lamp bulbs from the box and piled them on the shelf. Another empty carton for Rhoda. Thank goodness her move was almost completed. His arms ached and all he wanted was to go home and sleep. The shop would close in an hour and he would do just that.

The phone rang and he clambered down from his step ladder to answer it.

"Rhoda? The things in the loft?" He groaned inwardly. Not another evening of heaving and carrying! But the sooner it was finished the sooner he and Charlotte could get themselves sorted. "All right, I'll be there at seven."

A few hours later he saw Charlotte walking over the road bridge heading for the library as he was crossing the road to go once more to help Rhoda. They stopped and spoke like two strangers.

"Off to see my dear sister again, I suppose?"

"Well, yes, but she'll be out of there in a week and I won't be so tied up. What say we have a good night out? We haven't celebrated the new shop yet. In fact, why don't you come with me to Rhoda's now? There's only a few bits and pieces to pack, pictures and mirrors mostly, she doesn't trust herself to pack them safely. And there's all the baby things she and Brian bought. Stuck them in the loft we did, remember? They have to be disposed of. Come and help, it'll be painful for her."

"No thank you. I have other arrangements for this evening. I'm not so desperate that I'll hang around indefinitely waiting for you to come calling, Joe Llewellyn."

"Where are you going?" he asked as she walked away.

"None of your business," she retorted.

When Joe arrived at Rhoda's house he was struck by the drabness of it. Pictures and ornaments had been removed from the walls, rugs lifted, light shades

195

removed, shelves and floors scuffed and unpolished. The heart of a home had been broken and removed, he thought sadly. Rhoda had certainly been busy since his last visit a few days previously. Then he saw Ned Hardy.

"Hello, Joe," the constable smiled. "I had a day off so I called to see if Rhoda needed any help." He was whispering and Joe looked around to see if Rhoda was there. "I'm afraid I upset her," Ned went on.

"What happened?"

"She wanted the things brought down from the loft. I – I didn't know they were baby's things or I'd have waited until she was out of the house. She saw the box filled with toys and – well, she's in her room sobbing as if it happened yesterday."

The man looked so upset Joe almost smiled. "Don't blame yourself. It was what I came for. The same would have happened if I'd brought them down. But while she's out of the way, shall we get rid of them?"

"Good idea. But where will they go? She won't want them packed with the furniture that's going into store, will she?"

"We'll take them up to the Dragon," Joe decided.

"The Dragon?" Ned queried. Joe explained as he and Ned repacked the toys, clothes and the cot, and put it into the garage until they could arrange for it to be taken up to Mill House.

"Do you come here often?" Joe asked casually, seeing an opportunity to end his constant response to calls for help.

"I ring every day and call in whenever I have a

chance," Ned replied. "I'm – very fond of Rhoda, glad to help."

"Watch yourself, then, boy!" Joe laughed. "Beautiful she is, but expensive and very much the Dragon's daughter!"

Danny met Charlotte that evening in a prearranged date. Instead of catching the train to some ready-made entertainments, he took her beyond the railway, up on the lower hills on the opposite side from the hill of mills. The land was poorer here. A few smallholdings and isolated cottages were dotted around the sloping fields and almost barren scrubland. A few sheep roamed, grazing on the grasses. The earth was drained by stony soil and patches of unfertile gravel. Danny chose it because it was an unattractive place where few chose to wander. Privacy was what he needed.

In a dell caused by a wartime bomb, now recolonized by wild flowers and grasses, he sat down, offered her his coat to sit on and took out a bottle of gin. It was not his favourite tipple but he had learned that women liked gin better than whisky. To his chagrin, he was told firmly that Charlotte liked neither.

The evening, planned to lead to seduction and declarations of love, was not a success. Charlotte was uneasy; Danny's excuses for altering their plans from a cinema visit to a walk on these dreary fields seemed weak: that it was too warm and sunny to waste in the cinema; that they should enjoy the warm weather and flower-filled countryside while they could. It didn't sound like Danny at all.

Sensing the change in him, she was unable to relax. Tension increased as he began to kiss her, pressing his long body on hers, and her response was to become angry and a little frightened. She knew that if he wanted to force her he could, and she reacted by starting an argument.

"Get off, Danny, you're heavy and bony and you're hurting me."

"I'm sorry Charlotte but I find it impossible not to try and make love to you. You're so desirable you jangle my senses. Seductive, that's what you are. Seductive. And you're driving me crazy."

"Danny, I can't. I'm not made that way."

"You don't want to?"

"Of course I want to. But I know we must wait for some things in life and lovemaking is one of them."

"Wait for marriage, you mean?" When she didn't reply he went on, "Marriage is what I want, Charlotte. I have enough money to make a start. Nothing grand, mind, but better than that old butcher's shop! Say you'll marry me. Let's get engaged on my next shore leave, tell the world that we're together for always and always." His voice lowered and his lips touched her neck, his hands began once more to explore her body. But instead of succumbing to his caresses she moved away.

"I don't know, Danny. I think I love you but – "

"But there's Joe," he finished for her. He sat up and looked deep into her eyes. Experience had taught him this was effective. "Tell Joe. Tell him before I come back next time. I want us to start with everything straight and perfect between us. In the meantime, wear this." He handed her a ring, one he had used before to encourage a hesitant lover. "It isn't an engagement ring, we'll choose that together, although you might like to start looking. Anything up to a hundred pounds, how will that do?"

"A hundred pounds? On a seaman's wage?"

"I have enough to give you the best and the best is what you deserve." She kissed him then but without the intensity that would have given him hope. He sighed inwardly, pocketed the bottle of gin and walked her home. They wrapped their arms around each other but were isolated in private thoughts; Danny wondering if he had made a mistake by proposing to her: Charlotte thinking of Joe.

Joe spent so much time with Rhoda. Perhaps, if she did hint at an engagement in a couple of months' time, he would come back to her. But no, dishonesty wasn't her way.

It was still only nine o'clock when Danny kissed Charlotte good night and walked back to Bertha's house. He didn't go inside but sat on the bank near where he had found Lillian late the previous evening, and took out the bottle of gin. Two hours later he was still there. The level of gin was greatly reduced by the time Lillian appeared out of the darkness. Again he was reminded of legends of water nymphs as she glided slowly, heavily, towards him, bare feet hidden by the grass. Her dressing gown was swinging open, revealing her plump young body. He didn't see the face of a child above the mature curves. In his drunken state he saw only a desirable woman, offering herself to him, and he thought no further than that.

* * *

199

Charlotte's mother took the news of Danny's pro-
posal calmly. She did not want Charlotte to marry.
She knew she was being selfish but with Eric and
his "other family" to cope with, Peter ill and Rhoda
needing comfort, she was utterly dependent on
her elder daughter. Charlotte was such a good
organiser.

"Oh, well, it won't be a quick marriage in a registry
office like *that Joe* suggested. Danny at least will do
things properly, I'm sure. Next year is it? So there's
time to plan it all? Do it in style?"

"I don't know, Mam. I'm not sure I'll accept." She
showed her mother the ring Danny had given her.

"That's not an engagement ring, is it? A cheap old
thing like that?" Harriet was horrified.

"No, he said I can look for one costing up to a
hundred pounds."

"That's more like it. But where does he find that
sort of money, and him a seaman?"

"I don't know. He seems to have plenty of spending money but there's no explanation of where he
gets it."

"Well, at least he's got it, and not afraid to
spend it either." Harriet patted her solemn-faced
daughter and added firmly, "End of next year
then, say, October 1951, is it? Give us time to
sort things." Charlotte forced a smile and tried to
raise her spirits in preparation for telling her father
and her uncle.

In Vi and Willie's café, that great seat of learning,
Harriet announced that her daughter was about to
become engaged to Danny.

Charlotte was angry and worried. She should have

200

been given time to discuss it with Joe, warn him about what she was considering. She wanted to wait, and tell him when she was really sure – and she was far from sure.

A false gaiety became the pattern for the following weeks. Danny had returned to his ship and she saw little of Joe. She smiled, laughed and pretended that she was happy. Everyone she met offered their congratulations as news spread and her spurious joy increased with every word. She knew Joe had heard but on the rare occasions when they came face to face he did not refer to it at all. He simply asked about Peter and made no attempt to arrange to see her alone.

It was September before Rhoda's house was sold. To Charlotte's dismay, her sister returned to the family home. This only added to Charlotte's burden; an extra mouth to fill, another person to clear up after, even though Rhoda promised to do her share. The worst though, was having to share her room. She went home one day and found all her clothes in untidy piles in a corner of her bedroom. The drawers were no longer hers, the wardrobe was filled with Rhoda's clothes which, she insisted, couldn't be crushed. Shelves had been cleared to make room for Rhoda's enormous collection of shoes. Miranda found her a spare cupboard and dared Rhoda to commandeer it, and placed it on the landing for her outside the sisters' room.

But at least there was the consolation that, with Rhoda keeping her mother amused, there were frequent opportunities to spend time with her uncle and Jack Roberts.

Her father remained aloof from the minor complications of his first family. His only comment on her proposed engagement was a smile, a pat and a warning to be certain before putting the golden ring on her finger. It wasn't said with any real concern, Charlotte thought sadly. It was what he would say to any stranger.

A few friends gave her gifts to put in her bottom drawer and instead of excitement at the prospect of becoming Mrs Daniel Saunders, with five unofficial sisters-in-law and a baby brother, she felt that once more life was pushing her helter-skelter along a path she had not chosen.

The relationships were confusing. "Can I marry my own father's stepson? Will I be my father's stepdaughter-in-law as well as his daughter?" she laughingly asked Harriet. Her mother did not join in the laughter.

"Your father's second family are not legal and never will be," she said solemnly.

Charlotte missed Joe desperately. She wished he would come and drag her from her mother's house and take her away to a quiet place where they could talk, resolve all of their difficulties and float away on a magic carpet to a magical place where they would be happy. Not a palace, she thought with a wry chuckle, just their marble hall above the old butcher's shop.

She wondered, with a stab of pain, if it might be her sister who would actually live there one day. Joe and she seemed to be growing very close. Twice she passed the new shop to see Rhoda there, helping to serve customers. Joe had not mentioned the ending of their engagement and the beginning of her new one, although she was certain he must know.

"I see you have a new assistant," she said when she saw Joe standing in the doorway, checking on his display of wing mirrors and indicators. "I can't imagine Rhoda enjoying that for long."

"She was only minding the shop while I finished refilling the window," he said. "I've just cleaned it out."

"I know you always do it weekly," she said with a hint of nostalgia. "I did it for you once or twice."

"Rhoda hasn't your skill," Joe replied flatly, "you were able to pack more items in than I can, and without it looking overcrowded."

"Is business what you hoped it would be?"

"Great it is, but I miss the kids coming in with their bike repairs."

"Things change and some things have to be left behind, don't they?"

"So it seems," he said pointedly. "Like old loves being pushed aside for the new." He was referring to Danny but Charlotte thought he was referring to his new affection for Rhoda.

"And I hope she'll bring you happiness, Joe Llewellyn!" she snapped.

Joe frowned as she walked away. He had no desire to marry Rhoda. He considered Rhoda to be an empty-headed spendthrift, too much like her selfish mother. No, it was Charlotte he loved. He should have been strong and insisted on getting her away from her mother while he had the chance. But the fleeting moment had passed. Life moved on and things certainly got left behind. Like himself, he

203

thought wryly. Danny wasn't due home for several weeks so there might be a chance to put things right. Oh, if only they could talk. These days they were like strangers.

Charlotte, standing on the pavement, deciding whether or not to cross over and look at the shops on the other side of Main Street, was startled when an irate voice told her to –

"Shift yourself, can't you? Get on, woman, make up your mind. Talk about a ditherer!" The driver of a small, open-topped car had stopped to allow her to cross and was exasperated at her vagueness. Embarrassed, she didn't cross but walked on towards the road bridge.

He was right, that bad-tempered motorist. She *was* a ditherer and because of her inability to make up her mind, here she was at twenty-three having no job and wanting one, having lost Joe and wanting him, and practically engaged to Danny, whom she did not want.

"Mam," she announced when she walked breathless into the house, "you'll have to get Bessie back to help in the house. I am going to marry and soon!"

"Is Danny back already?" Harriet asked.

"No. I'm going to marry Joe!"

The following day she went down to find him. The smart new Motor Spares shop was closed and a notice explained that he would be back in two days' time. Following the path, she went to Auntie Bessie's cottage and that was closed up too.

"Gone away they have," Lillian chanted. "Gone away for to buy an action car."

"An action car?" Charlotte frowned.

"She means he's buying a car in an auction," Bertha chuckled. "Taking Bessie with him for a bit of a break. Barry Island they've gone to, would you believe? Come on in and have a cuppa while you're here and I'll tell you what I know."

"Danny's coming back," Lillian said, while Bertha busied herself with cups and saucers. "He's coming back."

"That's right," Charlotte smiled.

"See *me*," Lillian said. "See *me*."

"Yes, that's right," Bertha said. "Best to agree," she whispered through stiff lips, "or she'll keep on all day."

"Me and my nightie," Lillian insisted.

"That's right, love, you and your nightie." Bertha shrugged. "Never know what's going through her mind, poor dab. Half the time I just say 'yes' and hope for the best."

"I've been walking, and thinking about what I want to do with my life," Charlotte explained to Bertha. "I wanted to talk to Auntie Bessie Philpot. She's a good listener and she helps me put things right in my mind."

"Try me. I've known you and Joe all my life, remember. And your problems can't be worse than hers, poor child." She nodded at her daughter.

"Joe and I don't see each other any more and I miss him," Charlotte began.

"What about you and Danny then?"

"My Danny," Lillian muttered but they ignored her.

"I thought I loved him but I don't. He isn't for me.

I'll tell him when he comes next time. I – I don't want to tell him in a letter."

There was a telephone call two mornings later: Gaynor Edwards asking Charlotte if she knew why Jack Roberts wasn't at work. Charlotte had no idea but promised to make enquiries, but then said, "But surely you must have a better idea of his movements than anyone else? Isn't Jack your – lodger?" She couldn't resist the slight hesitation.

"Lodger he is and nothing more! I don't ask him to sign in and out!" snapped Gaynor. "He didn't come home last night and I haven't any idea where he is!"

Charlotte wondered whether the anger was concern for Jack's safety or whether they had quarrelled.

"I'll go into town and see if anyone has seen him. He and Kath Thomas were once very friendly, he might have told her where he was going."

"He wouldn't tell her and not me," Gaynor said, turning her previous protest on its head. "He went out to meet someone and didn't come back. It wasn't Kath or he'd have said."

"Don't you think we should call the police?" Charlotte suggested.

"If he doesn't turn up soon, yes, I think we should."

Charlotte put on a coat and gathered her umbrella. The day was a gloomy one, with rain slanting down from the hill, making mud of the surface, but she dressed smartly and in defiance of the weather. Joe was back and she wanted to look her best. After only a few minutes' walking on the glutinous surface she wished she had stopped to put on wellingtons.

206

Glamour came a poor second to comfort when you lived half way up a Welsh mountain!

The shop was open, windows lit to dispel the gloom of the day. She went inside, experiencing a poignant pang of memory as she glanced at the door which led to the flat above. Joe was standing at the counter serving someone with a battery. He didn't speak until the man had left.

"Hello my pretty, there's glad I am to see you. Got time for a coffee at Vi and Willie's café? I've still got the 'back in ten minutes' notice."

"Joe, Jack hasn't arrived at work and he didn't go home last night. What d'you think could have happened to him?"

"Let's go this minute and talk to the police. He might have been knocked down on the road, or fallen in a ditch."

Wordlessly, she went with him to see Ned Hardy, and listened as he gave the details of Jack's address and occupation.

Once enquiries were underway she seemed at a loss. "I ought to go back to Gaynor. She must be worried."

"As soon as it's one o'clock I'll come with you," Joe said. He hesitated. "Unless you and Danny are – "

"Danny isn't home for another three weeks," she said.

"Funny. He must have a double. Sure I am that I saw him yesterday when me and Auntie Bessie drove through Main Street."

"You were mistaken," she replied. Then, "You drove? You have a car, then?"

"Dying to show you I've been. But every time I

phone, the Dragon says you're busy, or out. You're making it very clear that you don't even want my friendship, Charlotte. Pity. I'd hate to think you weren't a part of my life."

"Mam didn't say that you'd phoned. She must have forgotten."

"Yes, that's right." He raised an eyebrow and stared at her. "Forgot she did. About a dozen times I've phoned and the Dragon forgot every time. Like when I had to alter an arrangement at the time Rhoda needed so much help. Forgot she did." In imitation of his aunt's deep, disapproving tones he said, "There's a memory for you, isn't it?"

By four o'clock when it was already dark and the rain was continuing to pour, they had still not discovered Jack's whereabouts. Police and volunteers began methodically to search the fields around Bryn Melinau, concentrating on the area around the factory. It was Joe who suggested looking at the other side of town.

"But no one goes up by there," the police sergeant said, shaking his head.

"Oh, some people do," Joe said, studiously avoiding Charlotte's eyes.

Joe had seen Charlotte and Danny returning from the barren area beyond the railway and, without thinking for a moment that they would find Jack, wanted to take her there himself, wipe out her memories of being there with Danny with memories of him.

Unerringly he led her to the hollow in the hill and looked down. "Charlotte," he began. But Charlotte was walking away, anger showing in the stiff-legged way she covered the ground.

"Wait," he called, "I want to explain."

She stopped then and, hands on hips, turned to glare at him. "You saw us, didn't you? And this is your stupid way of letting me know! So what, Joe Llewellyn? So what? I've been here with Danny while you and my sister have been – " Her voice choked on the words. She pushed him away as he attempted to put his arms around her and they all but fell onto the sticky earth. She recovered and hurried away, her eyes blinded by tears.

Jack was in hospital, in Barry. He had walked in there with injuries consistent with a fight but insisted that he remembered nothing. When the police found him he asked that a message be sent to Charlotte. He refused to see anyone apart from her. Joe offered to drive her but she refused and went by train.

Jack explained that he was not returning to Bryn Melinau or his job at the bookbinding factory. His wounds had been dressed and he was ready to leave.

"But why?" she demanded. "How can you leave us in such a mess? You know how little Uncle Peter can do."

He touched his face cautiously and said, "How many times do you think I want telling that it's time to move on?"

"You know who did this?"

"I know and I can't tell you. I wish I could, Charlotte." He stared at her intensely through bleary, bloodshot eyes and repeated, "I really wish I could."

For a moment Charlotte felt it was some sort of warning, but there was no one she knew who could do this to him. No, he was simply upset.

"Can't you tell the police?" she said.

He shook his head. "There's no chance of it stopping." He smiled at her then, his terrifying, distorted smile, and said more brightly, "So, now is the time for you to show what you can do, Charlotte my dear."

"Me? But that's ridiculous, you know it is. How can I do anything with Mam, and – "

"If you don't do something there will be no business to support you and your mother. Haven't I always told you that the job is one you'd do well? You're needed there, and your mother must be persuaded that it's in her interest for you to take over. Your uncle's days are numbered. Oh," he said quickly, when a protest sprung to her lips, "I know you pretend that it isn't so, but if he dies before you have a grasp of the day-to-day running of the place it will be too late. You'll thank me, Charlotte. One day you'll thank me for leaving you to deal with it all."

She left him, asking him to let her have his new address, promising to visit him again. As she walked down the cream-tiled corridor she saw a man enter from the outside. For a reason she couldn't afterwards explain, she slipped behind a half-open door and watched. It was Danny.

She saw him approach one of the nurses, heard him ask for Jack Roberts and heard the nurse reply that Mr Jack Roberts had signed himself out. An argument ensued in which Danny insisted on being told the man's address and the nurse, pale faced under Danny's anger, was equally adamant that he could not be told.

Charlotte remained hidden until Danny had gone.

She thought of Joe's conviction that he had been in Bryn Melinau on the previous day, and wondered why Danny had lied to her. Slowly she emerged from her hiding place, hurt and bewildered. Then she shook off the feeling of disappointment. What did it matter? She wasn't going to marry Danny. She had a job to do. Jack's words echoed round and round in her mind, obliterating Danny's deception and everything else. She had to take over at the factory where she was needed. All the confusion in her life had led her to this point. She was meant to take on the responsibility for Russell's. Once her position there was an accepted fact, the rest of her life would fall into place.

All she had to do was convince her mother. Saying it quick, it sounded easy.

Chapter Eleven

With Jack no longer working at Russell's Bookbinders and Restorers, Charlotte knew they faced a crisis. The staff did what they could but did not know how to make the decisions on which work to deal with next.

"Mam," Charlotte pleaded, "unless someone deals with it there will be no business. Without income, how long do you think you can continue to live here? In less than two months we'd have to consider selling Mill House. Maybe sooner."

"Now you *are* being ridiculous, dear." Harriet smiled with exasperating confidence. "Your father would never allow that to happen."

"My father? What has *he* to do with it? He's living in half of the house, but is separated from us by more than walls, and shows no interest in either us or our problems."

"It's only until he's properly settled." Harriet was adamant.

"Mam, he *is* properly settled. He lives with Miranda, Ellie, Isabelle, Louise, Petula and baby Matthew. He *doesn't* live with *us*."

"When he's persuaded me to forgive him, he'll come back to us and return to the factory and everything will be sorted out."

Charlotte sat back in her chair, where she had been looking through the order books, and gave a huge sigh.

"You go on believing that and by Christmas we'll all be homeless!"

"Always one for looking on the black side." Harriet touched the side table vaguely with her fingers and asked, "Fetch my tablets, will you, dear? I seem to have forgotten them again."

"I don't have time," Charlotte said grimly. "I am going to work." Without waiting for more of her mother's arguments she took a coat and hurriedly left the house.

It was half past ten on a Monday morning in September. The weather was cool, the air opaque with overnight moisture, but already the sun was peering through, touching the trees and the hills, bringing forth rich colours. The walk along the quiet lane always lightened Charlotte's heart and by the time she reached the factory she had left behind her bad humour.

Gaynor ran out to meet her as she approached the door and from her face it was clear she had bad news. Charlotte presumed she had heard that Jack had left. Preparing herself for an embarrassing conversation, pretending ignorance of how close Gaynor and Jack had been, she took a deep breath and said, "I know Jack has gone, if that's what you were about to say."

"It's your uncle. Oh Charlotte, I think he's dead."

With a wail of agony, Charlotte pushed Gaynor aside and ran into her uncle's office. He was sitting in his chair, head lolling as if he had fallen

214

asleep, but the sleep was one from which he would never wake.

She held him for a moment, arms around his shoulders, face against his cheek, unaware of the concerned faces looking around the door. She didn't cry then, but stood thinking how much she would miss him. A large part of her childhood had slipped away with his passing.

Gaynor came in after a few minutes and led her away. "Called the police and a doctor I have. Best we leave him until they come."

Charlotte began to shake, her arms beating a silent tattoo. Someone brought her a cup of tea, held it against her lips and she drank without even remembering she had done so. When the doctor was examining him, she rang Joe.

"Please Joe, come to the factory. It's Uncle Peter."

Joe was beside her when she went to tell her mother, holding her hand, sharing her grief. Harriet had her coat on to go out. She stared at them both as if they were tormenting her with a sick joke.

"Don't be ridiculous," she said. "It isn't true. Peter is fine." The arrival of the policeman followed by the doctor convinced her. She said nothing, just removed her coat, hung it on the hall stand as usual, for Charlotte to take upstairs. She took the tablets the doctor prescribed and went to bed.

The shock of Peter's death reverberated through the house. Eric looked bewildered, as if unable to believe what had happened to his brother. Harriet lay prostrate on her bed, easing away the disaster in sweet unconsciousness. Rhoda went away for a few days, insisting that after losing her husband so recently, she was simply unable to stay in a house of mourning. As always, it was Charlotte who was left to deal with the situation.

Joe stayed, leaving his Auntie Bessie Philpot to look after the shop and Charlotte briefly found ease and comfort in his arms. But as usual, everyone relied on Charlotte. Charlotte was the one who coped. Couldn't anyone see that in her genuine grief for her uncle she also needed to be consoled?

Eric seemed to be dazed by the event and came one night, late, when Charlotte was mixing her mother's cocoa. He stood in the kitchen, staring around him as if suddenly finding himself in a house of strangers.

"What will you do, Charlotte?" he asked.

"What do you suggest, Dadda?"

"It isn't for me to say. I gave up any right to advise you when I walked away from you so long ago. But Uncle Peter believed you could run the business. Why don't you give it a try?"

"Would you help me?"

"No, my dear. It isn't anything to do with me any more." He patted her shoulder and went back through the hall into his own part of Mill House, to his second family.

On the morning of the funeral a taxi deposited Rhoda outside. She wore a very smart and obviously expensive black suit, with a hat that must have cost enough to keep the factory going for a week. The suit was tight fitting, the skirt short, the neckline revealing the swell of her breasts. The jacket pinched in her twenty-two-inch waist smoothly, without a sign of a crease. Her stockings were nylon and her shoes high quality black leather. A tiny frill of white showed at her cuffs and was echoed by a frill on her black leather clutch bag. The outfit showed her figure to best advantage, Charlotte decided, while stopping just short of being salacious.

The funeral was a long drawn out affair. It was ten-thirty that night before Charlotte and Harriet and Rhoda were finally alone.

"What shall we do?" Rhoda said dramatically.

"I'm off to bed," Charlotte said, deliberately misunderstanding. "I have to get up for work in the morning."

"I meant in the future, how will we cope without Uncle Peter?"

"You're never going to the factory!" Harriet gasped in disapproval.

"Someone has to and I can't see you dirtying your hands."

Charlotte's sharpness was justified by tiredness. And besides the aching limbs and weary spirit she was suffering from the need to grieve. Tonight was not a night for sleeping.

The air was clear, the sky almost blue under a shining moon. She walked through the lane treading with care, afraid of disturbing the peaceful silence. Opening the door of the factory felt like disturbing a grave. Uncle Peter's presence was strong.

The keys in the locks were deafeningly loud. She shivered as she pushed back the door and switched on the lights. Although she planned to work in the small office, she put on the lights throughout the

217

whole building. She settled to try and make sense of her uncle's spidery writing. At seven the following morning, when the first of the work force entered the silent building, she had to face the fact that the bank account which should have held several thousand pounds, was empty.

She went home to get breakfast and attend to the routine tasks of the morning.

"Danny called for you last evening," Rhoda said. "Woke me up he did and I had to go down, make him a cup of tea and tell him you were out."

"Had he heard about Uncle Peter?"

"No. Well, yes, but that wasn't why he called so late. Wanted some information but I didn't ask what about. He was so dejected, not finding you home, but I looked after him, spoilt him a bit, so he wouldn't be too unhappy." She smiled dreamily as she explained and Charlotte wondered if Rhoda was beginning to show an interest in Danny. But that was ridiculous, so soon after losing Brian.

"All night you were out, Charlotte," Rhoda pouted. "Joe, was it? What will Mam say?"

"I was at the factory. Alone. Where's Danny now?"

Rhoda shrugged her beautiful shoulders. "We talked for hours. He stayed until about seven this morning, then, when he realised you weren't coming home, I gave him some coffee and some toast, with some of my butter ration on it, and he left. Lovely man he is, so easy to talk to. Did you know he was giving up working at sea?"

She smiled when Charlotte shook her head. "Well,

he confided in me. Fed up he is, of the long absences. Wants to put down roots he does."

Charlotte said nothing. Rhoda needed little encouragement to talk when she had something that interested her to convey. She was surprised to learn that Danny wanted to give up working away from land; he hadn't mentioned any discontentment with his career.

At ten o'clock, when Charlotte was back in the office, typing columns of figures in preparation for seeing the bank manager, Danny arrived.

"Where's Jack Roberts?" he demanded of Gaynor Edwards, before seeing Charlotte.

"Hello, Danny. Where did you spring from? Can I help?" Charlotte called.

"Hello my darling. I've come to see you, of course, but first I must speak to Jack Roberts."

"What about Uncle Peter? You did hear about his death?"

"Of course, and I'm sorry, but he couldn't have been having much of a life stuck in that chair."

What about *me*? Charlotte wanted to scream. I miss him! His apparent indifference to her beloved uncle's death and his lack of concern for her continuing anguish added to her determination to tell him she no longer loved him.

Danny had already turned back to Gaynor. "Where can I contact him? It's important, for heaven's sake!"

"Gone he has," Gaynor said firmly. "Gone and won't be coming back."

"Can you give me his new address, please?" Danny

said in a calmer voice. "I have private business with him."

When he was told that Jack had moved away and no one knew his address, he looked at Gaynor and with disbelief said, "Come on, Gaynor. Tell me where he is or I'll ask your husband. Threw him out, I bet. Husbands don't like lodgers who expect too many – er – favours, do they?"

"Danny!" Charlotte gasped.

Gaynor turned and walked away. Danny smiled at Charlotte. "Come on love, it is important. I have to see him."

Charlotte knew Jack's new address but something about Danny's agitated mood persuaded her not to tell.

"If I find out I'll let you know," she smiled.

"Come on then. Out from behind that desk and give me a proper welcome." Danny held out his arms.

"Not here Danny," she said as he advanced on her. "I have a business to attend to!"

They went out that evening, but at nine, Charlotte insisted she had to go home. In the dark, walking up the hill to Mill House, he tried to persuade her that loving someone was more than a good night kiss. She pushed him away from her, gently but firmly.

His face was disconsolate as he left her at the gate. She still hadn't told him how her feelings had changed.

Danny was crossing the road bridge when he heard a cry. On investigation he found Rhoda, hiding at the end of the parapet.

"Rhoda? What's up?" he asked. "Has anyone frightened you?"

"Well, you did," she said with a ladylike sob. "I didn't know it was you. You looked so huge, and dangerous, walking towards me. I ran to hide."

"Dangerous? Me? Never!" he laughed. "Come on, I'll walk you home. Damn me, I'll be wearing a groove in this hill with you and your sister!" He put an arm around her slender waist and she leaned against him as if recovering from a great shock. He felt her trembling. "On second thoughts, why don't we go and have a drink. From the look of you, you need it."

Later, as he walked once more up the hill, his arm around Rhoda, his fingers slowing seeking the soft swell of her body, he sensed that Rhoda, unlike her sister, was more than willing to satisfy his desires. They didn't need words, their footsteps taking them to a suitable spot where they could lie in reasonable comfort and gaze up at the stars. His hands began to explore and Rhoda began to guide them.

Still without words, she insisted that they remove every item of clothing, putting hers neatly and methodically beside them, regardless of the chill of the autumn night air.

When Rhoda walked back into Mill House, she was relieved to find all was silent. She irreverently thanked God that Charlotte was in bed and already asleep. This was a night for herself. It was private. She didn't want to talk to anyone, just relax and remember every magical moment.

Eric had knocked on the living room door at eight o'clock that evening and asked Harriet if she had a moment for a chat. When he was settled in the chair once favoured by Peter, with a cup of tea on the arm, Harriet sat and waited for him to explain his visit to her part of the house.

"Miranda wants to work," he said. "I don't know how I'll manage if she gets a job. I've sort of presumed that she would continue to stay home and look after the children, at least until Matthew starts school."

"That's asking a lot of a young girl, Eric." Harriet's voice was sharp, conveniently forgetting that that was what she had demanded of Charlotte. Sixth sense warned her what Eric was about to ask.

"I can understand," Eric said, "that she needs to get out with young people. She's eighteen and she'll be stuck here with a family with none of the fun a young girl is entitled to."

"So what will you do?"

Eric shrugged and put on a helpless expression. Harriet was determined not to be moved. "I can't give up my business," he explained. "Not yet. When I've finished expanding it will be worth a lot more and then I might sell and concentrate on the children. I'd like that, Harriet." He looked up and smiled at her, the familiar smile that swept away the years of his absence and brought back the happy years of their marriage. She found her face twitching in response and turned away. She was not going to be persuaded to help with the illegitimate children that had brought her humiliation and hurt. She was not!

"Miranda would do the morning school run. If I can find someone to take on Louise and Petula and Matthew until I get home from work, at four, when

I'll meet Ellie and Isabelle from school. I'd pay well."
He looked at her, waited for her to turn and meet
his gaze. "Do you know anyone who'd be generous
enough, Harriet, my dear?"

The following morning, Harriet looked at her eldest
daughter and said, "Your father came to talk to
me last evening. He wants me to look after the
children so Miranda can go to work." She was not
sure what response she expected, but it was not the
one Charlotte gave.

"I can give Miranda a job."

"You can? Charlotte, what are you talking about
now? Honestly girl, I sometimes think you're going
daft. One minute you're going to marry Joe, then
you're off out with that Danny. Then we're broke
and about to lose the house. Now you magic a job out
of the air for the daughter of your father's tart!"

Wincing at the unkind epithet, Charlotte warned,
"If we're to survive, Mam, we need to get the factory
back on course. Without Jack Roberts and Uncle
Peter, I need someone bright, quick to learn, reliable
and honest. Miranda would be fine, if she agreed."

"The factory!" Harriet dismissed it with a shrug.
"That can be run by Gaynor, she's been there long
enough!"

"Mam, I'm taking over the management. It needs
bringing out of the sad state it's fallen into and that's
exactly what I intend to do." Leaving her mother
searching for words to continue her argument, she
knocked on the door in the hall and asked to talk to
Miranda.

Two days later, it had been arranged. Miranda

was delighted to be offered a job as Charlotte's secretary-cum-assistant, Harriet had been pressed into agreeing to mind the three children, and the door in the hall separating the two families was propped open, at least for a part of each day.

Harriet began looking after the children, determined not to do more than she had to. She would care for them but with no treats and with strictly no enjoyment. When she found that she had to deal with meals without Charlotte's help, she threatened to abandon the arrangement.

"I don't know how you can be so thoughtless and selfish, Charlotte," she wailed, at the end of the first day. "I've been on my feet from nine o'clock."

"It's hard for us all, Mam," was Charlotte's response. "Now, what have we got for supper?"

"That is up to you! I've fed your father's little brood their dinner as you didn't come home, and I'm too exhausted to think about food for myself."

Charlotte began to climb the stairs. Without opening her eyes, her mother called, "Take my coat up, dear, it looks so slovenly hanging there."

"Then it will have to be cheese on toast," Charlotte said, grabbing the coat impatiently.

"Cheese is all gone," Harriet said.

"Then it will be Marmite. I have to get back to the factory: Joe is meeting me there to go through the books once more."

"You're going back up there, now? Leaving me to all this?"

Tightening her resolution and her jaw Charlotte said firmly, "You should have asked Rhoda to help before she went out."

"Your sister needs a break! Suffered terrible, she has."

"Out with Joe again, is she?" Charlotte tried to sound casual but was relieved when her mother replied, "No, not the repair man, she's out with that nice Ned Hardy."

Matthew was a good little baby who rarely cried. He cooed and smiled at Harriet in a way that melted her resolve within days. Louise, at four, was a little mother to her sister and baby brother, and endeared herself to Harriet in as short a time. But it was the toddler, Petula, the one who had offered her arms to be picked up on their first meeting, who really stole Harriet's heart.

The weather was capricious but, whenever possible, Harriet took the children up on the hill to picnic, not far from the house, but far enough for them to consider it an adventure. They became fatter, bronzed by the mild sun and the winds on the hill, and even more contented. Harriet felt happier than she had for years. If only Eric would show some sign of affection. He was polite, but so formal. After all the years of their marriage he was impossibly distant.

She avoided seeing him as much as she could, handing over her charges peremptorily when he came in with the two from school, and closing the door firmly once they had passed through it. Her life was split in two: the joy she found with the children and the solid wall of indifference between herself and Eric. During the hours she was with Louise, Petula and Matthew she was smiling, relaxed. Once her duties ended she returned to being the spoilt, selfish mother of Charlotte and Rhoda.

It was more painful than she had ever imagined. So close to Eric, yet still being locked outside the door in the hall. She became even more petulant and argumentative in the evenings, a time when frequent laughter was heard from across the hall.

Charlotte continued to spend many hours each day at Russell's Bookbinders and Restorers and quickly found Miranda to be a valuable assistant. She foresaw a time, not far into the future, when Miranda and she would work side by side. After all, she had not had much more experience than Miranda herself. They were both learning fast and with a sympathetic compatibility that augered well for the future.

Charlotte immersed herself in the work partly because she badly wanted to succeed and partly because she was missing Joe's companionship. He was clearly avoiding her. Rhoda and he went out occasionally and she felt a crushing hurt each time her sister told them some anecdote about their time together. Rhoda also met Ned on occasions but seemed less happy than when she went out with Joe. About her meetings with Danny her sister said nothing.

One evening, when Rhoda and Joe had been to the pictures, Charlotte waited until she heard his car bringing her sister home. She watched from the side of the porch as he called good night to Rhoda and closed the car door. She heard the engine change its note and he began to move away; there was a feeling of desperation as she called out to him:

226

"Joe, I don't know how to deal with the debts. Suppliers are demanding money that doesn't seem to be there." It wasn't what she wanted to say. What *did* she want to say? Joe, I want us to return to the loving relationship we once had? Joe, please don't fall in love with my sister?

"Oh, business is it?" he replied. He sounded as if the prospect was tedious. "All right. Tomorrow afternoon I'll go through the books with you, see what we can do." His words were curt, and cut her deeply. She watched the tail light disappear as he turned to go down the hill with unutterable dismay. Having plucked up courage to ask for his help, his cool response was a shock.

As she closed her eyes that night and tried to sleep she likened her life to that of a juggler, only instead of having all the balls under control, hers were defying her dexterity and going in every direction except the one she hoped. There was Joe, Danny, Rhoda, her mother, and her father with his new family . . . Everyone in her life was doing the unexpected. She knew that however efficient people thought her, she had allowed the wrong balls to fall to the ground. She slept and dreamt of Joe.

She arranged to have her long hair set during the lunch hour next day, and she carefully replenished her make-up. Today was important and she needed to feel as confident as possible.

Joe arrived, greeted her briefly and at once settled to examine the books. Silently he checked each column of figures. After two hours during which he hardly spoke, he closed the heavy books with a bang.

"It's gone, isn't it?" she said with a sigh. "The money that should be there, sufficient to pay our debtors and keep us going, has been stolen."

"It has to be Jack," Joe said. "I can't believe it but it has to be him."

"What shall we do? The police . . .?"

"Let's talk to your father first."

"He's made it clear he doesn't want to be involved."

"He might, when he hears how bad things are. He understands the business; it was his after all."

"Can we look once more in case there's a mistake in my figures?"

"I have to get back to the shop," Joe said, reaching for his jacket. "Rhoda's looking after it but you know how little she understands about things."

They arranged to see Eric that evening at six o'clock.

"Don't call the police," Eric said quietly, when he had listened to their story.

"But if he's a thief – " Charlotte frowned.

"I don't want you to involve the police. Please leave it to me." Eric's face had lost its placid expression. A frown deepened across his forehead and he said, half to himself:

"Such a mistake to come back. I should never have come back."

Three days later he handed Charlotte a cheque for a thousand pounds. "Tell me the exact amount and it will be paid," he said. There was no further explanation and, faced with her father's quiet intransigence, Charlotte stopped asking. The money was placed in the firm's bank account and was followed a week later by another that brought the books back to their correct totals.

Charlotte was uneasy about the whole thing and tried to talk to Joe, but each time she called at the shop, her sister Rhoda was there and she walked away in disappointment. She knew she had no right to complain if he chose to spend time with her sister. She still hadn't told Danny she wanted to end their relationship. She was using him, she admitted that, but she felt so alone that Danny's presence and the pretence that they would marry was a comfort.

"It isn't that I still love Joe," she told Miranda. "I don't want to lose him as a friend."

"If that's the case why do you walk away when you see him with Rhoda?" Miranda asked shrewdly. "If you don't love him, you can hardly be jealous. I think it's you causing the rift. You've stopped treating him like a friend."

"Nonsense," Charlotte said, but she cycled down to the town during her lunch break and went in to talk to him. He was sitting in the back room of the old butcher's shop eating a sandwich and going through his weekly order sheet.

"It's no good, Joe," Charlotte sighed, when she had brought him up to date about her father's cheques. "I can't just accept the money. I want to know why Jack stole it and why Dadda paid it back."

"Leave it, Charlotte. Forget Jack and his problems. Be thankful you don't have to close the business. Concentrate on getting new customers, regaining your lost reputation." He offered her a rather squashed egg sandwich.

"Is this the best you can do?" she laughed.

*   *   *

Danny came home a few weeks later and once again he enquired after Jack Roberts. Charlotte said nothing about the missing money or her father's replacement of it. He was as amusing and as attentive as usual but Charlotte sensed that he had something on his mind.

"What is it with Jack Roberts? Why are you asking everyone for his address?" she asked.

"Who told you I've been asking?"

"Joe's Auntie Bessie Philpot said you've been making enquiries in the shops and at the pub."

"It's nothing. He owes me some money, that's all."

She was tempted to tell him about the missing money then but the moment passed and the secret remained intact. It was no worse than Danny not telling her he no longer went to sea. But she knew it was the equivalent to a lie, not telling him when the subject was raised; now she never could.

Bessie's catalogue customers were a network of information, a spy system of great efficiency. Bessie was the co-ordinator and the dispenser of detail. She decided who to tell about whom and few were given the privilege of silence.

She was in town one Friday evening, early in November, walking around with her bag containing her collections on her shoulder, her catalogue tucked under her arm, when she saw Danny. She didn't like Danny. He had muscled in on her Joe, pushed Charlotte out of his life, got himself involved with that Rhoda too. Causing her Joe to be unhappy was a crime greater than murder.

230

To her enormous satisfaction, Danny Saunders was coming from the house of Sally Solomons, the local prostitute. This was something to pass on. Danny seeking favours from a "woman of ill repute". Joe must know about that. She'd make sure Charlotte knew too. Heaven knew what diseases that Sally Solomons was spreading. This wasn't gossip, she told herself righteously: it was her duty to warn Charlotte against the man.

She was about to turn away when she saw the door open, heard shouts, and curiosity halted her footsteps. She chuckled inwardly; this might be fun, grown men arguing over the favours of Sally Solomons!

The night had fallen, shadows distorted her view. Bessie slowed and watched; another figure emerged from Sally Solomons' door. It wasn't until he spoke that she recognised Eric Russell.

This was something to taunt Harriet with, but she knew she would not. There was a limit to spreading fascinating facts. Old snob she was for sure, but Harriet didn't deserve this: the implication that he preferred a prostitute to his legal wife.

Then other people appeared; men, women, even some excited children. Soon a queue of people stretched from inside the house to the edge of the river. Buckets and bowls were passed along the line and the last one threw the contents into the river. Further investigation revealed that Sally Solomons' house, built with its cellars too close to the river, had been flooded.

The facts were distorted by the time Harriet heard

231

them. She managed to grasp that Eric had been with Sally Solomons the previous evening and she gave him no chance to explain. Once the children were safely out of sight behind the hall door she slapped him hard on the face.

"You and your brood can leave immediately, Eric Russell, and I never want to see you again. Bringing gossip to my house. How dare you!"

"Harriet. What's got into you! I was passing and stopped to help, like a dozen others. Ellie was with me. I'd collected her from Girl Guides for heaven's sake!"

Being Harriet, she didn't apologize, but told him off again for walking past there on the way home.

"Perhaps it's as well I did," he said, when things had calmed down. "Danny was there and his *wasn't* an innocent visit. Not a word about it to Miranda, mind, but you'd better find a way of telling Charlotte before someone else does!"

The following morning it was Eric, not Danny, who looked guilty; he had a black eye. Harriet smiled. It seemed ironic that it was her wedding ring that caused it.

Chapter Twelve

One Saturday, Joe told Rhoda he would take her to Cardiff. This would give Charlotte a break from watching over her as well as the factory, but would also give him a much-needed opportunity: there were a few enquiries he needed to make. Mostly about Danny. He couldn't stop Charlotte from marrying the man, he knew that, but he was determined to find out all there was to know, so she would at least be prepared for any trouble. There was just something about the man that didn't seem right. He had too much money for one thing. There was a mystery about Danny Saunders and he was determined to find out what it was.

From Miranda, Joe had learnt that someone had cheated their mother, Gloria, out of her home. When their father was reported missing and then killed, in 1941, they had been living in a small terraced house not far from the docks and from Barry Island beach. Danny was then thirteen and Miranda was ten. Gloria had found herself without sufficient money to carry on. She took a lodger and managed to give up the factory where she packed food for the forces.

She had hated having a stranger in her house even more than going to the factory, and was delighted at her good fortune when someone with whom she had worked, offered her a solution. Miranda didn't query the wonderful offer. The man offered to lend her mother money on a weekly basis until the war ended, so she could live without fear in the house her husband had bought for her. He had asked that the agreement be kept a secret.

Gloria had been so relieved at the man's generosity that she signed the agreement in her sitting room without reading it. In her innocence she had signed away her right to the house. Somehow, the man had taken advantage of her confused, frightened and depressed state; grieving as she was for her young husband and trying to keep the family together. After a few weekly payments she was evicted.

It wasn't long after moving out into a sad little room at the other end of town that Eric had met her. He had taken her and the children into his care and, eventually, he had left Harriet, walked out of Mill House with only a brief note of explanation and moved into a new business, a new home and a new life. From what Miranda had told him, Joe understood they had been very happy.

Miranda had told him the name of someone who had lived next door to them. Joe had written to the man and today he planned to go and see him and try to find out a little about Danny. If he could also find the man who had cheated Gloria and her children, that would be a bonus.

Mr Hazel still lived in the terraced house not far from the Pleasure Beach in Barry. He opened the door and smiled a greeting.

234

"You must be Joe Llewellyn," he said. "Come in, the daughter's got the kettle on for a cup of tea and she's made us some Welsh cakes."

Joe was shown into a neat parlour where a fire burned brightly, brass shone its welcome and the table was set with an immaculate white cloth and fine china cups. Mr Hazel's daughter shook hands and, after pouring tea, left them to talk.

It had been Joe's plan to talk about Danny but, since hearing Miranda's story, he found himself asking first about the man who had stolen their home.

After introducing the subject, Joe asked if Mr Hazel had ever met him.

"It's too long ago for me to be any use to you if you're hoping to find him," Mr Hazel said at once. "Charming he was, mind. Real gentleman we all thought him. Smart, well spoken, respectable, you know the sort. If only we'd known what he'd done we might have been able to do something for Gloria and them children of hers. But she was proud, see, and never let on till later how she'd been cheated."

"You knew him?" Joe said in surprise. "Why wasn't he caught, then? Charged with theft, or fraud?"

"Yes, I knew him. Francis Culver he called himself. Wicked devil he must have been to steal from a war widow and her two children. But she wouldn't do anything about it. Who'd have believed her? People like Gloria are afraid of the police, the courts, solicitors and the like. She decided to forget it and start again. Brave little woman she was. Always cheerful. Never once moaned about her troubles."

"Can you describe the man?" Joe asked. "The

235

name you knew him by, Francis Culver, was probably false."

"Better than that. I have a photo. Not very good but it might help."

Joe tried not to sound too excited when he asked if he could see it.

"See it? You can have it, I've only kept it because Danny and Miranda are on it. Lovely kids they were."

Joe studied the photograph showing three people standing against a garden wall. Although it was a distance shot, there was no doubt as to the identity of the man with his arms on the shoulders of Gloria's children.

He hadn't learnt much about Danny but the visit was well worth the journey. His first thought was to talk to Ned Hardy and leave it in the hands of the police, but no, first he needed to talk to Charlotte. There was the money missing from the factory that had been replaced by her father. He could easily make things more difficult if he acted before gathering a few more facts.

Later that day, Joe drove up the hill to Mill House hoping to persuade Charlotte to go out for a drink and discuss what he had learned from Mr Hazel. She wasn't there when he knocked just after six o'clock. Harriet opened the door, with a crying Matthew in her arms.

"They've all gone out," she explained above the din. "Charlotte is off somewhere with Miranda and her father is meeting Isabelle and Louise from a party."

"Can I come in and wait?" he asked.

"You can help amuse the children while I bath Matthew then."

Joe settled the other children down by promising to read them a story. A fan of hands reached towards him, each with a favourite book and a demand to be first. Laughingly, he gathered the books, pretended to shuffle them and gathered the children around him. With a sigh of relief, Harriet took Matthew into the bathroom where the baby-bath stood ready.

It was almost eight o'clock when Charlotte and Miranda returned.

"Where have you been?" Harriet demanded. "Look at the time!"

"Sorry Mam, we had lots to do and – Joe!" Charlotte threw down the pile of order books and accounts she had brought home and sat beside him on the couch. "There's lovely. Mam made you a cup of tea, did she?"

"Have the children been good?" Miranda asked.

"It's very quiet," Charlotte said, "fed them with laudanum have you?"

"They've been bathed, read to and tucked into bed. And no thanks to either of you." Harriet didn't acknowledge Joe's help.

Miranda slipped through the door in the hall after a quiet apology and called for her father. Charlotte asked if there was any tea in the pot, Harriet shrugged, and Charlotte went into the kitchen to investigate. Joe stayed with Harriet, who avoided speaking to him by pretending to doze. He took out the photograph given to him by Mr Hazel as

Charlotte returned with a tray of tea and sandwiches. "Recognise anyone on there?" he asked.

Charlotte took it and smiled. "It must be Danny and Miranda. There's young they are. Where did you get this, Joe?"

"Anyone else?"

"Jack Roberts," she smiled. "I didn't think he knew them, did you?"

"Jack Roberts was the man who cheated Gloria out of her home," Joe said quietly.

Harriet's eyes opened very wide. "Show that to me." She studied the three rather indistinct figures, then shook her head. "Rubbish. Jack Roberts is nothing like that man. What nonsense you talk, Joe Llewellyn."

"Have you told Dad?" Charlotte asked.

"No, I haven't told anyone yet, but perhaps he knows. Jack was beaten up a couple of times, wasn't he?" He didn't mention Eric paying back the money. Harriet almost certainly hadn't been told.

"Now what are you saying?" Harriet demanded. "Are you accusing Eric of beating up Jack? Is that what you're saying?"

"No, but someone did, that's for sure. If he's the man who robbed Gloria of her home, then it might not be as inexplicable as it appeared at the time." He stared at Charlotte and added, "Danny would be another candidate for such an attack, wouldn't he?"

Harriet went to the hall door, the dividing line between her territory and Eric's and called him. He followed her back into the room, a frown on his face.

"What is it, my dear? No complaints about the children, I hope?"

"Tell him, Joe. Repeat what you've just said, if you dare." Harriet's voice was less harsh, Charlotte noticed. It always was, when Eric was around. She hid her frustrations and her complaints about the children from him.

Joe handed the photograph to Eric, who looked at it and frowned. "I don't understand," he said, looking at Joe for an explanation.

"Did Gloria ever talk about Mr and Mrs Hazel?"

"Yes, they were her neighbours. But how did Jack Roberts know Gloria's children?"

"I went to see Mr Hazel last Saturday and he remembered Jack Roberts well. Francis Culver he called himself then."

"Francis Culver? But that was the name of the man who – "

"– Who gave Gloria a simple form to sign and cheated her out of her home? Yes, that's what Mr Hazel said had happened. Gloria didn't have the confidence to fight, afraid of becoming involved with the police and having to give evidence and all that. The poor woman was told she must get out and did just that."

"Jack? There must be a mistake, he's never needed to steal. He earned good money and, living in lodgings, he's always had enough to buy all he needs."

Joe had been watching Eric's reactions and when Charlotte followed him to the door as he was leaving, he said, "I thought your father must have known. I suspected that it was he who attacked Jack and possibly demanded money from him. Now I'm not so sure. His surprise seemed genuine."

Charlotte was silent. Joe thought she was so

shocked by what he had discovered about Jack Roberts, a man she had trusted so completely, that she was stunned. "It's quite a lot to face, isn't it, Charlotte?"

"I don't understand. The attack on Jack Roberts couldn't have been anying to do with Gloria losing her house. If Dadda didn't know, who else is there? No one."

"Charlotte, my pretty, I hate saying this, but there is someone else. There's Danny."

"He doesn't know. How could he?"

"He's on that photograph with the man."

"But he was a child, Joe. They probably only met once."

She found herself defending Danny, once more putting herself on the opposite side from Joe. When would she be able to talk honestly about how she felt? Everything was clouded and indistinct. Why couldn't she just tell Joe that allowing Danny into her life had been a mistake? Until she had spoken to Danny and told him, it would be disloyal to talk to Joe. Yet Danny's disloyalty was clear to see. He had taken Rhoda out, she now knew, without bothering to explain or make an excuse!

Joe put her thoughtful silence down to concern for Danny but he coaxed softly, "He does flash a lot of money about, doesn't he?"

"I'm going in, Joe, it's very cold out here."

"Yes, go in, my pretty, and think about it. I'll see you tomorrow. Lunchtime?"

"Yes, I – perhaps." Leaving him to drive off without a wave, she closed the door and leaned back on it, her eyes closed. Danny beating up Jack

Roberts? Every new development made life more maddeningly complicated.

Joe parked the car in Main Street near his smart cycle and motor spares shop and walked along the footpath to his Auntie Bessie's house. Rain was falling, the drops icy cold and beating on his face like shards of glass. He bent his head and began to run, but the slippery surface made him slow down. As he reached the place where he caught sight of the lighted windows in the two cottages, a movement caught his eye and he stopped, screwed up his eyes and peered through the gloomy night.

At the edge of the river, a ghostly figure stood, white, insubstantial behind branches of scrubby willows. A slight swaying movement gave the form a fluidity and an undefined shape. He recognised the figure. With a shocked gasp he called, "Lillian, love, what are you doing out in this and you with hardly a stitch on you!" He went to guide her back to Bertha's house but she pulled away from him, tears trickling to add to the rain that trailed down her plump face.

"Come on, Lillian. This is no night to be out so late."

"Waiting for someone," she said between sobs.

"I know. What say we wait indoors? You can get something warm on, and if your Mam isn't up I'll make us a cup of cocoa. Right?"

Slowly, he approached her and finally suceeded in catching hold of her arm. She collapsed then and, sobbing loudly, she sat on the muddy ground, crying as if her heart was broken. Joe tried to pick her up but the ground was slippery and she was very heavy.

He managed to clasp his arms about but before he had taken more than a few steps, he tripped over a tree root and they both fell into a hawthorn bush. Lillian's nightdress was torn and Joe felt the prick of the branches through his own clothes.

"Auntie Bessie!" he called. "Bertha! Come quick!" He guided the howling Lillian home and thankfully handed her into the care of her mother.

"Never know where she is these days and that's a fact Joe," Bertha sobbed. "She went to bed hours ago and I thought she was sleeping fast." Soothing the girl, bathing her cuts, threatening her, scolding her and loving her, Bertha thanked Joe for his help and put Lillian to bed.

"Who was she expecting to come?" Joe asked.

"Her father," Bertha said sadly. "Or Father Christmas. It's all one and the same to her, poor dab."

Chapter Thirteen

Eric didn't know what to do. He had guessed that
Danny was blackmailing Jack Roberts. The man's
vague explanations, Danny's bruised hands, which
he himself had treated with vinegar and brown paper,
and the fact that Danny had more money than he
ought, all added up to blackmail.

Ugly as it was, he hadn't dreamed the truth, that
Danny had caught up with the man who had cheated
his mother and was making him pay the money
back. The fighting, or, to be more truthful, the
one-sided beating, he preferred not to think about.
How could a son of the gentle Gloria be capable of
such things?

The children who belonged to him and Gloria
he adored, Miranda he loved almost as much, but
Danny, he reflected, he had never felt close to.
Money had always been of great importance to him,
even as a small boy.

Refusing to explain it all to Charlotte, he himself
had paid back the money Jack had taken from the
bookbinding business to pay off Danny's demands.
He had hated covering up for the boy, but he had
done it as a gesture of his love for Gloria. He
couldn't, wouldn't, do anything more. He fervently

hoped Danny would soon leave Bryn Melinau and never return.

That evening, when Harriet and Rhoda were out, he came through the dividing door and called to Charlotte.

"Charlotte, when you have a moment, I have something to say to you."

She looked up from the accounts she was checking and smiled. "Just let me put these papers away and I'll come. No problem with the children?"

"No, the children are fine. It's you, my dear. When I came back I promised myself that I would never interfere with your lives. I'd interrupted them once in a quite devastating way and never want to do that again. But it's you and Danny. Tell me to mind my own business – it's what I should be doing anyway – but there are things about the boy that – well – he isn't as straight and honest as I'd wish."

"Can you explain, Dadda?"

"Sorry, but the story isn't mine to tell. Perhaps he will tell you himself, then I might think differently about him, but all I can say is, be careful, think before you put things on a permanent basis. Joe is a more admirable character. Bessie brought him up with a decent set of values. There. I've said it and I apologise for interfering. But please, my dear girl, make sure you don't make a big mistake."

"But you must tell me what's going on."

Again she cursed the situation she had made for herself by not writing to Danny immediately to tell him she no longer wanted to marry him. Now it might seem that she had decided Joe was a better-than-nothing choice. If ever Joe and she got together again she would hate him to think he was second best, as her father had for all the years of his marriage.

"Just think about it. If you can, avoid making a decision for a while, let things settle."

"What things? You can't half-tell me then walk off," she said as her father went towards the hall door, that insurmountable divide between her and his other life.

"One day I'll tell you, but I can't intrude that much, not now. Go and see Joe, he loves you and what you see is what he is, a straightforward, honest man. Danny is complicated and not altogether honest. There, that's all I can say." The door closed behind him, cutting off his rather sad smile. Charlotte stood for a while, staring at the door and wondering what to say to Danny when they met. She had to find out what he had done to make her father offer such a warning.

It was during the run up to Christmas when Danny returned. The shop windows were sparkling with multicoloured lights, bunting hung along the street from the station to the road bridge in great loops of red and green, with bunches of holly, ivy, and occasional bunches of mistletoe adding to the fun.

This time he had told Charlotte the time of his arrival and, even though the weather was damp and showery, she was waiting at the station to greet him. She wanted her father to be wrong about Danny. Somehow, it was a slur on herself if he was less than the happy-go-lucky, harmless individual she had thought him to be. She wanted him to jump

245

off the train and explain immediately that her father had been misinformed, that he was as transparent as the freshly polished shop windows, sparkling with innocence.

She tried to put the worry at the back of her mind. She must be patient. Allow Danny time to tell her what the problem was and let her decide on its importance. She began to prepare her speech in which she told him he was dear to her but she didn't love him enough to marry him. She wondered wryly if he would get round to mentioning that he had been seeing Rhoda, and that he no longer went to sea!

When she saw him, the words she had rehearsed vanished and all she could see was a handsome man bearing down on her with coat flying open, suitcase swinging wildly and arms held wide to greet her.

"My darling Charlotte," he said, holding her tightly against him. "I've missed you. There wasn't a moment to see you last time I was home. Apart from struggling into town with that sister of yours to buy wall-paper and paint, I never left Bertha's. I decorated her kitchen and scullery ready for Christmas. Did Rhoda give you the message? Oh, Charlotte, I felt deprived."

Her emotions were swamped. He hadn't been taking Rhoda out. He hadn't avoided seeing her. Oh, what a confusion of emotions! She was drowning in the pleasure of his embrace. She tried to pull away from his arms. What was the matter with her that she couldn't stay with a decision for more than two minutes?

The opportunity of bringing up the subject of dishonesty came almost at once, although it didn't

246

get her very far. As they walked through Main Street they saw Constable Hardy standing at the kerb beside a purring car, taking down some details in his notebook.

"Speeding, I'll bet," Danny chuckled. "It's about the only thing that ever gets written in that notebook of his. When was there anything wicked to report in this quiet town?"

"Have you ever been in trouble with the police, Danny?" she asked.

"Why d'you say that?" He stopped and stared at her.

She saw him frown in the neon light of the florists and greengrocers. "No reason, it's just that I remember being escorted home by a policeman once. When I was about six. Constable Hardy's father it was. He'd caught me climbing into an empty house."

"What were you doing?" he chuckled.

"I'd heard a cat crying and thought it was locked in."

"I suppose I was as mischievous as most when I was young, but no, my name isn't in any police file, as far as I know." He laughed again. "Not even for catnapping!"

"You would tell me, Danny? If you were in trouble of any kind?"

"Who's been talking to you?" he demanded, dropping his case and holding her arm.

"Talking? About what?"

"About me? Has something been said? Gossip is as important as bread in this place."

"Nothing's been said," she lied. But she knew from his fierce reaction that her father had been right, there

247

was a side to Danny that he didn't want her to know. "I just want to know everything about you." She looked at the suitcase. "Where's your kitbag?" she asked. "I haven't seen you with a suitcase before."

"I borrowed this, it fits on the railway carriage rack better."

So he still wasn't going to tell her he no longer had work. She covered her disappointment, smiled, took his arm and pulled him over to admire the magnificent display outside the butcher's shop.

"Come on, I will be in trouble if we don't get a move on. Not with the police, mind, with Bertha. She's promised to have dinner ready for me. I'll walk you home then borrow your bike to come back down."

"No, you go straight to Bertha's. I'll see you later."

Charlotte momentarily put aside her worries about Danny. She would tell him tonight.

"Tomorrow I want you to come out with me for the day," Danny said, as they pushed their way through the busy shoppers. He stopped when they reached the end of the lane. "I'll call for you at nine. Right?"

"Danny, I can't. You know I have to work."

"It's Saturday, the day before Christmas Eve! Please, Charlotte, it's important."

"I can't leave Miranda to cope alone."

Danny threw his suitcase onto the pavement again and stared at her. "There's always something, isn't there? Either your mother, or the factory, or some other urgent thing that demands your personal attention. When will I come first, Charlotte?"

Now was the time. It would be easy just to say,

248

"Danny, I think we should stop seeing each other". Instead she said, "Is it something special?"

"There *is* something special, yes. It's a pub that I want you to see. I've made enquiries. After doing a course in public house management we could run our own business. Looking at one or two will give us an idea of what we want. Please, Charlotte. It's important. It's our future, you must come." His lips tightened with insistence. Charlotte lowered her eyes.

"Sorry, Danny, I can't."

"Come on, Charlotte, no one is that indispensable. Christmas Eve, and you can't forget work for a couple of hours to do something towards our future?"

We have no future, she shouted inside. She still couldn't say the words. He'd be so hurt. How could she hurt him so badly? There was no real reason for telling him goodbye. Or not one that she could explain. "Danny, doesn't it cost a lot of money to run a pub?"

"Don't worry about that. I've enough."

"But where did you get it from? It will be hundreds, won't it? Have you arranged a loan? Or borrowed it from someone? Isn't that risky?"

"Leave that side of things to me. I've sorted it, that's all you need to know."

"You won't be borrowing it then?"

Presuming that was her worry, he said, "Come with me tomorrow and look at the place. I promise I won't be getting us into debt. I have enough cash to get us started. Then when you sell the business you can put your share in and – "

"Where did you get it?" she insisted.

249

"For God's sake, Charlotte! What d'you want? I have it. Isn't that enough for you?"

She shook her head. "No, Danny. It isn't. I need to know everything, don't you see?"

"I see a woman who's too scared to live. That's what life is for, Charlotte, living. Grabbing what you want and enjoying every moment. Are you with me or not?"

"Tomorrow I have to work," she said dully.

He swung away from her and she watched him walk along the path, quickly swallowed up by the darkness, without turning for a final wave. She almost ran after him, she was so frightened, standing there watching him disappear. She was seeing a future without Danny, without Joe. She might spend the rest of her life alone, or with her mother.

She loved Joe. And as for Danny, well, she was curious about her father's warning, and human enough to want to know how he could possibly have saved enough money to buy a public house.

What had happened to make her so confused? Once life had been straightforward and clear. She and Joe, together, working to build a business and have a family; it had all gone wrong and she didn't know how. A strong sense of duty perhaps. That might be the reason she had put emphasis on the wrong things.

She stopped and looked for a long time at the twinkling lights in the town below. The shop lights were going out one by one as she watched. The street lights were hazy and the people scurrying back to their families were lost to her sight once they left Main Street. Charlotte felt a sense of real despair.

* * *

250

Danny walked along the lane towards Bertha's cottage feeling less than happy. He could see his plans slipping away from him. He had hoped to marry Charlotte and be a part of the family at Mill House. He had doubts about Charlotte as a lover, she was too strong. Or she didn't love him enough. But there was Rhoda, she might still be fun, a worthwhile diversion once he had his feet under the table at Mill House.

The lights of the two cottages appeared out of the darkness and he could see through the curtains of number one. Joe's Auntie Bessie was preparing his meal. The door of Bertha's house was open, lights ablaze but with no sign of anyone there. He cursed. If he'd been wrong about Bertha having a meal ready he'd have been better going home with Charlotte.

The dinner that had been promised was there, ready to cook. Eggs, a rasher of bacon, black pudding, a small sausage and some bread. Near the fire a frying pan stood with a lump of dripping slowly melting.

"Bertha?" he called. "Anybody home then?"

"Mam's gone off to the church to do some flowers." Lillian sidled shyly into the room, a huge apron covering her ill-fitting clothes. Her grey corduroy skirt was fastened with a safety pin; her purple jumper was too small and so tight her arms bulged at the cuffs. "I got my clothes mucky playing with the hens and had to change," she excused, brushing imaginary dust from herself. "Mam says I've got to cook your dinner."

"Hello my beautiful! There's a surprise, being waited on by the best-looking waitress in Bryn Melinau." Lillian covered her face and giggled. Her

251

eyes were bright as she looked at him over her fingers. "Thanks Lillian, just give me ten minutes. I'll just go and have a quick swill." He gave the giggling girl a hug and took his case up to his room.

He stripped and began to wash in the bowl of cold water in his room. When he went down, his meal was cooked and Lillian stood proudly holding the plate.

"Look, Danny, I didn't forget and the egg isn't even stuck to the pan."

"That's just perfect, Lillian. Clever girl you are."

She put the plate full of overcooked food on the table and watched with shining eyes until he had eaten every scrap. Then, as he stood to take the plate into the scullery, she leaned against him, arms around his waist and pressed her plump belly against him. "A cuddle, Danny? I like your cuddles."

"Hang on, love, your Mam'll be back."

"Not for ages."

"We'd better not."

"A cuddle," she said with a hint of stubborness.

"A quick cuddle, then. Too tempting by half you are, lovely girl." He put his arms around the fat shoulders, and kissed the top of her head then pushed her gently from him.

"Make it happen again, Danny," she whispered. "Make it happen like before."

Suddenly it was impossible to resist. Her eyes so trusting and pleading for his loving . . . Life was hell at times, why shouldn't he give the kid a little pleasure? There was little likelihood of anyone else giving this sort of attention to poor, simple Lillian. Convinced he was only being kind, Danny bent his head and touched her lips with his own, saw the

252

fluttering eyelids and felt the shiver of ecstasy run through her and was quickly lost in the need for his own fulfilment.

They lay together on his bed for a while. He felt sleepy but daren't succumb. Lillian stared at the ceiling, her eyes glowing, her face so magically transformed that for a moment Danny thought she had been misunderstood, that hidden behind the childlike features was a normal, mature woman. He wondered if there had been others; she seemed to know instinctively how to please him.

"Have you cuddled with anyone else, Lillian? Come on, you can tell me. Friends we are, lovely girl." He felt her shaking and thought for a moment she was laughing, then she raised her tear-streaked face to him and said:

"Only Danny. I waited for you on the river bank. Mam was cross. She shouted at me. Waiting a long time."

He sighed inwardly. The child was back. The woman only a brief echo of what might have been.

"You didn't say who you were waiting for?" He crossed his fingers and said a quick prayer.

"Secret, isn't it, Danny?"

He let out his breath in a long, slow sigh of relief. "Our secret, for always and always, lovely girl."

Charlotte didn't see Danny that evening. She waited in, hoping, expecting him to call as they had arranged but he did not. The following day she went to the factory, watching the door, waiting for the phone to ring, but by lunchtime when the rest of the staff, apart from the loyal Miranda, had left to begin their

253

Christmas holiday, she had heard nothing. Before leaving the office to cycle home for lunch, she asked Miranda if she had seen her brother.

"No, but Dad met him last night. They had a drink together," Miranda said.

"Danny said something about going to look at a public house today. I wonder if he did go?" Charlotte tried to speak casually, as if it were nothing to do with her.

"Is he thinking of you and he buying a place, when you marry?" She glanced at Charlotte apologetically. "Sorry, is it supposed to be a secret?"

"It's no secret he's asked me," Charlotte smiled. "Miranda, can I ask you something?"

"Of course."

"Where would Danny get that sort of money? He's twenty-two and your mother had nothing to leave. He's hardly well paid. Sorry," she added when her companion didn't reply. "I shouldn't be talking to you about your brother."

"I think that's what Dad wanted to see him about last night," Miranda said. "I think Dad's accused him of something dishonest. I don't know what but it was serious. They quarrelled, I know that."

Charlotte sighed. It was all getting so complicated. Why, oh why, wasn't Joe there for her any more?

On Christmas morning Charlotte was the first to wake and she became aware of a strange sound. Children laughing, shouting, singing. She smiled as she dressed and went down to make the mince pies. She smiled even wider when she saw them already made, golden and delicious, on the cooling trays. Surely Rhoda

254

hadn't – but no, surprise after surprise, the pastry was her mother's handiwork. She began to hum a carol, accompanied by the radio, as she laid the table for breakfast.

After the presents were opened, Charlotte kissed her mother.

"Thank you for making the pies. I really was too tired to do them last night."

"I thought I'd take some in for Eric and the children," her mother said. "Your father always liked my mince tarts."

Eating the one solitary pie that Harriet had left for her, later that morning, Charlotte had another suprise.

"I've been talking to your father and I've decided that I'll ask Bessie to come back and work for us."

"Thank goodness for that, Mam. I don't see how we could manage for much longer without her."

"Well, we would have if you hadn't got difficult and insisted on leaving the house for hours each day."

Charlotte swallowed a retort.

"I'll write to her," Harriet added.

"Why don't you go and see her?" Charlotte suggested. "I might come with you to wish her and Joe a Happy Christmas."

They walked down on Boxing Day morning. Harriet complained at every footstep that she shouldn't have come. That the path was a disgrace, that wallowing in mud was for people like Bessie and Bertha and not the Russells of Mill House.

Bessie and Joe were out.

"Gone for a drive, they have," Bertha informed them. "Danny is out too but I'm making a cup of tea if you fancy one, and I've got a few mince tarts. Made with home-made mincemeat," she coaxed. Charlotte accepted and Harriet shuddered. With a continuing air of mild disapproval, Harriet accepted a seat on the old sofa, and one of Bertha's pastries and wished she had stayed home.

"Will you tell Bessie that I'm willing to have her back and she can start on Thursday?"

"She works for Kath on Thursdays," Bertha said.

"Then she'll change her day, won't she?"

"Yes, well, there you are then, I'll tell her and – I'll go and make the tea," Bertha mumbled as she left the room.

"The cup is sure to be cracked," she whispered to Charlotte through pursed lips. "Why did you make me come?"

When Charlotte helped Bertha to carry the plates back to the kitchen Harriet stood to leave. Idly she picked up an envelope that had been pushed behind a book on a shelf. She held back a cry. The writing was Eric's. Hands shaking, hoping Bertha wouldn't see her, she pulled out the single page and read it.

Here is the monthly payment as usual.
I hope you are both well,
Best wishes,
signed E.

So Kath's angry words were true, Eric *was* responsible for the daft Lillian! She picked up her gloves and hurried from the house, tears blinding her eyes. She couldn't stay. She mustn't stay; if she did she would scream and shout and let Bertha know she had seen the letter. Bertha and Eric! She was sobbing when Charlotte caught up with her near the road bridge. Charlotte pleaded and begged to be told what was wrong, but Harriet remained silent.

Danny regretted his quarrel with Charlotte and spent Christmas alone. There was some satisfaction in knowing that for Joe too, the celebration had been spent without Charlotte.

Much of each day was spent looking for Jack Roberts. He wanted more money. The money he had taken from Jack wasn't enough. If he were to marry Charlotte he needed enough to set them up properly.

Standing in the cold, damp lane near Gaynor's house, he waited for her to go out. If her husband was with her he didn't follow but when she went out alone he set off cautiously behind her.

It had been sheer luck that had led him to Jack Roberts the first time. The man who had cheated his poor, silly, trusting Mam, had literally bumped into him. He had stepped off the train at Bryn Melinau looking for Eric and his small step-sisters and baby step-brother, and as he walked up Main Street, Jack Roberts, or Francis Culver as he knew him, came out of Vi and Willie's café and cannoned into him. It had been that easy.

At first he hadn't recognised the man but the embarrassed look, the half-smile, the hurried departure had somehow made his memory click back to the day when he had been told by his mother this man was their saviour. The years between had changed the man, but the half-smile, the small moustache, the shifty, embarrassed look in the eyes, had instantly revealed to Danny the identity of the man.

He had done nothing that day, but over several visits to the town, had found out what name he was using, and all about his social activities, then he had demanded money. When Jack blustered and refused, he had beaten him up, pushing and punching him along the dark path until they reached the gates of Bessie's and Bertha's cottages near the river. His muscles tensed with remembered pleasure.

He had intended to stop once the value of his mother's house had been paid back, planning to give it to his siblings, but somehow, perhaps because the man was so easily frightened, he had gone on demanding more.

Once he found him again he would demand money just once more. He'd promise Jack it would be the last time and he would keep his promise. He just needed a little more to enable himself to get a place of his own and start a new life with Charlotte. He had to do better than a flat over a shop.

Following Gaynor still seemed his best chance of finding Jack. He'd write to Charlotte, tell her how miserable he'd been and how he regretted their quarrel. He'd assure her that if she didn't want to buy a pub, then he'd get them a house and work with her at the factory. Danny wanted stability in his life. He would steer clear of trouble with Charlotte at his side. He wanted to go and talk to her but decided it was best to stay away from Mill House and let Eric's rage cool.

Eric's rage when he learned that Gloria's son had

been blackmailing Jack Roberts and was a thug to boot, was nothing compared with the rage Harriet felt at what she had learnt at Bertha Evans's cottage. She wanted to burst through the hall door and scream at him but she held back. This was not something for others to hear. It was nothing short of a miracle that it hadn't been general knowledge before now. Angry and humiliated she might be, but she wouldn't risk the secret being disclosed after eighteen years.

Her opportunity came later on Boxing day when Charlotte had gone for a walk on the hill, Rhoda had gone looking for Ned, and Miranda had taken the children to a pantomime in town. Eric was alone with baby Matthew.

"You can leave my house tomorrow and don't pretend not to know why!" Harriet had pushed open the door and confronted Eric the moment Miranda and the others had stepped into the taxi.

"Harriet, what's wrong? Is it the children? Surely they haven't upset you. They think so much of you."

"Stop it! Stop it, stop it!" she shouted. "I know! After all the years you kept your filthy, sordid little secret, I know!"

"What do you know, my dear?" Eric asked mildly.

"Don't you dare 'my dear' *me*! How could you? As if this Gloria affair wasn't enough for me to face. With Bertha of all people. That skinny, grubby little woman. How could you?"

"How could I what?" But light was dawning and Eric lowered his gaze. "Sit down, Harriet. There is something you should know . . . Lillian isn't my daughter, if that's what you're thinking."

For a moment she was taken aback but she rallied and repeated her list of epithets. "Filthy little slut. A skinny, unwashed, uneducated peasant! That's what Bertha Evans is!"

"Lillian was the child of a man who left Bertha to cope alone. I helped. I've been paying a monthly sum which I intended to stop when Lillian reached fourteen and could leave school." He still spoke quietly and Harriet stared, still unconvinced. "She was so slow, poor love, that there wasn't a chance of her earning a living, so I have continued these small payments."

"You expect me to believe that?"

"I hope you will, because it's true."

"Why?"

"I love children, Harriet. At least you must believe that."

"So do I – my own. Why should you help that Bertha woman, taking money from our daughters to do so?"

"They had sufficient. Every child is entitled to a happy childhood. So many miss out on that very ordinary expectation. Without my help there's a strong possibility that Bertha would have put Lillian in a home. I didn't want that. I can't help every child in the world but I could help one. So I did."

"And that's it? You paid for someone else's mistake for eighteen years?"

He shrugged.

"I never knew."

"I wish you hadn't found out. Will you promise me not to tell anyone, please, Harriet?"

Bemused, ashamed of her outburst and ridiculously

proud of him, Harriet could only nod. How little she knew of this extraordinary man to whom she had once been married.

Rhoda was tired of her mother's constant refusals to go out with her to wander around the shops as they used to.

"You never have time to keep me company any more," she complained that Boxing Day tea time.

"In case you haven't noticed, Rhoda, I have children to mind, meals to see to."

"Who comes first, your own daughter or my father's illegitimate offspring?" She burst into sobs.

"You'd be better off working instead of hanging around being looked after by me. A grown woman you are, Rhoda, though no one would ever think so. See what young Miranda does in a day and compare it with what you achieve."

"Mam!" Sobbing loudly, Rhoda ran into the hall, heading for the stairs and her room and a good long sulk, but her father, entering at the same time, stopped her.

"What's the matter?" he asked, pausing with his hand on his door. "What's happened?"

"You Dadda. That's what's happened, if you must know."

"What have I done?" He smiled. "Recently I mean."

"You bringing your – those children here. Making Mam work all hours and having no time for the rest of us."

"You mean, no time to go out with you. Charlotte never did have much of her time."

261

"All right. I'm grieving for my Brian and she expects me to spend hours on my own."

"Get a job. You aren't stupid, you'll find something interesting, I'm sure. You can't waste the precious years of your youth idling away the hours. Best you use them. Go and look for a job."

Sobbing louder than ever, Rhoda ran up to her room and slammed her door. Before Eric disappeared through the dividing door, Harriet came out and asked, "What did you say to Rhoda?" Her eyes sparkled with incipient anger. How dare he upset the girl?

"I told her to get a job," he said quietly.

"Oh, now there's a thing. So did I!"

Chapter Fourteen

Harriet told no one about Eric's contribution to Lillian's welfare. It was extremely difficult for her not to boast about his secret generosity. Eric was a very special man. She felt the glow of pride and began to see why it was important not to tell of kindnesses. Such an honourable man was Eric. She had almost forgotten how he had abandoned her in her joy at his noble act.

It was good sharing his secret. It gave them something in common, an excuse for a shared glance now and then when something bordering on the subject came up. Oh, if only he would show some sign of real affection! She must have impressed him with the way she had dealt with his return with those children of his. Soon Harriet felt sure, he would talk to her and beg to return to his rightful place as her husband.

When Danny was not in Bryn Melinau he was usually in Barry. He lived on an old boat from which all the paint had gone, bleached by the weather to a pale, bare wood. The old craft was fairly sound, apart from a few small holes and one large gash in the hull where the rudder had once been. An examination proved it to be weatherproof, and it was strongly partitioned, so that it was possible to choose his accommodation. He had created a warm and cosy place, safe from cold winds, rain and snow. With a few added comforts he now called it home.

He had money and could have afforded to rent a reasonable room somewhere but until he had that final payment from Jack Roberts he didn't want to spend a penny more than he needed to.

He was quite comfortable and, considering it was the depths of winter, surprisingly warm. There had been a rusted up pot-bellied stove which, once cleaned up, had lit with minimum fuss and, when it had been going for several hours, glowed fiercely and looked fit to burst. His bed was a shelf that at first had smelled strongly of rotting fish but repeated scrubbing had reduced this to acceptable levels. He bathed regularly in the public baths in the town and hoped the smell did not linger.

He worked in a small public house, doing the menial jobs like cleaning the cellar, organising the empty barrels for collection, restocking the shelves and rearranging the stock when necessary. So far, he hadn't been allowed to serve in the bar but the work he was allowed to do was already giving him some idea of what running a public house of his own would entail.

Enthusiasm for this occupation had rapidly dwindled, as did his life with Charlotte. Coral, a pretty, red-haired divorcée who worked in the bar, had eliminated all thoughts of marriage to the girl he once thought would make the perfect wife. Coral made him feel strong, capable of anything.

He still planned to find Jack and demand a final

payment for his silence. Then he could show Coral what a catch he really was!

Early in March he left his simple home, and caught the train once more to visit Bryn Melinau. A letter to Bertha told her to expect him and he set off carrying a few gifts for Bertha and Lillian. What good fortune that he hadn't told Charlotte he no longer went to sea; it saved complicated explanations of what he was doing when he wasn't in the town.

One Saturday afternoon after he had been at Bertha's cottage for a few days, he set off along the muddy path. Like a rather poor farce, Danny was following Gaynor and he in turn, was being followed by Lillian. The day was dull, a mist covered the mountain and was draped like a sad veil over the town.

Lillian was soaking wet. She had seen Danny set out and without a thought of keeping dry had walked out after him without changing from her slippers or collecting a coat. He had hurried along the path to Main Street and there had stopped and looked around at the scurrying shoppers. He was in luck; Gaynor was among them.

Lillian was puzzled to see him in pursuit of Gaynor. What could he want with her, and, with his long legs, why didn't he simply catch her up? Her slow mind grappled with the problem and she realised that he didn't want to be seen. She giggled, eyes as bright as the raindrops sparkling on her hair.

Gaynor, unaware of the two people in her wake, led them through the school grounds and on, past the railway line to a quiet part of town not far from the river.

Jack Roberts came out of a house in the middle of a small terrace and walked quickly towards Gaynor. Lillian saw Danny's rapid approach. An argument ensued which she didn't hear, but which frightened her. It was that Jack Roberts from the factory, she realised with a pout of anger. She'd got a job there cleaning once and he'd sacked her, said she was slow.

Danny left the man and walked back towards where she stood.

"You don't like him, do you?" she said suddenly, startling Danny.

"Lillian, you startled me!" he said, recovering quickly. "What are you doing so far from home – and look at you! You're soaked!"

"I don't like that Jack Roberts either. Stopped me sweeping up in Russell's, he did."

"Come on, borrow my coat. We'd better get you home before you catch cold."

Danny walked with her back the way they had come.

"Found her right down past the station," he told Bertha, who was talking to Harriet. "Going for a walk, she was, would you believe! I gave her my coat and brought her home."

"Who took you down there?" Bertha demanded, ignoring Danny and shoving the girl's shoulder. "What have I told you about wandering off? Who did you go with?"

"Not me, I promise you that," Danny laughed. "I'd have made sure she had a mac and wellies! No, there wasn't anyone with her. She was on her own."

"We don't like him, do we Danny?" Lillian said.

266

Danny shrugged and smiled sympathetically at Bertha. "Poor dab," Bertha said sadly, as Lillian left them and set off home down the lane. "Will you be all right without a coat, Danny?"

"I'm so wet it doesn't matter. Charlotte in?" he asked Harriet. "I think I'll go and see if she's free of work for once." He looked at Harriet, sheltering under a dripping umbrella. "What say we have a taxi? You can't walk all the way back up that hill." Taking her packages, he ushered her to the taxi rank. "Come on then. If I get any wetter they'll make me sit on the roof!" Harriet laughed.

"Don't get tea for me, Mrs Evans. I'm hoping to persuade this charming lady and her daughter to come out with me," Danny called back.

For once Charlotte agreed to leave her work. The elegant surroundings of the restaurant was a thrill. Charlotte, Danny reflected, was far from beautiful but her manner and dress sense clearly signalled money and good breeding. He envied Harriet's confidence, her dealings with the waiters. He must get used to such places. He was going up in the world, thanks to that two-faced Jack Roberts.

When it was time to pay, he took out a large roll of notes and smiled at the surprised look in the waiter's eyes. If he lacked breeding and manners, money was a good sustitute. He left a generous tip. There would be more money soon; he could afford the fun of throwing it about once in a while and it had certainly impressed Harriet.

It was still raining when they left the railway station and began to look for a taxi to take them up to Mill House.

"We can walk," Charlotte said. "Don't spend any more money tonight, it will do us good to walk off that wonderful meal."

They walked up Main Street and had just reached the taxi stand when Danny saw someone walking ahead of them. He said hurriedly, "Here, you and your Mam go on, I'll catch you up, there's someone I have to see."

"Danny, where are you going?" Charlotte called but Danny was running up towards the lane in pursuit of a man she did not recognise. She got into the taxi and, frowning, watched as both men disappeared into the distance. The rain thrumming on the roof of the car blocked out every sound, the raindrops distorting every sight. Cocooned within the small vehicle, they left the town and climbed the hill.

"Who was it, did you see?" Harriet asked.

"I don't know. He seemed very anxious to catch him up." She smiled a reassurance she didn't feel. "He'll be joining us in a while and I'm sure he'll explain." But Danny was very good at not explaining, she thought with a frown.

Danny ran after the man who was heading towards Bertha's cottage and caught up with him not far from her gate.

"Looking for me, are you?" he panted as he touched Jack's shoulder and came threateningly close. "Got something for me I expect."

"Yes, I have something for you." Jack spoke calmly, and seemed unperturbed by Danny's hand pushing against his shoulder, making him step closer and closer to the river.

"Let's have it then." Danny held his hand out.

"I have words, not money. There won't be any more money."

"Don't kid me. You can't risk my telling what I know about you, stalwart member of the community. The police won't consider it too late to charge you for cheating Mam, mind. That Mr Hazel is still alive, he'll remember it all."

"I'm not paying you for silence any more, Danny. I regret many things I've done but I won't regret this."

"You think I won't do it, don't you? You think I'll say nothing, that I've been having you on all this time. Well, you're wrong."

"Oh, I believe you, Danny. You'd enjoy it. And in a way I can understand that. Pulling down someone who had no right to be standing upright, someone who should be grovelling and ashamed."

"I will tell." Danny's voice was losing its authority, he was no longer sure how to handle the situation. He racked his brains trying to think of something to add to his previous threats. He moved closer to the man, pushing so Jack's feet were on the edge of the river bank, slipping and sliding on the wet grass and surface mud.

"It's no use trying violence either. I'm leaving Bryn Melinau. You've won that victory at least."

"Leaving are you? We'll see about that. I'm going this minute to see the police."

"Go then. It doesn't matter any more."

Danny, shook the man by his lapels and walked off, then, his frustration overflowing, he turned and pushed Jack backwards into the river. He watched as the man swam to the bank.

"I hope you choke on it, you stubborn old fool!" he called before running through the dark lane back to Main Street.

As Jack slowly hauled himself further away from the muddy edge, a shadow emerged from the bushes.

Lillian said: "We don't like you," and pushed the exhausted Jack into the water once again. "Danny doesn't like you," she called after him, before the splash had subsided.

This time, Jack's head struck a remnant of the old bridge as he passed. He was carried unresistingly downstream, under the road bridge, past the town and was brought to rest in the garden of the house that had once been Rhoda's.

Bertha returned from visiting Kath Thomas and sighed as she picked up a soaking wet nightdress and put it in the washing basket. Lillian had been wandering around in her nightie again! She began to fill hot-water bottles to put beside her; the poor child must be frozen. What was going to become of the girl?

"In the spring, you can have some bantam hens, and a fine little cock. Beautiful they'll be and something for you to look after," she promised the next morning when, bleary-eyed and sickly, Lillian came down for breakfast.

"Oh, Mam, I'd like that. Perhaps my Dad'll come then, and make me a proper coop for them. Will he, Mam? Will he?"

Bertha sighed. "No, lovey, I don't think so. We'll have to get some boxes from the greengrocers and make it ourselves, like we always do."

"Mam, can I take Danny's breakfast up? It's his last day."

"No you can't. He'll come down and get it. This isn't some posh hotel!"

Jack had been found late the previous night by the new owners of Rhoda's house.

His recovery was slow and steady but there was about him an air of sadness, of utter defeat. He seemed no longer to care whether he got well or not. Once, when Gaynor visited him, he whispered. "How would you feel, Gaynor, if you knew someone hated you enough to kill you?"

"What d'you mean?" she asked. "Are you saying someone pushed you into the river? Jack! Who was it? I'll speak to Constable Hardy now, this minute. Oh, Jack!"

Gaynor had defied her patient husband, who did not want Jack back, and prepared a room for his convalescence. He never used it. On the third day he developed a temperature which led to a fever. That night he died.

"We didn't like him, did we, Danny?" Lillian said, when Bertha had told him the news of Jack's accident, and he was amused at the thought of the man being in hospital after floating down the river like a log.

A few days later, when further news reached him of the man's death, the joke turned bitter and Danny's mouth filled with bile. He was convinced it was he who had caused the man's death. He was shocked and very afraid.

"I didn't know the man very well. I met him at Mill

271

House a few times, that's all," he said to Bertha. "Fell in the river you say?"

"Didn't like him, did we?" Lillian insisted. "Pushed him."

"Who pushed him? Talking rubbish you are, Lillian!" Bertha said, hushing her daughter. She tutted at Danny. "Too much imagination and not enough sense, this one, for sure."

Making the excuse that he had to see Charlotte, Danny went straight out. He was in a panic. He couldn't have killed him! He couldn't have! He remembered seeing the man swimming strongly towards the bank. He remembered looking back and seeing him standing there, dripping, spluttering, coughing water out of his mouth: remembered calling back "I hope you choke on it, you stubborn old fool." Whatever had put him back in the river had happened after he left; Jack's death was nothing to do with him. But the feeling of dread wouldn't go away.

When Jack Roberts' will was read it caused quite a stir in Bryn Melinau. When Charlotte walked into the house with Danny, she realised that something momentous had happened.

Her mother was cuddling Petula, her father sitting beside her with Louise and Isabelle on his knees. Rhoda was on the floor between them. Miranda was there too, nursing Matthew and listening to Ellie read her school book. Her parents looked stunned.

"Danny, we've been waiting for you." Miranda stood up, gave the baby to a startled Charlotte and hugged her brother tearfully.

272

"What's going on?" Danny demanded of Harriet, who said nothing. Danny turned to Eric for explanation.

"It's the will, you see," Eric said. "Jack left all his money to us."

"What d'you mean, us? Who's 'us'?"

"He left it for me to use to make a home for you all."

"There can't have been enough to do that."

"Several thousand pounds," Harriet said. "Apparently he had a large bank balance as well as owning six houses, in Barry and Cardiff. They are to be sold and apart from a few small bequests, the money is to be used to give Eric and the children whatever they need."

"Several thousand!" Danny gasped. Damn me, he thought, with a wave of anger, I could have been set up for life with some of that money.

"What bequests?" he asked, dry-mouthed. God, he needed a drink.

"Charlotte is to receive some money and with it goes the hope that she will continue to rebuild the family business. The church and the youth club gets a mention too."

Charlotte hugged her mother. "Mam, why the long face?"

"I'm tired, that's all; funerals at this house seem to be becoming a habit. If you'll all excuse me, I'll go to bed." She gently kissed Petula before handing her to Miranda, and left the room. After a while, the others went to their own part of the house and Charlotte went up to her mother.

Harriet was in bed, sitting wrapped in a frilly shawl,

a book in her hands. Charlotte guessed she was not reading, from the angle it was held.

"What's the matter, Mam? Don't you want them to leave? Is that it?"

"Of course I want them to leave. Rhoda, you and I will be glad to get back to normal. Such a lot of work and muddle their presence has caused us all."

"You can talk to me, you know."

"There's nothing to say! Your father and his brood are leaving Mill House and I'll be thankful to forget they've ever been here. Now go and get me a cup of tea, will you? I need to take my tablets." She dug around in a drawer, searching for the sleeping tablets she hadn't needed for weeks and glanced at her daughter. "Go on then, fetch my tea or I'll be asleep before you make it."

Downstairs, Danny confronted Eric. "Was he really that rich?" he asked Eric. "I wonder how many others he cheated to get it?"

"Miranda agrees with me that before we do anything else, we'll instigate enquiries about the previous owners of the houses, in case there were others who had been fraudulently deprived of their homes," Eric said solemnly.

"That could cost a lot of money."

"It would be well spent."

"What will there be for Miranda and me?" Danny asked.

"Miranda will share in whatever I do, but you, Danny, you are not included."

"That's not fair." Danny spoke reasonably, smiling as he added, "I'm more entitled than your children, aren't I? I was the one thrown out of my home, me and Miranda. I'd have turned out different if it hadn't been for that."

"Making excuses now, Danny?"

"It's the truth. He owes me."

"There was a letter for me, held by the solicitor to be handed to me after Jack's death. In it he asks me to make certain you do not benefit in any way."

"And you'll do that? Cut me out of money that would set me up with a job and a place to lay my head?"

"I think you've had your share, don't you? Jack believed you were capable of taking care of yourself. Danny, I think you ought to leave Bryn Melinau, don't you? Rumours and talk of someone pushing the man into the river haven't faded. Ned Hardy is an intelligent young officer . . . he wouldn't need much of a hint."

"You believe I killed him?"

"I think he was pushed into the water that night, yes, and there's no one else who'd want to, is there?"

"Gaynor's old man, that's one for a start off!"

"He doesn't have your barely contained violence, Danny."

"You're threatening me now! You're no better than *me*, you aren't."

"If I believed that," Eric said quietly, "I'd shoot myself."

Harriet didn't take the tablets and she didn't sleep. She lay against the pillows wondering how soon they

275

would leave and how she could persuade them to stay without losing her pride completely.

One of her worries was that, moving to a place where she was not a part of his life, Eric might find someone else. He didn't want her, that was clear, but he did need her. But the situation was precarious. Not wanting her meant there was a chance he would meet someone he did want. Thank goodness the government had withdrawn their plan to make a seven year separation grounds for divorce. At least she still held that advantage.

When Charlotte went down to make her mother's cup of tea, Danny was dressed, ready to leave.

"Oh, Danny, you aren't leaving? I need to talk to someone about all this."

"Tomorrow, Charlotte. I'll meet you tomorrow."

"I'll be at the factory all day."

"I think I'll go to Bristol tomorrow then and see if I can find myself a job."

"In Bristol? But why not here?"

He glanced at the dividing door and whispered, "Best you get away from your Mam while there's still a chance, my lovely one."

"No, Danny. I'm needed here, both at the factory and, if my father leaves, Mam will need me at home."

"Then this might be goodbye." He walked out and Charlotte gave only token protest. In truth she felt only relief. It was over and she hadn't had to say the difficult words after all.

Chapter Fifteen

At Bertha's cottage, the oncoming of spring had told its own story. Eventually Bertha took Lillian to the doctor and had her fears confirmed. Lillian was only weeks away from giving birth. She blamed herself bitterly for not having noticed Lillian's condition, her burgeoning stomach concealed by her vastness. Gentle questioning failed to reveal who was responsible for her pregnancy and Bertha didn't know what to do. She kept the girl in, refusing to allow her to go further than the hen coop, where she sat for hours each day watching the birds and dreaming of when she would have her own family of bantams.

"Shutting the stable door after the horse has bolted, I know," Bertha sighed one morning when she had rather reluctantly confided in Bessie Philpot. "It isn't a punishment, she doesn't know what she's done, poor dab. I can't let her wander about in her state, the doctor says she has only a few weeks to go."

"She might lead you to the one responsible if you let her go out, mind," Bessie suggested.

"She's been wandering off a lot lately, there's no doubt she's been meeting someone. With hindsight, it's very clear she was meeting a man, but all hindsight does is make you feel very stupid! I must have been stupid. There she was, wandering around at night after I'd put her to bed, and me thinking it was just her usual dreaming about her father coming home."

"Wandering at night yes, but she was always on her own," Bessie excused. "You had no reason to think she was seeing a bloke."

"Out there in the freezing cold, standing watching the path, wearing nothing more than her nightie. Danny found her on the river bank frozen and soaking wet one night and brought her home."

"He didn't see anyone with her?"

"No, she was quite alone. Waiting for someone, she told us. All this time she's been talking about waiting for 'him', and I thought she meant her father. She was talking about this man, and if I'd been sharper I might have found out who he was. Bessie, who can it be?"

"Just the once Danny brought her home, was it?" A quirked eyebrow added suspicion to the question.

"Give over, Bessie! You can't think that Danny would want to bother with a poor thing like our Lillian!"

"Crafty he is for sure, whoever he is. Seems to have made certain he wasn't seen." Bessie poured another cup of tea for her friend and asked, "Can't you remember her mentioning a name? She must have talked about him sometimes."

"All she talks about is her father coming back and about the bantams I've promised her."

Lillian came in and Bessie held out her arms for the girl to come and sit beside her.

"Tell Auntie Bessie Philpot who you've been – er – fooling about with, Lillian," Bertha pleaded.

"You've been doing naughty things, haven't you?" Lillian lowered her head and began to cry in a crooning tone, but she said nothing.

"Naughty girl. That's what you've been," Bertha said, her voice raised in her distress. Lillian began to wail louder.

"Will I still have the bantams, Mam? Even if I've been naughty? I won't be naughty again."

"Who was it, girl? You must know who you spent – naughty times with." Bertha racked her brain for a better way of saying it but failed. She had constantly warned her daughter against being "naughty" but without explaining what she meant by that versatile word.

If she had used the word "cuddle" she might have seen a reaction. Cuddling was something Lillian understood. Naughty was when she forgot an errand or lost money or fell asleep and allowed food to burn; not something she associated with the precious moments she and Danny had shared. She continued to cry, worried that this unknown naughtiness of which her mother complained might mean she didn't have the hens and the fine bantam cock in the spring.

"When will it be spring, Mam?" she asked, a sob pouting her lips. "When will I have my hens and the beautiful cockerel?"

Danny had, himself, realised Lillian's condition; her persistent attention meant he noticed more about the girl than her mother, her patience worn thin, did. Now that Bertha knew, Danny had to leave his comfortable lodgings. Every moment he was there was like living with a time bomb. He had to get away from Bertha and Lillian before the fact of his involvement was revealed. He knew it would. Lillian was too innocent to be clever. If someone asked her the right question she would answer truthfully. He had to stay calm though and not move out too soon. That might give the sharp-witted Bessie something to dwell on. No, he'd find work too far away, just as he'd told Charlotte. That would clearly make staying on at Bertha's impractical.

He wished Charlotte was more keen to marry him. If she wore his ring proudly he would be even less likely to be considered as the father of Lillian's child.

He went up to see Charlotte one lunchtime when he knew Eric wouldn't be there. She was surprised to see him, hoping that he had gone from her life, but she smiled brightly.

"Danny! Just through the door I am. I'll make us all cup of tea and a sandwich, shall I?"

"Go and sit down," he said. "I have something to say to you."

Charlotte glanced at the clock and asked, "Is it important, Danny? I have to get the chips prepared ready for Mam or we'll never eat tonight."

"Tell Rhoda it's her turn to cook."

"What a hope," Charlotte laughed. She lowered her voice. "I suspect that when Brian was alive, he dealt with the food, she seems to have no idea."

"None so dull as those who won't learn!"

"She can't help it, she's – "

"I don't want to talk about your sister; I want to talk about us. Marry me, Charlotte. Forget about

280

running a pub. I'll find something. When Eric has gone, perhaps we could stay here. We could look after your Mam, spoil her rotten between the two of us. Couldn't you find me something at the factory? I'm a fast learner and I'll soon be invaluable."

"You have a job, haven't you?" she asked, giving him the opportunity to tell her he no longer went to sea.

"I can soon give it up; the charms of going to sea, being from home so much, are fading. I want to be here with you. Say the words and I'll resign."

Saddened at the continuing lie she said, "I can't afford to pay anyone for ages. Stay with your ship and perhaps in a year's time when I get the place buzzing again – "

"What about the first question that you neatly fielded? Marry me, Charlotte, now, before your father moves away and Harriet becomes a twenty-four-hour headache again."

"You don't like my family very much, do you?"

"Love 'em. I love them all! The Russells are wonderful! I love your Dad for the way he looks after the little ones, I love your Mam for her generosity in giving them a home, I even love your pretty, idle Rhoda. There. I love you and your family. Marry me."

Laughing, Charlotte stood up and shook her head. "I'm needed here for a few months at least. If Dadda leaves, Mam will need a lot of support."

"Damnit, Charlotte, let me help. Together we can give her all the love and support she needs. Flatter her, I will. Tell her she's wonderful, three times a day. There. Marry me."

"Sorry, Danny. I can't."

"I'll go to Bristol then. I have a few friends there who might help get me started. I'll come back as often as I can and persuade you what a good catch I am."

"Danny." The words she so dreaded saying came out as her heart thumped and colour suffused her cheeks. "Danny, I can't marry you. I – I think I still love Joe and – "

"Charlotte! You can't prefer boring old Joe Llewellyn to me? Please say you're joking?"

"I'm sorry. I feel guilty at having led you on, but I'm not the wife for you. You need someone more carefree than me."

"Don't tell me what I need, Charlotte, I know what I need, and it's you." He had to persuade her to stay with him. They had to be considered a couple, at least until people had given up searching for the father of Lillian's baby. She had to save him from that.

He knew the people of Bryn Melinau would never forgive him. As far as he could run he'd never feel safe. Someone would find him, as he had found Jack Roberts.

"Marry me," he said again. As she began to shake her head he added, "Then at least don't tell anyone it's off between us. I don't want people offering their sympathy." Like an actor in a melodrama, he added sorrowfully, "Don't put me through that, I – I couldn't handle it at the moment. I was so proud to have you for my girl. You're far above anyone else I've ever met and I thought the Gods were smiling on me. Oh, Charlotte." It was the best he could do.

Charlotte thought he was bravely holding back tears and she put an arm around his shoulders and whispered, "I'm sorry."

He left soon after, and Charlotte prepared the chips and unpacked the pies she'd bought from Vi and Willie's café. She was tense and tearful herself. Telling Danny she no longer loved him was the most unpleasant thing she had ever done. He had been so distressed.

Why hadn't she fallen in love with him? He was fun to be with, rather handsome, and he attracted her physically. What more was there? As usual, she longed to talk to Joe.

Later that day, Eric saw Danny at the pub. With deep trepidation Danny forced a smile.

"Danny. I want a word."

Eric's appearance made Danny feel like a little boy caught stealing apples. "Well, I can't stay long, Bertha'll have my food ready. Steaming away on a pan of hot water, and hot water's what I'll be in if I'm late," he joked.

"I wanted you to know that you don't have to worry; I've paid back all the money Jack stole to pay your demands."

"What? Mr Russell, what are you on about? I thought we'd sorted all this."

"Not quite. Two thousand pounds is a great deal of money. Far more than I can afford. But I paid it because I loved your mother. I couldn't bear the thought of your name – her name – being besmirched."

Danny was looking at him, open-mouthed. "Two

thousand? Hells bells, where did you get that from? Two thousand?"

"A thief, is what you are, although blackmailer is nearer the truth."

"Off your head you must be," Danny laughed. "All them kids have driven you round the bend, have they?"

"It's no use bluffing, Danny. I paid the money back into the factory accounts. Not for you. For your mother's sake. She had so little, but she never resorted to anything even slightly dishonest. She'd have been so ashamed."

Danny said nothing for a while. Eric saw that he was smiling and anger flared in a most distasteful way. He had never been a violent man and Danny wasn't going to change that. He swallowed his drink and asked calmly when Danny was leaving the town.

When Danny spoke it was not in answer to Eric's question.

"He owed it to us," he said at last. "He it was who robbed us of the house. He who made Mam sign away her home."

"I know," Eric said quietly. "I can understand your need to make him pay back what he took from you. I could still have understood if you'd demanded double. But two thousand pounds. There's no justification for that amount, and all you've done is deprive the children again. I had to pay back that amount and it was put aside for their education."

"You aren't seriously telling me I got two thousand pounds from Jack Roberts? Two thousand? Where did you get that figure from, a Christmas cracker quiz? I never took more than he owed us plus a couple of fifties to help me get started."

It was Eric's turn to stare.

"I swear it, Mr Russell. If there was two thousand missing it was nothing to do with me."

"Then the money he left us in his will, it was simply paying back what he had stolen from *us*!"

Later that evening, Eric invited Joe to call and when the children were in bed, he went into Harriet's side of the house and, avoiding Danny's part in it all, told them what he had learnt about Jack Roberts' money.

"I found out that he had robbed the factory and I paid it back believing, wrongly as it happened, that I was protecting someone."

"So the will was a farce? He was giving you money that was yours anyway? Is that what you're saying?" Harriet gasped. "His generosity – that so impressed people – it wasn't for you and the children, he was simply paying a debt?"

"An unacknowledged debt, yes."

Harriet looked away from Eric and asked almost casually, "Does this mean you won't be able to afford to buy a house and move away then?"

"There are the houses to be sold, unless we find that they were stolen, like everything else. About our staying, I'll discuss that with you later, Harriet, if I may," Eric said in his polite way.

"What could he have wanted the money for?" Charlotte asked. "He had plenty."

"I think I can answer that," Joe said. "I found this photograph among his things." He took it out and showed them. It was a crumpled, faded photograph of a shabby, tumbled-down shack built of mud and corrigated iron. Windows and doors hung at odds with the walls. Rubbish was piled against a broken gate. Outside the door were two figures, a shabby, shapeless woman with her arm around a small boy.

"Who is it?" Harriet asked, shuddering at the unpleasant reminder of how some people had once lived.

"The boy is Jack," Joe said. "He's written on the back:

'Home.
Me with my beautiful mother.'
February 1890'

I suspect that all his life he'd been trying to live down his childhood poverty. He dedicated his life to acquiring money in any way he could. There were several newspaper items in his possessions. Names of companies he worked for, with amounts written beside them. I think the books and newspaper cuttings might have been his black memoirs, details of people whom he had cheated. It's possible we'd be able to find them, perhaps compensate?" He looked at Eric, who nodded. "He bought houses . . . and from what I've discovered so far, cheated two, possibly three, women out of their homes. He robbed firms he worked for and quickly moved on, buying more houses, increasing his various bank accounts."

"But he lived like a pauper, renting one small room," Harriet frowned.

"He was so afraid of being without money he

couldn't spend it or enjoy it. A sad and wasted life."

"Greedy more like!" Harriet said firmly. "How can you eulogize the man and pretend he was justified to cheat and steal? The man was a thief and confidence trickster and we're lucky to be shot of him!"

"How did you find out?" Charlotte wanted to know. Joe and Eric exchanged glances and Joe nodded, giving his approval for Eric to continue.

"Joe did a lot of the detective work." He paused and smiled at his daughter. "You won't like what I have to say and I hate saying it," he said with his slow smile. "Sorry, Charlotte, my dear, but it concerns Danny."

"He didn't know Jack Roberts," she protested.

"He recognised him as the man who had cheated his mother out of her home. He's been blackmailing the man."

Joe moved a little closer to Charlotte and put his hand over hers.

"So that's where he's been getting the money," Charlotte gasped. "I knew he had too much."

"What are we going to do?" Harriet said.

"That's up to Charlotte, I think," Joe said.

"Up to me?"

"If you're going to marry the man we can't go to the police with this, can we?"

"I'm not marrying Danny."

"Thank goodness for that!" Harriet said.

"Do we inform the police?" Joe asked. Charlotte shook her head.

"If Jack had lived I would have insisted," Eric said, "but now, it all seems so pointless. I suggest I take the money he owed me, repay the children, compensate any others we learn about, and hand any that's left to a charity. A children's charity would be my choice."

The others agreed.

"What about Danny?" Charlotte whispered.

"We'll leave that to you. Whatever you decide we'll go along with it."

"He's leaving. I've known for a long time that it was a mistake, but I've found it so difficult to tell him. I could never marry him."

"And you, Eric? You'll stay here – until you find a suitable place?" Harriet asked.

Eric nodded. "Until I find a suitable place, thank you. I know it's too much for you and I'll do my best to get out before the summer."

Harriet wanted to beg him not to go but she merely pointed to the teacups and asked Charlotte if she was going to make another pot of tea, or did she intend to watch them all die of dehydration?

Eric knew he had to get away from Mill House. He had already stayed too long. Harriet was beginning to rely on them being there. She had used his beautiful children to fill her empty life and if he didn't move out soon he would be compelled to stay.

Harriet needed them but – they no longer needed her. After walking out on his family so cruelly, leaving Harriet to face the gossip and speculation and, he suspected, the jeering laughter of the town, he had walked back into her life, asked for her help and received it generously. Now he was having to leave her again. But he had to go, and soon. Delaying would only make things more difficult. He had to do what was best for his lovely children. To remain would be to commit them to a life-style over which he had less and less say, and himself to misery for the rest of his life.

It wasn't that Harriet was wicked, but he knew he wouldn't be free to do what he wanted for them. Without anyone realising it, Harriet would manage them, lead them down the path she wanted to go.

It was only then, as his tortuous thoughts struggled to explain to himself the enigma of Harriet, that he became really aware of how Charlotte had suffered. He knew how hard she worked, doing far more than her share of running Mill House and trying to rescue the business from the edge of insolvency, but looking at Harriet with complete honesty, he saw too how Charlotte had been forced along a path she had not chosen. From the little he had heard of Joe, he guessed, in that flash of understanding, that he and Charlotte would have married but for Harriet's determination that they would not.

Bertha's rule that Lillian was not to leave the house or garden was not strongly enforced. Bertha had always found Lillian to be obedient. She simply instructed her not to go out and did nothing to ensure she stayed in.

Lillian stayed at home for almost a week. Then, one morning, she woke and the rule was forgotten. Mam was out, Auntie Bessie Philpot was out, so she went for a walk. She didn't go far the first time, just lay in the new grasses at the edge of the river.

The weather was perfect. A gentle breeze filled the air with the sweet fresh scents of spring. The sky was blue, patterned occasionally with birds flying above her, carrying beakfuls of food for their young. Primroses and violets spread their carpet of colour along the banks under the bushes. There was a warmth and excitement in the air. Lillian laughed aloud at the sheer happiness of it all. Soon she'd have her new hens and the beautifully coloured cockerel. She had to find Danny, tell him about the bantams. He'd be so pleased. Perhaps he'd cuddle her again. She had to find Danny. He hadn't been home for such a long time. Mam had told her he was back on his ship. That was too vague a concept for her to understand. A ship was something she'd only seen in picture books. She had often seen him running up the hill towards Charlotte, who kissed him. That was where he would be.

The sun was getting stronger each day and she puffed as she climbed the hill. Charlotte opened the door to her knock.

"Talk to Danny," she said.

"Danny? He isn't here, Lillian. He's working now a long way off. And what are you doing so far from home? Didn't your Mam tell you to stay in?"

"Danny. I want to see Danny." A pout appeared on the plump face and perspiration gleamed on the girl's forehead, Charlotte took pity on her.

"You'd best come in. I'll get you a drink and you can have a rest before walking back."

"It's Lillian, Mam," she called, and Harriet came into the kitchen and gave the girl a hug.

"My goodness, Lillian, there's a lot of you to cuddle these days!" Harriet laughed. "You've put on weight, young lady!"

"Danny gives me cuddles," Lillian said. "Where's Danny?"

"Daddy?" Harriet misheard. "How would I know where your daddy is, Lillian? Go home now, there's a good girl. Don't come again, we're too busy for visitors, aren't we Charlotte?"

"Did you say, Danny gives you cuddles?" Charlotte whispered, when her mother had disappeared.

"Lovely cuddles." The girl's eyes glowed. "When Mam's out." She placed a finger against her mouth to denote the secrecy of her words and went on proudly, "I cook Danny's tea I do, I watch the pan careful, I don't forget what I'm doing. I don't burn a thing. Then, we have cuddles. Secret," she whispered, giggling, her fingertips in her mouth, her eyes sparkling with joy. "Where's Danny? I want to tell him about the bantams. Beautiful they'll be."

"I expect he'll be coming to see you soon," Charlotte said, with a sick feeling in the pit of her stomach. Not Danny, she pleaded of the Gods. Please, not Danny and this poor simple child. He couldn't be responsible for this too?

A few days later, Eric announced that he had found a place for himself and the children. A small cottage not far from Bessie, who had promised to help with the children. Harriet said she had a headache, searched for her pills and went to bed.

"Get someone to help in the house, someone who'll be company for your mother," Eric advised. "Don't let fate push you where you don't want to go," he pleaded. "We've all done too much of that and it's brought nothing but unhappiness."

"Bessie refused to come back and she'll have warned off the rest of the possibles within a ten mile area!" Charlotte sighed. "It isn't that easy to get help any more. I suppose I'll have to give up the factory. I can't see any other way."

"What will you do for money? You'll have to work somewhere, you'll still be leaving her all day, the same as you do now, but with less satisfaction for you."

"We'll buy a smaller house, we'll manage."

"Don't give up so easily, Charlotte. There must be someone who'd like the job."

"And put up with Mam?"

"What about Lillian?"

"Lillian? Her baby's due any moment. Besides, she'd hardly be company for Mam!"

"She'll tell your mother how beautiful and clever she is. She'll admire the house and take a pride in keeping it spotless. An obedient, adoring slave. I think she'll suit your mother perfectly."

He took her hands in his and smiled at her but there was sadness behind the smile. "Charlotte, my dear, you've had plenty of shocks over the past months, and I'm so very proud of the way you've coped with it all. Please will you help me over this next one? Your mother will be devastated at my leaving. I know she hoped that we'd get back together. That isn't possible, you must understand that."

"Couldn't you try?" Charlotte pleaded. She saw her last, tiny chance of a life to call her own fading, like the final autumn leaf falling from a tree, fluttering, twisting, now rising, now flying, trying to defy gravity but dropping inexorably onto the earth.

"My dear, I have an obligation to my children and

292

it's a far greater one than my debt to your mother, large as that debt undoubtedly is."

"Will Miranda still help at the factory?"

"I'll help too, when I can. I'll start by giving you a day each week to help get things on a firm footing. Will that help?"

"Will you teach me to deal with repairs and restoration? You and Uncle Peter used to do wonderful work. Remember how I loved to watch and admire?"

"Better than that. I've been making enquiries. There's a man I know, retired now, but willing to come in to do any such work that you are offered."

"That's wonderful! I'd love to rebuild that side of the business."

"Don't thank me. I owe you that and much more."

When all had been discussed, it was Charlotte's turn.

"I have a shock for you, Dadda. I believe that Danny is the father of poor Lillian's child."

"I suspected as much." He frowned. "Charlotte my dear, I have to do something for the girl. If she could come here, be a companion to your mother, it would help them both."

Charlotte smiled but thought the windmills on the hill would start turning again first!

"Mam," Charlotte said a few days later, "I have to work. Either at the factory where I can rebuild our business, or in an office or shop. We need some money coming in. The other thing is, you need someone to help with the house and keep you

293

company. I have someone in mind but first there's something else. Danny has been lying to me, he isn't scrupulously honest and, he's been seeing other women."

"What? And that man came into my house, sat in my chairs, drank from my best china cups? Heaven alone knows what we might have caught from him. Oh, Charlotte, how could you have encouraged him?"

Charlotte rushed her mother on to the problem of housework; she didn't want to discuss Danny. "You need some help here and I want you to consider Lillian," she suggested softly. "She needs work and someone understanding. Bertha needs a break from her and Lillian could come here daily, while I'm at the factory." She didn't wait for her mother to reply, but walked out of the room, leaving her considering the preposterous suggestion, hoping she had touched a chord.

"Lillian here to help with the housework?" Harriet shouted after her. "Lillian? I couldn't stand the girl around me all day. Sorry for her I am, poor dab, but really, Charlotte, you do have some odd ideas."

"Can I at least ask her to come and talk about it. You see, I have to work and I don't like to think of you alone here all day."

"No!"

"Sorry Mam but she's on her way. In fact, I think she's at the door now." Not giving her mother a chance to argue further, Charlotte showed Lillian in and Harriet had to listen when Charlotte offered the girl the job.

"Me, work here with you? Lovely it is, Mrs Russell."

Open-mouthed, the girl stared around her in wonder. "Lovely things. You wouldn't shout and tell me I'm slow, would you? I know I'm slow, but I do things well. Mam says that."

To Charlotte's complete surprise, her mother agreed.

"Just for a week to see how we get on," Harriet added.

"Oh no," Lillian said anxiously. "I can't come for a week. I have to go into hospital next week. Mam says I'm going into hospital."

"What for?" Harriet was all concern. "Are you ill?"

"No, not ill. I'm going to have a baby, as well as bantams and a beautiful cockerel."

"What is the girl talking about?" Harriet asked irritably.

"She won't be able to start for a few weeks, not until after her baby is born," Charlotte replied.

"A baby? Lillian's going to have a – oh, good heavens, yes! It's as plain as plain. Why didn't I see for myself? Then what are we talking about? How can she work?"

"Bertha will look after the child, until she finds out who the father is."

"Get her out of here! Charlotte, everyone seems to think Mill House is a place for waifs and strays! Get her out!"

Chapter Sixteen

Rhoda was in a bad mood. Her parents and her sister had pointed out with unnecessary sternness that she had to find something to do. More than that, she needed to earn some money. It was so unfair. She'd never worked. How could Brian have left her in this mess? Why couldn't her family see how impossible it was for her? She still grieved for Bri and needed time to adjust before making any decisions about her future. How could she consider work? The word was such an ugly one, with connotations of poorly dressed, grubby-handed people. A career, now that was better.

She thought about it while hand-washing her precious nylons and drying them on a soft towel. As she re-polished her nails, she still hadn't come up with an idea. If something didn't happen soon she might have to marry Ned Hardy!

On cue, the doorbell sounded and there he was, P.C. Hardy, honest face looking as if it were scrubbed twice a day; a pleasant, sincere, unexciting young man, but, he was there!

"Ned. How lovely. Make a cup of tea while my varnish is drying, will you? Mam's out with the children and I've so much to do. My hands will be ruined with all the washing." She touched her brow with a beautifully manicured hand.

Ned took her hand and kissed it reverently. "Hands like these should never have any work to do," he said shyly. Silently, she agreed with him.

"Come for anything special, have you?" she asked.

"I'm wondering if you'd help with the scouts picnic this year."

"I'd love to, Ned, dear, but when is it? So many calls on my time, things get so booked up, don't they?"

"Yes, I remember how disappointed you were when you weren't able to come to the Jumble Sale," he said, not seeing the grimace of distaste appearing briefly on her lovely face. "Still, this is on a Saturday. Two weeks' time."

She frowned prettily and pursed her lips. "I'll have to check with Mam of course, I'm sometimes needed to help with the children while Miranda and Dadda do the shopping." She smiled, and touched his smooth cheek. "I want to help you, Ned, dear and I'll come with you if I can, I promise."

"Thanks."

When he was about to leave she shuddered in a ladylike manner and asked herself if she could manage to survive a lifetime of being Mrs Ned Hardy, with the limited social life that this would offer. No eating out, no dances, apart from those run for pimply members of the youth club. Then there were scout meetings, jumble sales, choir practices and fund-raising committees. The alternative was work, so she decided she could.

His kisses were always brief. Almost formal. More

like an uncle kissing a baby. Today, she would add a bit of "zing" to them. If she couldn't wake him out of his respectful torpor today, she'd go and look for a job.

He gave the usual light touch of his lips on hers but this time her arms went around his neck. She felt his shoulders go rigid with shock but held him close, her fingers ruffling his hair, and refused to separate her trembling lips from his. When she finally allowed him to break away, his eyes looked down at her like those of a startled owl. She looked at him, closed her eyes and waited for a repeat. It was a long time coming and she almost dispaired but he kissed her again and this time there was less of the uncle and a little more of the impatient lover about him. She sighed contentedly.

Charlotte saw very little of Joe. The engagement, or understanding, she had had with Danny had been over on her part as soon as it had begun, but as she had waffled and wavered and been unable to tell him she didn't love him, she was now having to suffer the consequences. Joe must certainly think she had loved Danny and was unhappy at his leaving. How could she expect him to believe otherwise? Why hadn't she spoken out, explained to both Danny and Joe how she felt? Now it was too late.

She went along Main Street one Saturday morning and bumped into Joe coming out of Vi and Willie's café.

"Hello my pretty. Are you in a hurry, or can you stop and have a cup of tea? I've bought some buns, look." Lowering his voice in mock imitation of his

Auntie Bessie he said, "Now there's a thing. I must have known I'd bump into you."

"Put the kettle on, will you, while I serve? You'll see I've put everything ready."

There was no cubbyhole of an office in the new premises, but there was a small, neat kitchen behind the shop. A table and two chairs, a shelf for china, a shining new kettle and a new cooker made it easy for her to find everything and when Joe came in the kettle was just starting to steam.

"Still four sugars for you?" he asked with a grin.

"Joe. You know I don't take any," she smiled.

They began to eat the buns and drink their tea. Charlotte served someone with a torch and another with a replacement wind-screen wiper, a third with a new headlamp.

"Thanks," he said when the rush was over. "We always did work well, didn't we?"

"I've missed you," she said quietly. "There's so much to deal with and no one to discuss it with."

"Talk away, I'm always here to listen." He searched under a curtain hiding a set of shelves. "Damn notice, where's it gone?"

"You don't still have your 'Back in ten minutes' notice!"

"It's here somewhere." He grinned at her. "What say we put it up and have another cup of tea? Go to the café if you like?" She shook her head. "No, you'll miss some customers. If you let them down once they might not come back."

"There's a businesswoman talking," he said. "How is business at Russell's Bookbinders and Restorers?"

"Dad is coming in once a week and he's found

someone to do any restoration or repair work, not that we've been offered any yet."

"That's great! Once people know Eric Russell is there you'll soon see an increase in that side of the business." He touched her hand, "How are you, my pretty? Not too much for you, all this, is it? Danny leaving you and all?"

There was the chance to say, I never loved him, it was all a mistake, but the words wouldn't come. "I love working at the factory, but Rhoda doesn't do much and – " She stopped, wary of criticising her sister in case she and Joe were still seeing each other. "I mean, I could do with some help at home."

"Don't rely on Rhoda. Advertise for someone. My Auntie Bessie can't oblige as she's promised to help your Dad and young Miranda with the children when they move out of Mill House."

"She wouldn't come back anyway," Charlotte smiled. "She's been a saint putting up with Mam all these years, but she won't come back."

"Housework is getting a bit too much for her, bless her heart," Joe said. "The children will be hard but at least it'll be a change."

"Here we are, sitting talking like two old women!" Charlotte said, rising and putting the cups in the shining white sink.

"Come again," Joe said. "I miss you."

There it was again, the chance to start putting things right betwen them but still she couldn't say the words. Afraid of being hurt, of hearing him say it was no longer her he wanted, that he found Rhoda more exciting, more fun, she swallowed any attempt to explain about Danny.

"Goodbye, Joe." She left the shop and hurried up the street without glancing back.

Lillian walked up the hill to Mill House several times in the weeks that followed. She would arrive weary and breathless at the door and ask for Danny.

Charlotte spoke kindly to her, invited her in and, on one occasion, when the girl refused to believe Danny wasn't there, allowed her to walk through the big house, examining every room. Lillian lumbered through the rooms, fascinated by the attractive home, gasping at its size, the comfort of carpets and the big upholstered chairs and highly polished tables. She was particularly interested in the electric cooker and the fridge, neither of which she had seen before.

Harriet was more abrupt when she spoke to the girl, telling her to go home and stop pestering them. She would close the door the moment she had said her piece.

It was on one such occasion that Harriet realised Lillian was unwell. As she was about to shut the door, she saw that Lillian had been crying.

"What's the matter, girl? What are you thinking of walking all this way and you in that condition!"

"Got a belly-ache that hurts right through to my back," was Lillian's explanation. "I want to go home."

"You shouldn't have come, silly girl," Harriet remonstrated. "Hasn't your mother told you to stay near your house? You'd better come in and wait. I'll get a taxi to take you home."

"A taxi?" The idea appealed to Lillian. She smiled through her tears and sat obediently while Harriet

302

telephoned and put on her coat. Between the pains she looked around the sunlit room and saw a thin layer of dust on the dark oak table which held a vase of flowers. Surreptitiously she lifted her skirt and used it to polish the surface with a look of pleasure on her podgy, red face,

While they waited for the taxi to arrive, Harriet didn't sit with Lillian. She busied herself putting away the dishes they had used at lunchtime and setting the table for the evening meal, jobs she usually left to Charlotte, but which she preferred to the task of amusing poor Lillian.

Lillian cried on and off. When she went to see what was the matter, Lillian shook her head and said it was nothing, she just wanted her Mam.

While Harriet clattered about ineffectually in the kitchen the girl began to wail, yelling occasionally, then returning to a wailing, sobbing moan. Harriet decided it was simply for attention and ignored her. Then a loud shriek startled her and she went in to see the girl lying on the floor, curled up and panting. Her eyes were wide and terrified.

"Make it go away!" she cried. "It's hurting me. Where's Mam? Aaahhh!"

"The baby!" Harriet's shriek was almost as loud as Lillian's. Harriet put a cushion under the girl's head when she had calmed between contractions and ran once more to the telephone. The number of the factory was engaged. "Where's Charlotte?" she asked the world at large. "Where *is* the girl! How can I be expected to deal with this?" The taxi arrived at the same time as the ambulance and close behind them was Miranda with the children she had met from school.

It was too late for Lillian to be taken to hospital for the birth.

"How long has it been hurting?" the ambulance man asked.

"Long time. Mam give me ginger for the belly-ache," Lillian sobbed. "Bad belly-ache this time."

When Lillian eventually held her daughter, and was taken in the ambulance to the hospital, Harriet went with her.

"Are you sure?" Miranda asked. Charlotte had told her how Harriet hated hospitals.

"I can't let her go on her own, she's so frightened and doesn't really know what's happened."

"Then shall I go?"

Harriet shook her head. She knew Eric would be pleased if she did this and pleasing Eric was important to her. "Best I go, Miranda, dear. She knows me and there's no time to go for her mother. Ring Charlotte will you? The number was engaged when I tried. Tell her to go down, now, this minute, and tell Bertha where her daughter is." Harriet sat in the ambulance holding Lillian's fat hand and looking down at the tiny mite in the girl's arms.

"My baby," Lillian said, bemused. "Will Mam still let me have the bantams?"

"I'm sure she will," Harriet said softly. "What are you going to call your baby?"

"Danny."

"That's a boy's name. You have a baby girl."

"I'll ask Mam, then."

"What about Danielle? That's a pretty name for a girl," Harriet suggested.

"Will she be pretty? She won't be slow, will she?"

"She'll be quick and clever and so beautiful you'd never believe," Harriet said softly.

News of the birth of Lillian's baby spread with the town's usual efficiency. The headline news was that it had been Harriet who had assisted at the birth, on the floor of Mill House. The name Danielle, which Bertha dismissed as too fancy, but on which Lillian was determined, added to the speculation of who the father was. Miranda held her head high and insisted that the name Danielle had nothing to do with her brother. Harriet was pleased to have her suggestion accepted. Eric said nothing.

To everyone's surprise, Harriet was enchanted by the baby. She visited Lillian in hospital each day and when she was home, continued to call at the cottage near the river with gifts and advice.

"It's all right," Bessie grumbled one day in Bertha's cottage, when Harriet was showing Lillian how to "burp" the baby after feeding. "We all know how to get a baby's wind up for heaven's sake. And who d'you think fed and winded and looked after yours if it wasn't me!"

"I've asked Eric to get the pram down out of the loft," Harriet said to Lillian, patting the baby and ignoring Bessie. "Tomorrow I'll bring it down and we can take the baby for a bit of fresh air." She gave the baby one final kiss, handed the sweet-scented bundle back to her mother, and left.

Rhoda and Ned announced to the world that they were courting. She appeared at the youth club and sat watching with barely disguised boredom while he showed his prowess at table tennis and snooker. She refused to dance to records, insisting that it was much more fun to watch. At the pub she even sat through a game of darts, clapping when someone shouted double top, even though she knew little about what that meant and cared even less. She was quietly confident that, within a few months of their marrying, she would persuade Ned that the time was better spent with her.

Harriet still refused to consider having Lillian as a companion. One morning, as she was setting off for the factory, Charlotte pleaded with her to at least consider it.

"Honestly, Charlotte! What conversation would there be? She'd gawp at me, only understanding half of what I said, even if I spoke to her like a child of four! I need someone to talk *to* not talk *at*!"

Charlotte didn't altogether agree, but she was determined to continue working at Russells. "Give it a try," she pleaded. "Just a week or so to see how you get on. The baby will be with her," she coaxed.

"There you are then!" Harriet said with satisfaction. "That's what you want me to do, look after that child and give her a chance in life. You weren't thinking of me at all!"

"No one could care for her better than you," Charlotte said. "And think how much poor Lillian would benefit, living here with you."

"You can forget the whole thing and please don't

306

mention it again. Your father will be staying and the household is large enough as it is. I won't have time for Lillian and Danielle, not with your father and his children."

"Mam, Dadda's been looking at a cottage further along the river, past Bertha's and Bessie's."

"Rubbish!" Harriet glared at her daughter. "Your father is staying here, at Mill House. He needs me to help him and how can I help if he moves all the way out there? Use your brains, girl!"

"You have to face it Mam," Charlotte insisted. "Dadda, Miranda and the others, they're moving out, and soon."

"What if he does?" Harriet spoke bravely, although she was trembling inside. "There's still you and Rhoda."

"I think Rhoda will marry Ned. And as for me, well, perhaps I won't marry now, but I'll be out all day. You'll be lonely Mam."

"Stop fussing over things that might not happen. I've never known such a one for looking on the black side!"

One lunchtime, Charlotte cycled to Vi and Willie's café.

Joe was there and as he was about to begin his beans on toast, he invited her to join him. "You'll have to hurry, mind," he warned. "They'll be closing at one."

She ate the beans on toast and accepted Joe's invitation to have a cup of tea at the shop. Before they reached the Cycle and Motor Spares, they saw Willie, his white apron tucked up across his middle, followed by Vi, darting through the traffic, arguing, shouting instructions and eventually pushing their way into the crowded restaurant where they regularly ate.

Joe took his notice off the door and they went into the small kitchen. Joe filled the kettle; Charlotte set out the cups and all the time they were aware of each other so the very air crackled. Charlotte was at the back of the room looking out into the rain-misted yard, while the kettle began to sing and Joe came to stand behind her.

"When are you coming back to me, my pretty?"

"Joe, I've never really left you," she whispered.

He turned her to face him and kissed her gently, with such tenderness that she felt tears seeping from under her eyelids and running down her cheeks.

"Oh, Joe, how I've missed you," she said, as she curled into his welcoming arms.

"Not half as much as I've missed you, my pretty. Let's put that ol' notice back and spend ten minutes saying how much we love each other, shall we?"

The notice was up for an hour and at the end of it, Charlotte was still anxiously telling Joe he was not to consider himself, second-best.

"Wasn't it ever good between you and Danny?" he asked. "It won't make any difference to the way I feel about you, nothing ever could. I'd just like to know."

"He was different, like a breath of fresh air, and a lot of fun. He flattered me and made me feel special, but although I was happy in his company, something held me back."

"He didn't make your heart swell with happiness like you make mine?"

"Something held down the strings and stopped it

singing." She stared at him earnestly, wanting him to believe. "You were never long out of my thoughts and the attraction for Danny was a brief and foolish thing. Don't think you're second choice, Joe Llewellyn. That was how Dadda felt all through his marriage. It was never like that with me. I thought you'd left me for ever, and Danny seemed so set on marrying me I didn't know how to tell him I didn't love him and never could. I know it was cowardly. And all the time there was Mam demanding my time, and Dadda with his new family. My own feelings were pushed into the background. There was no time to think clearly about what I wanted – and –y "

"It's all right, my pretty . . . I've been here all the time, patiently waiting for you to remember where you belong." He looked at her seriously and said firmly, "I know how hard it was for you to hurt Danny, I know how you hate defying the Dragon. But, don't you see, I'm the one who cares for you. I should have been the one you couldn't hurt. Don't put anyone before us again, will you?"

"Sorry, Joe, I've been so weak."

"I knew you'd eventually realise what Danny was like and I've put up with your mam hating me for so long that her opinion doesn't matter. I've been waiting for you, willing you to come and terrified that you wouldn't."

"Why *does* Mam hate you so much?" she asked.

"You mean you don't know?"

"You mean you do?"

"It's to do with your father being second choice. It's true, he really was. Your mam was engaged to my father, Joseph Llewellyn, local dance hall owner

309

and wealthy entrepeneur – or at least until the police caught up with him! He came to her one day and told her he'd been seeing someone else and as she was expecting a child he had to marry her. He left your mother and married my mother, and they parted a few months after I was born. Your Mam, the Dragon, has always believed that if she hadn't married on the rebound, and waited, he would have come back and married her. It's my fault, see. My fault she married your father and not the man she really loved."

"I never knew!" Charlotte gasped. "Oh poor Dadda!"

"Poor me," Joe laughed. "She wishes I'd never been born!"

Rhoda and Ned announced their engagement soon after Joe and Charlotte got together again. Harriet could now clearly see the gap Charlotte had warned her about opening up.

"You'll live here, of course," she said to Ned when he and Rhoda showed her the engagement ring. Rhoda pouted prettily and looked at Ned.

"Ned wants us to live with his parents," she said, "in their little house in town, so convenient for people to call in when they want to see Ned, you see."

When Charlotte told Joe her sister had set a wedding date he said, "Don't let her upstage us. Come away with me, let's get married without telling a soul."

"Joe, we couldn't!" He looked at her quizzically and she added with a gasp, "Could we?"

"Why not? We're both of an age where parental permission isn't necessary. What about it? We can go now and arrange it for three weeks' time and tell no one."

Two days later they had it all arranged. A quiet wedding at the registry office in Barry followed by a brief honeymoon in Tenby.

Mill House was filled with wedding talk, as Rhoda began her preparations. Quietly, Charlotte made hers. She carried clothes down into town and deposited them in Joe's shop. Gradually the larder of the flat was filled, ration books surreptitiously prepared for the change of name and address. Extra items of equipment were added to the pieces Joe had already bought and a week before the date, everything was ready. Then, Eric moved his family out of Mill House and Harriet took to her bed and refused to eat.

"Joe, I don't know what to do," Charlotte said.

Stiff lipped, Joe asked, "What d'you want to do, my pretty?"

"I can't leave her like this."

"Can't you?"

"Well, Rhoda isn't much use,"

"Isn't she?"

Charlotte looked at Joe and saw a steely brightness in his eyes. This was a test of her love and she was failing it.

"If I'm not there – " she began.

"If you're not there?" questioned Joe warningly.

"If I'm not there – then Rhoda and Mam will have to cope, won't they."

"And they will, my lovely girl. They will." Joe hugged her.

*   *   *

311

Two days before the secret wedding, Lillian pushed the pram given to her by Harriet up the steep hill to Mill House. A film of sweat covered her face and the baby was crying when Rhoda opened the door to her.

"Charlotte's at work and Mam's in bed," Rhoda said, trying to close the door. But from upstairs Harriet had been disturbed by the child crying and had gone to the window, hoping it was Eric with young Matthew.

"Let her in, Rhoda, I'll be down in a minute." Surprised, Rhoda widened the door and watched as Lillian struggled to get the pram into the hall.

"Silly girl," Harriet scolded, coming down the stairs in her dressing gown. "You should have left the pram outside." She picked up the baby, and groaned. "Small wonder she's crying, poor love, she's dripping wet!" She soothed the baby and demanded a clean napkin. Lillian handed her a bag of fresh, clean clothes. While Rhoda kept well away, she efficiently removed Danielle's soaking clothes and, after washing her carefully, re-dressed her, all the time explaining to Lillian how it should be done. The child was dressed cleanly but in clothes that were ill-fitting and well worn. "Is this the only dress she's got to put on?" she asked. Lillian mumbled about her Mam trying to make one ready for Sunday and the Christening.

When Charlotte returned from work that evening Harriet said, "I'll have to have that Lillian here, for a while at least. She and Bertha haven't any idea of how to look after a child. It's my Christian duty."

"That's wonderful Mam," Charlotte said.

"It won't be hard, with you here to help."
Charlotte was on the point of telling her she wouldn't
be there after the following Saturday, but held the
words back.

"I'll go to the Christening, buy her a decent dress
to wear. Bertha will have to make me Danielle's
God-mother," Harriet went on. "I'll see she's brought
up properly. Your father will help. He'll be pleased
I've taken charge," she added. Charlotte guessed her
mother still dreamed of a day when she and her father
were together again.

On Saturday morning Harriet over-slept. Charlotte
hadn't called her. "What's the matter with the girl!
Gone to that damned factory again, I expect," Harriet
grumbled as she woke Rhoda.

There was a knock at the door before either of them
were dressed and a sleepy Rhoda answered it. "Hello,
Lillian, you'd better come in, we aren't ready to go
just yet, and didn't my mother tell you to meet us in
town?"

"Mam says to come here and stay till she comes.
Gone out with Auntie Bessie she has. I'm to stay
with you and Mrs Russell, for the day," Lillian said
nervously.

Harriet tried to find out where Bertha and Bessie
had gone but Lillian seemed not to know. They all
walked down the hill to town, Harriet pushing the
pram. They passed Joe's shop and there was a notice
on the door. It read:

Gone for more than ten minutes!
Back a week Friday,
September 8th.

313

"Gone off with his Auntie again, I expect," Harriet said. "I wonder if Charlotte knows?"

They completed their shopping and delivered Lillian back to her mother. Bertha was goggle-eyed and smelled of sherry. Bessie's cottage was empty and silent. Puzzled at not knowing where Joe had gone, she wondered if he and Charlotte had argued again. That would explain her daughter's non appearance at breakfast. She always went to the factory when she was upset.

At ten o'clock, when Charlotte had still not returned and there was no reply at either the shop or the factory, Harriet went to her room to see if her daughter had come in while they were out and gone to bed.

Charlotte's clothes were gone.

On the pillow was a note.

> Sorry Mam, but Joe and I were married
> this morning at eleven o'clock.
> We will be away for a week, then
> you'll find us at the flat – our
> marble hall.
> I love you all,
> Charlotte.
> (That is, Mrs Joe Llewellyn.)

Bessie and Bertha were witnesses and Bessie's only regret was that they didn't marry on a Friday so she could spread the news as she made her collections.

Lillian moved into Mill House and to Harriet's delight, settled in remarkably well. She was proud to be living in such a beautiful place and soon learned to care for it.

Harriet glowed in Lillian's admiration and the approval she earned from the town. So far as she was able to be, Harriet was happy.

Joe walked through the beautiful historic town of Tenby in a dream. The sun shone, the sea was an unbelievable blue and worries about Bryn Melinau were far away.

"I don't think I could be happier," Charlotte said to Joe on the day they were to leave.

"Don't you? I have a suggestion that might change your mind."

She smiled at him. "What can you tell me that would make my life more complete?"

"I've had an offer for the business and, if you agree, I want to sell it."

"Why, when it's doing so well?"

"One reason is that I miss the kids coming in to have their bikes repaired. The new owers of my old shop don't want to bother. I'd like to get a shed somewhere and go back to doing that. The other reason is that I've been talking to your father and he thinks you and I could work together at Russells Bookbinders and Restorers. He'll help me get started and, only if you agree mind, I'd invest the money I get from the shop to buy some new equipment and – "

"Joe!"

He was unable to continue, stifled by Charlotte's hug. "Oh Joe you were right, I could be happier. Joe and Charlotte Llewellyn, together, running their own business! It will be just wonderful"

"You and me, Charlotte we'll really make the place hum."

Harriet was waiting for Charlotte and Joe at the station, a taxi purring beside her.

"Come on, you two," she smiled. "Come up to Mill House, Eric and the others are there to welcome you home and wish you well."

Bessie and Bertha were on the porch, the proud passers-on of the secret wedding plans. Eric and Miranda gave them both an affectionate hug. As they walked into the hallway, voices reached them and they realised to their surprise and delight that half the town was crammed into the house.

"Damn me," Joe whispered later as they walked back down the hill to their 'Marble Hall', "I think your Mam has finally forgiven me."